SUSAN SHAW

HOUSE OF SERENITY

Complete and Unabridged

ULVERSCROFT
Leicester

First published in Great Britain in 2005

First Large Print Edition
published 2008

The moral right of the author has been asserted

British Library CIP Data

Shaw, Susan, *1950 –*
House of serenity.—Large print ed.—
Ulverscroft large print series: general fiction
1. Self-confidence—Fiction 2. Legacies—Fiction
3. Domestic fiction 4. Large type books
I. Title
823.9'2 [F]

ISBN 978-1-84782-368-7

Published by
F. A. Thorpe (Publishing)
Anstey, Leicestershire

Set by Words & Graphics Ltd.
Anstey, Leicestershire
Printed and bound in Great Britain by
T. J. International Ltd., Padstow, Cornwall

This book is printed on acid-free paper

HOUSE OF SERENITY

Family life, for Emily and her mother, had meant being in the thrall of her domineering father. She'd been compelled to go to university and then forced to marry a student friend, Howard. But her husband is too much like her father, and the marriage is a disaster. But then, she discovers a grandmother, and that she has inherited a legacy. Things are about to change for Emily . . .

Books by Susan Shaw
Published by The House of Ulverscroft:

ELEANOR
DREAMS OR REALITY
TOO MANY WASTED YEARS

To my husband, David, heartfelt thanks for becoming a house husband allowing me the time to complete the novel.

1

Emily thanked the day the M62 had been built. Once she reached it after weaving her way through the heavy traffic of Bolton in Lancashire, she was on the start of her journey to Hornsea. Her travels had never taken her to the East Coast. As far as she could recollect she had only travelled on the motorway as far as Leeds. It brought home to her how little she had actually seen of her own area, so during these next few days, at least some of that was going to be rectified.

Her parents in a way, she supposed, were to blame for her passion for foreign travel. She had been fifteen when her father had booked their first family holiday abroad to Majorca. That was it; they'd all been smitten with the travel bug. Anybody looking at her father around that time, when few people were daring enough or could afford to travel abroad for pleasure, would have taken him to be the Bournemouth type of holiday maker, going back there year after year relentlessly.

Emily herself, if she had not known better, would have made the same assumption that her mother and father did just that and dragged along a rebellious child — her. If her father hadn't had to travel the world so much because of his profession, she was certain he would never have considered such a radical move as venturing to foreign parts.

As a scientist it was often necessary for him to attend conferences around the world. But always on his own, not with his family, much to their disappointment. So he'd decided to compensate them with regular holidays abroad.

Even after Emily's marriage her parents had carried on the tradition of the foreign holidays, with just their two selves, right up until the time of their untimely deaths in Greece. It was an irony that they were both killed instantly on a quiet jaunt into the countryside, an area they loved. On top of that it was another tourist who had killed them, despite people saying the Grecians were crazy drivers. The road had many sharp bends and Emily was sure her father, a cautious person, would have been driving with his usual care and attention. According to the police her parents' car was at a blind bend when a car came around the corner at top speed on the wrong side of the road. The opinion was that her father must have instinctively pulled the steering wheel to the right to try to get the car as near into the edge as possible. The other car had hit them at high speed, sending them off the side of the road and down the steep drop. The car had rolled over and over, coming to land on the road below, which thankfully was deserted. The one thing Emily felt relieved about was the fact the car had not caught fire on impact. She would have hated the thought that they'd gone up in flames, if there had been the remotest chance of any life, however small, left in either of them.

The other driver and his family had escaped unscathed. He blamed it on the fact he was a tourist and he had suffered a momentary lapse of memory to which side of the road he should have been driving on. This excuse never fully convinced Emily and by what she had always understood she'd imagined the police would deal with him harshly and even impose a custodial sentence. Instead, he was given a caution about which side of the road to drive on and a fine for speeding — which he had admitted. Two precious lives lost and that was it, a free man with no blemish to his name.

He had got in touch with Emily and said how sorry he was, but that hadn't brought her parents back or taken away any of the grief. Emily gave a slight shiver as though someone had walked over her grave. This nudged her into hoping once more that he lived his own nightmares of what he'd done, as she had many times since their deaths. The dreams, often so vivid she could have well witnessed the accident, but realistically she knew it was her imagination playing tricks with the details she had been given.

She gave herself a shake deciding it wasn't a good thing to be having such thoughts when she was on the start of a long journey through heavy traffic. But there again, she didn't expect to be going up and down any long and twisting roads like the one in Greece. She'd been led to believe that much of the eastern part of the country was flat.

She became aware of intense hunger pangs in her stomach as she had been too stressed by Howard's comments to bother with breakfast. When her parents had been alive, and they'd come to Bradford to visit her mum's cousin, Stella, they'd always called at Friar Tucks for a fish and chip treat.

Emily only hoped she could find her way there once again as it had been a long time since her last visit. Long before her parents' deaths. Howard had scoffed at such acts stating bluntly, with no thought for anybody's feelings, 'How common, having fish and chips — a working class man's meal.'

She heaved a sigh of relief as the familiar

4

sign came into view. She'd had a horrible thought that, like so many things in her life, it could have changed or no longer existed. She eased the car into a vacant slot at the rear of the building. Her father had always insisted that they ate their fish and chips in the comfort of the restaurant.

Emily felt something of a rebellious emotion churn up inside her as she decided she was not going to do that. Howard very rarely travelled in her car so he'd not smell the lingering odour of the meal.

Getting a drink, buttered tea-cake and fish and chips, saturated in vinegar, she marched back to her car with a defiant walk. She'd never known they could taste so good. She made her mind up, however much Howard protested, she would do this again. She was more thankful than ever that Howard had refused to have a couple of days' leave from work in order to come on this journey with her. He'd been indignant saying, 'It'll be a waste of two holiday days for such a futile trip.'

Replenished, she headed onto the motorway. This time there was need for full concentration as the road became very busy around Leeds. At the Goole signpost she edged into the inner lane watching out carefully for her exit. It was with a sense of relief that she left behind the motorway, and was on country lanes enveloped by fields. It was a glorious summer's day and now on the quiet roads it dawned on her how warm and sunny it actually was. It brought home to her that when England is seen in sunshine it outweighs many of the foreign places she'd visited.

Her first port of call was Holme on Spalding Moor. The desire to own an old house and modernise it had been quashed many years ago when Howard had flatly refused to do any such thing, stating, 'If I do get a place of my own it will be built from scratch. Everything shining and spanking brand new, for me. I don't want anything secondhand.' Here he gave a sneer, 'After all, that's why I chose you because you were not used goods.' He gave a cruel laugh when he saw the hurt expression on her face.

Emily knew better than to protest in order to avoid further confrontation. She'd become accustomed to the fact that he only spoke of his wishes, as if all they jointly owned were his alone, her needs and desires totally ignored.

Her next destination was Beverley and she had been assured by her work colleagues this was well worth a short browse around. Being Thursday, she pondered whether to stop or not as it would have been the market on a Wednesday that she was interested in. Because markets were another of Howard's pet hates she very rarely had the opportunity to browse around any. They held a fascination for her as if creating an atmosphere of another era. She promised herself a visit at a later date.

She approached a large area of unfenced grassland with young bulls grazing and made an instant decision to stop and take in the scenery.

Plenty of cars were parked and an ice-cream van, displayed a sign 'Burgess Ice-cream'. For midweek there seemed to be a lot of people around, Emily supposed many were on holiday.

She pulled over onto the grass. She didn't need to be at her destination until early evening, so leant her head back against the head rest, shut her eyes and let out a loud sigh.

2

Emily had been born to George and Iris Lambert after they had been married many years and given up all hope of having a child. Then, when in her late thirties her mother found herself pregnant they had been over the moon. Her father had convinced himself that the baby would be a son.

When Emily appeared, he had found it very difficult to hide his disappointment. He was of the generation that believed it was a man's duty to produce a son to carry on the family name and traditions. Not to do so he considered to be a failing on his part. He had often made it quite clear to Emily his resentment that she was a girl. Not that it stopped her loving both her parents deeply.

Her father could have been taken for a military man with his stern, upright bearing and cool reserve, he could often be harsh with both his wife and daughter.

Iris was of small stature and her build gave the impression of being feeble. She was a timid lady who couldn't stand up to her domineering husband both on her own account or Emily's. Knowing how weak her

8

mother was, her father often played on this with cruel jibes, just to get her mother upset and let her know who was in charge, which he was without a doubt. As Emily grew older there was many a time she had to offer comfort and support to her mother, rather then the other way around.

When Emily had been informed of their deaths she had been heartbroken, it seemed incredible how much she had loved this oddly matched couple. It was the end of an era. Even now she would still think to herself or say to somebody, 'I'll have to give my Mum a ring and ask if I ever went there as a girl,' and so on . . . Then she would remember she could no longer do that. She was the only one left with memories whether she could actually still recount them or not.

When she'd had to break the family home up for disposal, it had a devastating effect on her. Howard was adamant he didn't want any of their tat, as he called it, in their luxurious home. But it didn't represent tat to Emily — it was so much part of her life.

Her parents had lived in the house on the outskirts of Preston since their marriage. Emily had to admit it was rather a nice three bedroom semi, although not traditional. It had a large, square entrance hall in the centre of the house that could easily have been another room, with a lounge, dining room, kitchen and cloakroom going off it; and upstairs, another massive landing that a double bed could have easily fit on. There were three very large bedrooms and a bathroom. Her father was very reluctant to spend money on decoration so over the years it had become very dated, although always spotlessly clean. The only disadvantage to the house had been that the garage was on a road at the back of the house. It didn't belong to the house; her father had to rent it. The only two concessions her father had made to modern day living were to have central heating installed and the row of steps removed at the front of the house to create a steep, narrow driveway. She only wished her father had thought to have the heating installed whilst she'd still lived there, as even now the thought of the cold winters sent a shiver through her.

Emily had always understood that it was the intention of her father that she should attend University. She'd accepted this until she was in her early teens and heard some of her friends discussing how they would be able to leave school at sixteen, get a job and have some money of their own to spend as they wished. She had gleaned that to work in a bank she only needed to pass 4 'O' levels and decided that shouldn't be too difficult for her as studying had always come easy and she sat exams with no trepidation whatsoever.

When she broke this idea of hers to her father, she'd never seen him as angry and thought he was going to have a stroke as he blew his top at her.

'But it's a respectable profession,' stammered Emily, amazed that he was taking this approach to bank work.

'I'm not saying it isn't, for the right people, but it's not for you.'

'But I'll have a chance to earn some money,' pleaded Emily.

Once again these words brought her father's wrath down on her head. 'And why do you need money? I don't keep you short do I?'

That was one thing Emily could never accuse him of, being mean with her and she quickly reassured him on that score. 'No, Dad, you are more generous than most of my friend's parents.'

'So who put this idea into your head of leaving school at sixteen?' he demanded.

'Nobody,' Emily stuttered beginning to feel nervous how the conversation was going.

'Don't lie to me, girl. Credit me with more sense. I'll ask you again what is it all about?'

'Well,' she stammered, 'I've heard quite a

11

few of the girls at school talking and saying they're leaving at sixteen so I thought about it and it seemed a good idea.'

'You can forget that notion straight away. You are staying on at school for your 'A' levels then on to University. Have you got that clear in your head? I want to hear no more nonsense about leaving school at sixteen, understand?'

Emily replied meekly, 'Yes, Dad,' knowing she was beaten.

After that she accepted that University was the way forward for her. As she grew older she still had one or two minor rebellions against it but none got her very far. So in a resigned manner she knuckled down and studied hard for the examinations she knew she needed in order to gain entry to University.

She didn't follow in her father's footsteps at being good at the science subjects. Although George would have liked his daughter to study science he did acknowledge that everybody had their own different abilities and then if English was Emily's, so be it.

There were no congratulations from her father when she passed the required 'A' levels and gained entry to University. He simply said, 'It is no more than I expected of you.'

Out of earshot of George, Iris said, 'Well done, dear. You've done a lot better than I ever could have done with my studies. I'm proud of you.'

'Thanks, Mum,' replied Emily knowing it had taken a real effort on her mother's part to go against her husband and say these words.

Emily felt lonely at University for the first year and found it difficult to make friends, due to her shyness. Unfortunately none of her school friends had applied to the same University and she spent much of her time in lectures or in her room. She was accepted gradually but knowing she couldn't let her father down by slacking on her studies she invariably refused invitations but on odd occasions she accepted. Initiated into a new world of lighthearted fun and pleasure, she was dismayed at how much some of the students drank and made a silent vow to herself that she'd never drink as much as them and show herself up.

A firm friendship developed with Barbara Wiltshire, who was also an only child like herself with an outgoing personality. As they entered their third year of the course, Barbara started going steady with Ian, who she'd been seeing on and off for the last couple of years. Knowing this once more left Emily on her own she suggested they make a foursome and

Ian would bring along a friend. Emily was reluctant to agree as the thought of a blind date petrified her. But Barbara could be very persuasive and at last she conceded defeat.

That was her first meeting with Howard, who was in his final year of studying architecture. He was tall and attractive; Emily supposed all one could hope for in a blind date. But something in the tone of his greeting set Emily's nerves on edge and made her wary.

'Hello, so this is your little lonesome friend, Emily is it?' he asked in a condescending manner.

Emily being as timid as she was only wished she had the guts to answer for herself but she remained silent as Barbara answered, 'It is,' then gave a small laugh as if they were sharing some private joke at her expense.

It soon became a regular occurrence for the foursome to go out despite Emily's protests to the contrary stating she'd too much studying to do. This was brushed to one side. Howard suggested an evening out on their own. Emily was petrified. Not that he'd been anything but polite to her but she always felt there was a hidden agenda in most things he said. He could also be very persuasive and against her better judgement she agreed.

Once the precedent had been set, he

expected this to continue. It became normal for Emily and Howard to go out on their own. As students neither had much money available to them, so in the summer months it simply involved a walk to a nearby beauty spot.

To Emily's horror Howard began to make suggestions that he would like to meet her parents. She'd not wanted the relationship to go this far as she only saw Howard as a companion in her student days. But it became obvious he expected more from her and was keen to meet her family.

She wasn't sure how her parents would react to her taking a young man home, particularly her father. She was sure he'd say she was too young for any relationship and should be concentrating on her studies and future job. As he'd invested in her education, he must want some return from it.

It was with amazement that she heard her father bark over the telephone, 'Good show, you bringing a young chap home. I'm looking forward to meeting him. You've been a sly one not letting on before that you were courting.'

Emily quickly tried to clear any misunderstanding up before it got out of hand. 'It's not like that. We're only good friends.'

'Pull the other one. How many times have I heard that before? By the way what is he studying — English?'

'No, he's studying to be an architect.'

'That's excellent, well done. Looking forward to meeting him,' he repeated in his usual abrupt manner.

She'd actually hoped her father would refuse to meet a young man and then she could put Howard off by telling him. Now she'd have to arrange to take him home, despite her feelings to the contrary.

Once she told Howard her father couldn't wait to meet him he said, 'You see, I told you he'd want to meet me. I don't know what all the prevarication has been about.'

She might have known her father and Howard would hit it off straight away. When Emily saw them together she realised how like her father Howard was.

Her mother, finding an opportunity to speak to Emily on her own said, 'A nice young man, but do be careful, dear. Don't be persuaded to do anything rash against your better judgement.'

It shocked Emily to hear her mother speak in such a manner and made her study her in a slightly different light.

When her father had a few minutes on his own with her he stated, 'Excellent choice, I couldn't have chosen anybody better for you myself.'

16

'No, Dad, I told you before there's nothing in the relationship. We're only good friends. No doubt once we leave University I'll never see him again.'

'I don't think Howard sees it that way and I can only stress I want it to be more than that for you. Just make sure you hang on to him — do you hear?'

Emily, like her mother couldn't argue against her father when he spoke in this tone of voice and replied meekly, 'Yes, Dad.'

'That's what I like to hear.'

She had no option but to let the relationship flourish and develop. Not that Howard made any suggestion at all that they do anything remotely wrong. The most he did was give her a kiss which was devoid of any great passion, much to Emily's disappointment.

Towards the end of his course Howard said, 'I want to go to see your parents again soon. I've something I want to ask your father.'

It had come as an immense shock to Emily when her father, after his and Howard's little talk, gathered her mother, Howard and herself into the lounge and said he wanted to propose a toast.

'What to?' asked Emily innocently.

'Why, your engagement of course.'

'Engagement?' Emily repeated.

'You didn't know you were marrying a parrot, did you Howard?' Her father roared with laughter at his own supposed joke.

Howard had not asked her if she wanted to marry him. Nobody had asked her. She tried to put her point of view forward, 'Who says we're getting engaged, this is all news to me.'

'Of course you are. Why do you think Howard wanted this visit? It most certainly was not for the pleasure of my company.'

'But I hadn't thought about marriage just when I'm finishing University. I want to get a job now and start my career,' she protested feebly.

'Well, you can start thinking now. We've agreed you'll get engaged in the summer when you've both finished your courses, then married in a year's time. That will give you all the time you need to settle into your career, Emily. Although I don't suppose you'll be teaching for very long once the family comes along.'

Emily could feel all colour leave her face and she felt quite faint, she'd been handed a fait-accompli.

Emily's eyes suddenly jerked open as she became aware she was feeling chilly. She gave a gasp of surprise as she saw the time and

18

realised she had better make a move if she was to find any accommodation for the night. Otherwise she'd have no alternative but to sleep in the car which she didn't fancy.

3

It was approaching the end of the term at the local college where Emily worked. She had been there since leaving university, although initially it was a stop gap. Her original aim had been to teach in a school but for some reason there didn't seem enough teaching jobs to go around the year she left university. Already at that time Howard had taken control of her life by telling her to look for a job handy to Bolton, as that was where he proposed they lived after they were married.

Fate stepped in as Emily met a fellow student from the year above hers. Anne went on to tell Emily how she'd found some part-time work at Bolton College, as she, like Emily, couldn't find a school vacancy. She enjoyed her work at the college and they were looking for more part-time staff. She successfully applied and had worked there ever since. Howard hadn't been bothered about her taking the part-time job as he kept stressing it was irrelevant what she did, she wouldn't be working for very long.

Emily was sure that was the one aspect her father wasn't too keen on, the knowledge she'd have to give up her career for children. She knew he'd said differently but he saw it as a waste of a good education and, of course, his money. Emily had to admit his eyes had shown how proud he was of her at her graduation ceremony, despite the fact he still couldn't manage the words to express his feelings. For all Emily's shyness it was the one moment in her life that she enjoyed showing off as she walked up to the rostrum in cap and gown to receive the degree.

On this particular morning Emily had no time to think about any aspect of her life. She was in too much of a rush to get to work.

'Here,' Howard said as he thrust an envelope towards her as she rushed into the kitchen. 'A letter for you. I wonder who could be writing to *you*.'

It actually quite amazed Emily that he'd simply not torn the envelope open and read the letter for himself. He was quite capable of it as he'd proved in the past. Emily decided that despite his sarcastic tone he must actually be in a good humour.

'I haven't a clue,' she said ramming the letter into her handbag.

'Aren't you going to open it?' he queried.

'Not now, I've got to rush. I'm late as it is. We've got an employers' breakfast today so we can tout for more students.'

21

'The college seems to have a lot of money to waste on these kinds of things nowadays,' he said in a caustic tone.

'You know why they do it. I've explained it all to you before.' He'd no interest in her career, he never had. Yet he expected her to be fully supportive of his own career which had flourished. When he wanted the little woman at his side, then he saw it as her duty to be there whatever her own work commitments. They often clashed over this, as they did over most other things.

'I'll be in at teatime,' she threw over her shoulder as she went out of the door.

Tuesday had usually been one of her late evenings but as all the students had finished their course work there were no more night classes. As Course Co-ordinator she was expected to chair all those exam boards relevant to her course. She always found these very draining as special concentration was needed for long spells. The decisions of the board could influence some students' future lives — so it was imperative the correct results were awarded for the work.

Emily moved straight from the working breakfast to the exam board and totally forgot about the letter in her bag. Just as she walked into the staff room, prior to her lunch break, a colleague called out to her, 'Ah, just in time, your husband is on the phone.'

'Howard?' she asked in amazement, it was a rare event for him to trouble ringing her at work.

Emily heard a laugh from somewhere around the staff room, 'How many husbands have you?'

'Just the one,' she replied as she picked up the phone.

'About time too,' a curt voice spoke down the receiver. 'They obviously give you too much free time there, as it seems a lot of frivolity is going on.'

'Howard, I'd only just walked into the staff room straight out of an exam board which I've attended all morning. I'd hardly call that spare time. Anyway what are you ringing for?' she asked with curiosity and a slight feeling of worry that something might be wrong.

'What was in the letter?' he enquired impatiently.

'Which letter?' asked Emily puzzled.

'The one that came in the morning post,' he replied getting exasperated with her.

'I haven't a clue,' she replied. She had too many things going on to give a thought about it.

'You mean you've not troubled to open it yet?'

'I've already explained I've not had a

moment to spare.'

'Yes, well if I were you I'd open it soon as it looked official,' he snapped.

'It'll be nothing, more like an advertisement put in an envelope like that to fool people into opening it, just for the reason you've said.'

'Please yourself.' With that the phone went down abruptly at the other end of the line.

Emily let out a sigh of exasperation, because it was always like this with Howard, if she stated her own opinion he lost his temper as if it was a personal affront against him. Mark, who sat opposite her in the staff room, asked with concern in his voice, 'Is everything all right?'

'Fine, just as it always is,' replied Emily, giving nothing away.

It was one of the rare occasions that she actually took her lunch break and she went into the town centre, her mind feeling so much anger at Howard's uncalled for attitude towards her. She found a quiet spot and sat down for a moment to study the envelope. She felt a certain reluctance to open it as some inner sense made her feel as if she was on the edge of some great change in her life. Realising how silly she was being she tore open the envelope. The words on the top of the letterhead — Brian Nicholls, Solicitor.

Her heart really did miss a beat with trepidation and panic. Slowly, as her mind came out of the daze she read the words:

Dear Mrs Cartwright

I would like you to contact my office at your earliest convenience in order to make an appointment to come and see me. I have some information to give you that will be to your advantage.

Can you kindly bring some proof of identity with you? A passport or driving licence will suffice.

I look forward to meeting you.
Yours sincerely
Brian Nicholls.

Emily was nonplussed. Sinister thoughts went through her head but then sense took over as she realised it couldn't be anything bad if it was to her advantage.

Before she'd reached any conclusion what to do about the letter it was time for her to go back to college and another examination board.

★ ★ ★

Howard was late in but his first words were again asking about the letter. Emily realised it seemed to be causing him uncalled for concern. Her first instinct was not to put him out of his misery and tell him what it said, but it was not in her nature to be so unkind.

'You were right, it was an official letter,' she replied.

He seemed to blanch at these words and asked with impatience in his voice, 'So what is it all about?'

'I'm not really sure, to be honest,' she admitted.

'Oh really, Emily, are you trying to say you can't read a letter now?' he asked sarcastically.

She ignored his jibe and carried on, 'It doesn't really say. It's from a solicitor and he's asked me to make an appointment to see him in order to tell me something to my advantage.'

'So when are you going?'

'I don't know when I'll have time for a while,' she said.

'You mean to say you haven't made contact?'

'No, I haven't. I've had other things on my mind.'

'Oh, Emily, at times I don't think you've the sense you were born with. Make sure you ring him first thing in the morning,' he ordered her. 'Surely you can nip out in your lunch time to see him?'

Emily was fingering the letter and then glanced down at it to notice something she'd not seen before, so she stated to him, 'No, I won't be able to do that.'

'For goodness sake,' Howard exploded, misunderstanding what she meant. 'The college won't fall apart with you out of it for an hour.'

'It's not that. His office is at the other side of the country in Hornsea,' she said with satisfaction in her voice at catching him out.

Now it was Howard's turn to look perplexed. 'Why from Hornsea?'

'I haven't a clue.'

'Have you any relatives there?'

'Not to the best of my knowledge.'

'So what is this all about?' he sneered at her.

'I haven't a clue,' she repeated, then added, 'I didn't think to look in my crystal ball.'

'That's right, always little miss righteous, who's never done anything wrong. You must know. You just don't get a letter out of the blue like this. I see now why you didn't want to open it; you had a good idea what it contained.'

'That isn't fair. I've told you the truth, I've no idea.'

'Oh, shut up with your whingeing excuses. I'll find out soon enough.' Then his tone changed, 'Would you like me to ring up and say you're too busy to go and that I'll pay him a visit on your behalf.'

'I don't think they'll tell you because they said I'd to take proof of identity.' Emily felt relief that she could put him off going, as she didn't want him probing into her business until she knew what it was about herself.

⋆　⋆　⋆

At last Emily saw the signpost to indicate she'd arrived at Hornsea. It had taken her longer than she'd expected on the small country roads and she was getting rather concerned that she'd find a room for the night. She saw the sign for the seafront and was slightly dismayed that it only looked a small place. She just hoped there were boarding houses there. She could only see 'No Vacancies' displayed. Panic setting in once more she was just about to turn the car when out of the corner of her eye she saw a vacancy sign in a house tucked away. She noticed the clean net curtains and the unusual name. It was called Wade Bank. It seemed like an omen because it was just what she'd been looking for, not a traditional hotel.

She timidly pulled open the door and rang the bell on the small reception desk. All this was a new experience for her as Howard had always been in charge of organising anything they did. It suddenly struck her that she'd never actually stayed at a hotel on her own.

A no nonsense middle-aged lady, wearing a pinafore, appeared. 'Yes, can I help you?'

'I wondered if you had a single room available for a couple of nights,' she enquired timidly.

'I've only got a double.'

'Oh,' said Emily, her face dropping.

'Look, it had been booked for the night but it's just this minute been cancelled. I doubt I'll let it at this late stage, so I'll let you have it for the price of a single.'

'Oh thanks, that's kind of you.'

'Nay, get away with you, not kindness just good business sense,' replied the woman abruptly, but not unkindly.

It was as Emily imagined it would be, clean and tidy with no frills, but more than sufficient for her needs.

'Breakfast is between 7.30 and 9.30, dear. Do you want a sandwich now? I'm afraid dinner has just finished.'

It was a long time since her fish and chips. 'Yes please, that would be very welcome.'

Emily felt better after she'd eaten the

sandwich and snuggled down into the comfortable double bed. Despite the tiredness her mind remained too active to sleep.

She thought about the phone call she had made to confirm she had received the letter. She had told them she wouldn't be able to attend for an appointment for a few weeks due to work commitments. Mr Nicholls, the solicitor, would be away himself for a couple of weeks after her end of term and it was mid-August before the appointment could be made. Her curiosity getting the better of her she did try to tentatively ask Mr Nicholls' secretary if she knew what it was all about. She was obviously well trained in discretion as she replied, 'Mr Nicholls only has me do the letters, I don't always know the reason why.'

Emily knew she would get no more out of her and would have to be patient until the meeting. As she lay in bed her impatience was getting the better of her now the meeting was coming so close. But with the exhaustion of the journey she finally slept.

4

Emily woke up refreshed, ate her deliciously cooked breakfast and was ready for her meeting with the solicitor. She became quite excited at the thought she was going to hear something to her advantage.

She asked Mrs Sewell, as she now knew her to be called, if she could direct her to the street the solicitor's office was in. Much to Emily's surprise she asked no questions about where she was going. She certainly wasn't nosy.

It was easier and quicker to find than she'd thought. She studied the building; it was obvious it was an old terraced house that had been turned into offices for the firm. Emily imagined she was going to enter an old fashioned reception and waiting area. Much to her surprise it was totally modern and up to date with very bright, cheery decor.

The receptionist asked her to take a seat, once she'd rung through to Mr Nicholls to let him know Emily had arrived.

As Emily entered the office she saw a pleasant young man behind the desk and for a moment she thought she'd entered the wrong room. She was sure he couldn't be old enough to have completed his studies.

But the figure sitting at the desk said, 'Come in, Mrs Cartwright and take a seat.' He shuffled his papers on his desk and looked rather embarrassed at what to say next.

'You're here about, er, um, your Grandmother's will,' he stammered.

Feeling as if there had indeed been a big mistake made Emily cut in before he divulged any more to her that was none of her business. 'I think you must have made a mistake and contacted the wrong Emily Cartwright.'

'No, no mistake has been made,' he said determinedly.

'But there must have been. All my grandparents lived in Lancashire, besides which they passed away many years ago.'

'Oh, dear, I seem to be making a complete mess of this. I knew I would. You see, it's very complicated. If you'll just bear with me I'll try to start at the beginning and take you through events so you might have a better understanding.'

'Oh, yes, right,' Emily responded, now all at sea as to what this man was trying to tell her.

'It's like this. My father, also Brian Nicholls, used to attend on Elena Robertson to assist her in her legal affairs. She was a spinster who had stayed at home to look after her parents in a rambling Victorian house. Of course, in those days there were servants to help her out. But in the last few years, as the money ran out, I believe she ended up only having a part-time cleaner to assist her. On my last visit to her, before she died, I've got to admit the house was run down and not over-clean in parts.'

Emily sat trying her best to concentrate on what was being said as none of this was seemed to have any relevance to her.

'Miss Robertson asked me go to the house because she wanted to make sure I'd been fully instructed by my father regarding all the bequests I had to do upon her death. My first priority was to contact you, which I did. She always kept us up to date with an address where you could be contacted.'

'She did?' queried Emily, wondering who on earth this woman could be. It was turning out to be a bit spooky that this old lady had kept track of her.

'Yes, she always knew where you were from the moment of your birth. Anyway, as I was saying she stressed we must make contact with you straight away after her death — which I did. For one reason and another I've to admit this meeting took longer to organise than I'd hoped. Anyway Miss Robertson was your mother's mother, therefore your grandmother.'

'That's impossible,' exploded Emily. 'I've already told you, I knew her mother, my grandmother very well. I used to go and stay with her. In fact we were very close and my mother always said I took after her.'

'I'm sorry to say that was your mother's adoptive parent. Miss Robertson became pregnant with your mother and in that day and age it wasn't allowed for the girl to keep the baby. Her parents sent her to the other side of the country to give birth and have the baby adopted. That's how come your mother wasn't raised around these parts.'

'I can't take all this in,' said Emily, astounded by what she was hearing.

'I'm sorry, it must be a shock to you,' the solicitor said kindly; showing his own embarrassment at having to explain all this to her.

'But my parents are dead so I can't even ask them if what you've told me is true,' she said in disbelief.

'There's no need for anybody to confirm it, it is true enough. I'm pretty certain your mother knew she was adopted but never the background behind it all. As far as I am aware no contact was ever made between Miss

Robertson and your mother.'

Emily had to admit, 'Neither my mother or grandmother spoke a lot about the past. Maybe that's the reason why.'

'If your parents had still been alive when Elena died I hadn't to make contact with you at that point, but only after they'd died. She felt it would have been too upsetting for your mother to have her past raked up at this late stage in her life. Besides she wasn't sure if your father even knew about it. She never stopped regretting she'd had to have the baby adopted. I think that's the reason she never married. From photos I've seen she was a very pretty young woman. Even as an old lady she had a dignified bearing.'

'So this is what the meeting is all about, me getting to know my mother was adopted. I wonder why she wanted me to know?' queried Emily.

'That's only part of why I wanted to see you.'

'There's more?' Emily asked in amazement.

'Yes, your grandmother has left you her house and whatever money was left, which I have got to say is very little. The house swallowed up the money in upkeep over the years. There was no income as such coming in, only from her meagre investments. In honesty, I don't think there was much left over when her parents died as I mentioned before.'

'She's left me a house?' Emily stammered, still absorbing the part about the house never mind the money.

'Yes, but I've already told you it's in a bad state and needs a lot of money and loving care spent on it. I know Elena would have loved to bring it up to date but she hadn't money for essential repairs or anything else.'

'When can I see it? I presume I can?' demanded Emily still convinced there had been some mistake.

'Of course, once we've done all the formalities it will be yours lock, stock and barrel. As for you seeing it, I've left tomorrow morning free so I can take you there. I thought you'd have had enough to take in today but at the same time I was certain you would want to view it.'

'Yes, I do feel exhausted, to be honest as if I'm recovering from shell shock.' Here she gave a small nervous giggle. 'I suppose I am in a way.'

'It's a shame your husband couldn't be here with you then he could have seen it at the same time.'

'Er, yes he's rather busy at work at the moment,' she responded hoping he believed this excuse.

Brian quickly worked out from her nervous look that it wasn't the reason at all that he was not at his wife's side, when she was in need of his support.

'Just a formality, but I hope you brought your passport along.' Then he laughed, 'I'm rather presuming you have one.'

'I have and I did,' replied Emily feeling on safer ground now.

'I'll just confirm things, although you look very like your grandmother when she was younger, there's no mistaking who you are.'

Emily felt a slight tingle of delight go through her that she resembled this old lady who had left her so much. She'd already worked out that the house meant far more than just a house to her.

Brian's voice interrupted her thoughts, 'If you would just tell me where you are staying I'll pick you up in the morning. No point in going in two cars.'

'I'm staying at Wade Bank, Mrs Sewell's the landlady.'

'I know it; you've made a good choice as she's not one to tittle tattle tales like a lot I know.'

After they had finalized the paperwork Emily walked out of the office in a bemused state and straight past her parked car. Her legs continued walking as her mind was

37

recounting all she'd just been told.

She came back to the present with a sharp jolt as she heard the squeal of car brakes, a horn and a few aggressive words shouted. She realised they were directed at her as she'd stepped into the road without looking where she was going. She felt herself going red and mouthed 'Sorry,' to the driver. A slight tap came on her shoulder and she looked up to see an old gentleman as he asked, 'Are you all right, dear?'

'Yes, fine, er, just miles away.'

'Doesn't do not to be thinking where you are these days with all these young lunatics on the road,' he said giving a glare at the offending vehicle.

Emily wanted to give a giggle as the man who had been cross with her for stepping in front of his car must have been sixty if a day.

Then it came to her what a fool she'd been as she'd left her car parked outside the solicitor's office. She only hoped she could find her way back to collect it.

Once settled in the driving seat she drove with extreme caution until she found a quiet place on the sea front to sit and gather her thoughts about how she was going to tell Howard all this news she'd just received.

She'd found a quiet car park near some static caravans. The high sea wall took away some of the pleasant view, yet none of this matttered as she sat in deep contemplation of recent events.

★ ★ ★

When Emily explained to Howard what it had all been about there was a silence at the other end of the line. Emily held her breath waiting for an explosive comment and she finally let it out with relief as he said calmly, 'Is that it? You've been left a rundown old place that will be worth next to nothing in that God-forsaken place.'

Knowing better than to challenge him she agreed equally as calmly, 'Yes, that's it.' She continued, 'I'll stay on here an extra day as I'm going to see the house tomorrow and I don't know what time I will be finished. I don't fancy driving home afterwards.'

'Ugh, I hope you have left me enough food.'

'I have, it is all labelled and in the freezer.'

'Make sure you have a good look at the place. Assess its worth — we might as well make as much out of it as we can,' he told her.

Emily felt she was reliving previous events. That was what he had said about her parents' home. All the money they had got from the sale of the house had been sunk into his pet project. He'd had them built a very modern, minimalistic house with all the up to date gadgets imaginable. Emily had not been given a say in the design and hated it. Despite all the modern heating it felt cold to Emily, as if it was devoid of any feeling or character.

She wasn't going to argue with him, she was just determined he was not going to get his hands on any of this money. She had already made up her mind. She could use the house as a retreat to get away from Howard when things became too much to bear.

★   ★   ★

She had no interest in the delicious cooked breakfast she was offered as she was more impatient for Brian to arrive and take her to see the house. During the night she had built up all kinds of images in her head of what it might look like. She'd decided it must be of a good size to have had servants working there in the past.

Even so, when Brian drove up and stopped outside what she could only assume was the property, she decided it could only be described as a mansion. So shocked she gave a gasp of disbelief. 'This can't be it?'

'It is. I told you it was large,' he laughed at her dismay.

'But it is huge,' she exclaimed once again.

'Don't get too carried away. I think you'll be disappointed when you see inside.'

Emily quickly decided they must both view the property differently as to her it was beautiful inside and out. All right, there were signs of neglect and wear and tear but it had character, a feeling of warmth as if inviting people in. There were a variety of rooms downstairs — lounge, dining room, study, library, drawing room, all with original period features.

Although Emily was no antique expert she could appreciate some of the lovely items of furniture that only needed a good clean up. Scattered around the walls were a lot of oil paintings. Maybe some were worth something?

'Let's see the heart of the house,' she said to Brian.

He looked puzzled.

'The kitchen,' Emily laughed.

'Oh, yes,' he blustered knowing he must appear foolish not to know what she meant.

Here Emily gave a gasp of dismay. 'My Grandmother was never using this place, was she?' she asked, looking at the antiquated stove and the rest of the fittings, what there were of them.

Now it was Brian's turn to laugh, 'No

— she did have the butler's pantry fitted out as a modern kitchen, some years ago now. But it's still very serviceable.'

Emily had to admire her grandmother's taste when she'd chosen this kitchen. The units were of light wood in a style that was timeless. There was a built in split level oven and hob, fridge, freezer, washing machine and most surprisingly a dishwasher hidden behind one of the cupboard doors.

Seeing her look of surprise, Brian said, 'She was a very modern old lady. I'm sure you'll find some photographs around of her and you'll see what I mean.'

Upstairs there were six bedrooms, then a further floor of four attic bedrooms. Outside there were extensive grounds which had obviously, at some time, been beautiful gardens although neglected. Emily felt certain they were not past all redemption to bring them back to their former glory. There was also a large garage that could have easily been mistaken as a separate small dwelling, with a staircase leading to a store room above.

Brian asked, 'I suppose you'll want to discuss the pros and cons about it with your husband before you put it on the market. If you don't want to travel back here, give me a ring and I can organise all that for you. Although I suppose you will have to come back to sort through the things in the house. No doubt most of the stuff will have to go to auction to be sold. That's unless, of course, you want some of it for your own home.'

'Good gracious me — no, it wouldn't fit in that house. My husband would have a fit. It's all new and modern for him. But I won't be bothering you to put it on the market.'

'It'll be no bother, I assure you,' he smiled cheerfully at her.

'No, you misunderstood me. What I mean is I've no intention of selling it.'

'Oh, I am surprised. What are you going to do with it then?' he asked puzzled.

'I'm not quite sure to be honest but I'll get it all sorted out. All I know is I want to keep it,' she stated boldly.

'What will your husband say?'

'Ah, I have no idea,' Emily replied but would not be drawn any further on the subject. It once again struck Brian how like her grandmother she was — not only in looks but in personality and strength of will. Something that Emily would never have recognised in herself.

5

'Well this is a turn up for the books,' mused Howard. 'Fancy, little miss prim and proper's mother being a bastard.' The last said in a snide tone of voice.

'Hey, I wouldn't go as far as to call her that,' protested Emily, feeling the need to defend her mother. 'At least she was adopted and her adoptive parents were married.'

'That may be the case but the birth certificate must show no father so that makes her a bastard in the eyes of the law.'

Howard seemed to be getting great delight by the way he kept repeating the word 'bastard', knowing it was hurting Emily at hearing it. Seeing Emily's disbelieving expression he carried on, 'Look at her birth certificate yourself, that's if you can find it among all the junk you've accumulated over the years,' he snapped.

Emily was a bit dubious. To do so may well prove Howard right and he'd keep on and on about it. At the same time not to find it would mean he'd probably carry on calling Emily names — maybe even a coward.

He could be so cruel and Emily wondered

how he'd managed to keep this part of his nature so well hidden when they were courting. It came so naturally to him, that he must have had to contain himself with tremendous care in those early days together.

Finding he wasn't appearing to get under Emily's skin as much as he would have liked he changed tack. 'I wonder what your righteous and pompous father would have made of all of this. If he'd known he wouldn't have touched your mother with a barge pole.'

'You can't blame my mother, it wasn't her fault,' protested Emily.

'But she could have been tarred with the same brush,' he said, sounding cruel.

Emily knew from years of experience it was no good answering him back, that would just goad him further. She kept quiet until he'd finished his snide remarks.

She said in a low voice, 'It was good of her to leave me the house.'

'Good! I see nothing good about leaving you a derelict property in some run down seaside resort.'

Emily now wished she hadn't brought the subject of the house up, but seeing she had she felt the need to defend it and Hornsea. 'It's not derelict, just in need of some tender, loving care to put it back in order. As for Hornsea, it's a very pleasant little place with all amenities you could wish for. I've got to say I'd not thought of it as a holiday resort I'd have liked to have gone to, but that was before I'd seen it. Now I am taken with it and think it very attractive.'

'Well, I doubt you'll be seeing it again. You can leave it all up to the solicitor to sell everything off, but I suppose he'll charge you an arm and leg for the privilege.'

Emily put off the moment of telling him the truth, she was too tired to cope with the angry tirade that would follow. Instead she prevaricated with, 'Actually, I'd like to sort through the possessions myself.' Here she gave a small nervous laugh, 'It might be educational for me in my interest in antiques.'

Howard jumped in before she'd time to finish, 'I shouldn't imagine you'll find a genuine antique in that place — maybe just the plumbing.' Here he gave a laugh as though he'd made some kind of joke, and then carried on, 'If there had ever been any antiques there I should imagine they have been sold off years ago to keep the house going. No, don't waste your time going back there again.'

Emily said nothing knowing she would not have the opportunity to go to Hornsea again until the October half-term. Plenty of time for him to get used to the idea of her paying another visit. Maybe she would tell him about her intention to keep the house as a 'get away' place, she mused.

She found herself busy before College officially started with her own preparations for the courses she was teaching. College holidays were shorter now that the College had gained corporate status and new contracts had been signed by the staff, besides which they expected staff to go in prior to the college commencement for some days, once the exam results were out.

Once college started properly then it was enrolment week. On the first day back there was no time for chit chat to each other about their own holidays as a formal departmental meeting was called at 9 a.m. The College Principal liked to have a meeting with all the staff present to keep them up to date on new developments. There was no time for anybody to eat lunch before 12 noon when the doors opened for the masses to swarm in to enrol on the courses.

Emily could remember the days when the doors hadn't opened until 2 p.m and most of the staff had stayed in the staff room to have a sandwich prior to this, giving them opportunity for an exchange of holiday gossip. At that point in her career there had been a feeling of camaraderie amongst all her colleagues. Now it was each for themselves as they coped the best they could with the workload.

For two of the three enrolment days she'd not finish until well past eight o'clock. On the last couple of days of that week it would be her duty to finalise timetables for the courses she co-ordinated, so staff could be allocated to teach each course that had enrolled sufficient students. Then there were the staff meetings to ensure each course would run as smoothly as possible.

The importance of this was constantly rammed home by management, it was 'bums on seats' that earned college fees. Emily felt sad for the happier days that had passed when a teacher had control of their own students and more so herself as course co-ordinator. She'd had the authority to make decisions about who stayed on a course or not. This was no longer possible.

Howard was getting sadistic satisfaction from hurting her with continuous jibes about her mother.

Finally Emily did pluck up courage and look at the birth certificate, but much to her disappointment it only said her mother's name — Iris Robertson and where she was born. Emily could only glean from this that her grandmother must have registered the birth herself prior to the adoption as she had put her surname on the certificate. Obviously at some stage her adoptive parents had changed this name. Thinking the piece of paper might quieten Howard's taunts she showed it to him, but was quite unprepared for his reaction.

'Oh, we'll soon sort it out. I'll send for a full birth certificate.'

'Can you do that?' Emily asked in all innocence not aware of the procedure.

'Oh really, Emily, I often wonder where you've been all your life. Your nose has been stuck in too many books — that's the problem. Of course you can request one for a fee.'

Emily felt the need to defend herself and stuttered, 'I only meant can you, as son-in-law, request it or has it to be me as nearest relative, her daughter.'

'I don't see why I can't do it as your mother certainly can't request it.'

She should have known he would never let go once started. Of course, typically the post would arrive after she'd gone to work so he was the first to see the envelope and open it.

With glee he showed her it one evening and pointed out, 'Look, father unknown, just as I told you.'

'I can't see it makes any difference to what we already know.'

Emily knew straight away she'd said the wrong thing. Howard's face turned bright red, as it always did when he was angry.

'What's this then, the little woman trying to challenge her husband?'

'Of course not,' Emily replied back, in her timid voice. Each time she did this she cursed herself for being so weak where he was concerned. She was confident enough in her job and with the staff. Howard had only to speak like this and she turned to putty in his hands, being totally obedient. Emily had to admit she'd never known him so bad, he just kept on and on with no let up in continuous nasty comments.

On top of this she'd got one of the worst classes she'd ever had to teach. Not that most of them came from poor backgrounds, just the opposite in fact. She'd never had a class before where so many in one group had received a private education. Most of them had already jobs promised and organised through their parents. Therefore they saw no real benefit to being at college and used it as a way to make new friends and have some fun along the way, at the expense of the staff.

One lad even had the nerve to say to her, 'Emily, what kind of car do you drive? My father drives one of the new Mercs.'

She was so taken aback at being referred to

by her first name outright, never mind the question, she only just managed to gulp and evade answering by saying to the whole class, 'Let's get on with some work, time is moving on.'

As the students settled down she felt herself looking at them with distaste. 'Why am I in front of a class who are only here to waste time? What is it all about? What am I doing with my own life?'

These questions were coming far too frequently into her mind for her comfort. She'd always known when she started to feel like this, instead of loving the job, it was time to get out.

More and more she sat staring into space and dreaming of the house in Hornsea, returning it to its former glory with her living in it. She kept doodling with figures on how her money would eke out for such a proposition.

She wasn't quite as dependant on Howard as he supposed. When her parents had died Howard and she had both been led to believe there was no money left, only the house. But when Emily started sorting their possessions out, which Howard had no interest in helping her to do, she had found a Building Society pass book with over thirty thousand pounds deposited there.

She had hidden it from Howard and sorted out getting the money transferred into her name. She had silently thanked her parents and tucked it away. She was sure some day the opportunity would present itself for her to get out of her present unhappy life.

Howard was always meticulous in his bookkeeping and controlled her income but whenever she could she added to these savings.

She was in a career she no longer enjoyed, it had got to a point that she almost hated it. She was trapped in a loveless marriage and now she thanked her stars there were no children to take into consideration or cause complications. Thanks to her parents and grandmother she'd been provided with the perfect get out.

For once she felt strong in her determination to take control of her own destiny. She was going to hand her notice in and request to be released without serving the full notice required. She would pack up and go, only leaving the solicitor's address as a contact point for Howard. Howard was quite capable of calling in the police and telling them a very convincing tale that she was a neurotic and he was worried about her being missing — possibly starting off a nationwide search.

After years of loyal service the College

administrators were not pleased with her request and told her in no uncertain terms that she would never be employed again by them.

She couldn't have given a damn, she was so relieved to be leaving and knew she'd never want them to employ her again. With the money she had she could repair and decorate the house and then she must surely come up with a solution for how such a spacious house could earn her some money in order to survive. Her needs were small; she didn't need much to live on.

She'd never been so positive about anything in her life and for the first time the decisions were down to her, nobody else. There would only be herself to blame if her plans were a failure.

The thought that she would be free of Howard gave her the impetus she needed to move forward to a better, happier life.

6

Events seemed to be working in her favour. Howard had to go away for a few days on business during college half term. He never gave a thought to the fact Emily was on holiday and could have gone with him.

Emily made no mention that she'd left her college post and with the knowledge it was her holiday he was none the wiser. She'd been wondering how she could pack up all she wanted to take in one day and be on her way before he came home from work and fate gave her a hand. There was no need for haste. Not that she'd a lot to pack as she had already made her mind up she didn't want any possessions to remind her of her life with Howard. She was going forward to a new life.

There was enough furniture in the house in Hornsea although some was shabby. To Emily that only added to its charm.

She knew Howard would not bother to phone whilst he was away. He never did, but she was well aware of the reason why — he'd have other things to occupy him. She'd no illusions. She'd come to accept that she was out of sight and, as the old saying went — out of mind.

Packing took quite a time as she carefully looked through her personal possessions and shed a few tears when she studied the photos of her parents. How she wished they were here now. It seemed a never ending grieving process that didn't diminish with time, as people had told her it would.

By the time she'd finished packing the things she was to take into her little car; it was laden down. She'd never thought for one minute it would have taken so long to pack the meagre things, she was grateful that Howard had gone away.

With her last act of thoughtfulness she made sure there were plenty of pre-prepared meals in the freezer. If anybody had asked why she'd done this she wouldn't have known how to answer. She supposed it was partly habit, and had learned to her cost that if there was food prepared for him it seemed to appease his temper.

Her final act was to write a letter which proved the hardest task of all. Finally she decided the least said was the best:

Dear Howard
I think you must agree that for a long time we haven't seen eye to eye and I don't

make you happy. Therefore I think it is best if we now call it a day and have a parting of our ways.

I have resigned my college post and it may surprise you but I left the last day of half term.

She gave a smile as she could imagine his fury that she had given up the job — as he saw it, not career — despite his constant request that she'd do this from early in the marriage. Now she'd given it up on her own terms, not because he'd told her to. They'd had numerous arguments over this as Howard had felt her place was in the home, despite the lack of children. That was one thing she'd always stuck firm on, more so if she brought to mind her father's delight when he saw her in her cap and gown. Howard had never credited her with a very active brain that needed stimulation in the form of a career.

As she thought about it she realised he had not asked for the address of the house in Hornsea. Typical of him not to be interested in anything that belonged to her. She realised that since Hornsea was not a large resort he would have no problem tracking her down if he was determined to do so and added to the letter:

If there is any need to communicate with me, do this via Brian Nicholls, Solicitors . . . Hornsea.

You will notice I have only taken my personal possessions. I will not be coming back for anything else nor will I make any further claim on you regarding money.

I know you love this house. You designed it and had it built to your requirements, so I do not want you to sell it or give me any money from it. It is yours to do with as you please.

Emily

P.S. There's plenty of food prepared for you in the freezer.

Emily left without a backward glance. She'd always hated it and it was no great loss to be leaving it now. The more she thought about it, she wasn't leaving anything behind that meant any importance to her life.

She wiped away a tear as she felt sorry for herself realising what a lonely and sad life she'd been leading with only this to show for it. She was sure this is what her unknown grandmother must have intended by leaving her the house but the old lady couldn't have known her unhappiness.

She didn't dawdle on the journey, she felt the need to put as much distance from Bolton and Howard behind her as she could. She knew this was silly as Howard wouldn't be home for another day.

The further she got way from Bolton and nearer to Hornsea, the fear receded and changed to excitement. She'd had the foresight to ring Mrs Sewell and book herself in for a week with the proviso this could be extended if needed.

Emily glanced at her watch and found it was still too late, despite the good time she'd made getting there, for her to call at the solicitor's office.

She had not phoned ahead to Brian Nicholls to organise picking up the keys as she felt by doing this she might be inciting fate to make things go wrong. Howard's trip away could have been cancelled so she couldn't have left as planned. Everything seemed to be working in her favour.

Once in Hornsea she was impatient to see the house and it was already dusk when she arrived. The drive gates were shut and she parked her car in a quiet cul de sac.

Looking around cautiously, as if she was a

naughty school girl, she opened the gate and went through. She tried her best to look in through the windows, but there were too many shadows to see much.

A voice suddenly boomed in her ear, 'Can I help you?'

'Er, no, I'm fine,' she managed to stutter recovering from the shock.

'You'll not find anybody at home,' the voice said abruptly.

'I know.'

'You do, do you. What are you doing then, casing the place out?'

'No, I'm not,' replied Emily indignantly.

Now as the moon came out from behind a cloud Emily could see the person speaking to her more clearly. She realised he wasn't as old as she'd imagined from his voice. He was actually quite good looking in a rugged sort of way with an unruly mop of dark hair falling over his eyebrows. From what she could see he appeared to be of similar age to herself.

'May I ask what you are doing?' he asked abruptly still sounding suspicious of her intentions.

'Not that it is really any of your business but this is my house now,' she replied indignantly at his arrogant attitude.

Now the voice mellowed as he replied

calmly, 'Sorry, I was just keeping an eye on things. There's been odd youths hanging around the grounds since Miss Robertson died.'

'Oh, did you know her?' asked Emily beginning to feel they were on more mutual ground.

'That I did and she was a fine old lady. Anyway I'll leave you now but if I were you I wouldn't hang around here much longer in the dark,' he said, abruptly.

'I won't, I'm going now,' Emily replied, rather put out as it was none of his business what she did.

'Let me see you out of the grounds.'

Emily wasn't sure if the offer was made as a kind act or because he still didn't trust her.

At her car they parted company, the stranger saying, 'We'll no doubt meet again if you're going to be around a while.'

Emily felt sorry to be leaving his company as he was rather attractive, despite his tone of voice. She gave herself a mental shake. She'd not come here for anything like fancying an unknown stranger. She'd had enough of men in her life.

Mrs Sewell made her welcome and told her she was still in time for dinner. There was only one couple besides herself in the dining room. Emily had expected it to be quiet now the summer season was over, although it was half term week and that could attract people for their last break of the year.

Emily was lucky Brian Nicholls had a gap between appointments when she called at his office unexpectedly the next morning. As she looked around the reception area she acknowledged it was very tastefully decorated.

Brian Nicholls was surprised to see Emily, 'What can I do for you?' he queried.

'I've come to sort the house out.'

'Ready to put it up for sale?'

'No, I mean for me to live in.'

'I'd have thought you'd have wanted your next holiday in it during the summer,' he said, still misunderstanding.

'I'm not here on holiday, I've moved here for good.'

'Oh, and what does your husband feel about moving here?' he asked cautiously.

'He's not coming. I've left him,' she stated boldly.

'I'm sorry.'

'Don't be. I should have done it years ago. Now I want to sort out my own future. So could I have the keys to the house?' she asked impatiently.

'Of course, but you do realise it will cost you a lot of money to make it properly habitable.'

'I know that, but I have some money saved.'

'Good, good,' he said rather embarrassed that he seemed to be prying so deeply into her personal affairs.

'Do you know if the utilities are switched on?' Emily asked, getting down to business.

'They're not. There didn't seem any point with nobody living there, but I'll get it organised straight away for you. You'll want to do some of the work before you move in, surely?'

'I suppose so. Oh, by the way, I left your name and address for a contact for my husband if he does need to get in touch. I doubt he'll bother. But if he does, please don't tell him the address of my house.'

'I couldn't in any case for client's confidentiality. Are you expecting trouble?' he enquired kindly.

'That's not Howard's style,' she reassured him.

'Right. I'll just get you the keys, but if I can be of any further assistance let me know immediately,' he said.

As soon as Emily had the keys she was impatient to go to the house. She gave an involuntary shiver as she entered the hall, but not with fear, more with the chill of the day and happy anticipation. She walked from room to room trailing her hands across furniture and leaving finger marks in the dust. She looked at the radiators and began to think Howard had been right in his sneering way, it was antiquated. As winter was approaching that had better be one of her priorities, getting an effective heating system in the house and also making sure the roof was sound.

She felt satisfied with her first inspection and went into Hornsea to buy all the cleaning equipment she would need. She decided to get the kitchen, library, a bedroom and bathroom functional, and then she could move into the house.

As she started to assess how much she might need to spend, it dawned on her that every night she stayed in the guest house was another night she was eating into her savings.

She put her effort into cleaning the house and it was as if she was purging Howard out of her system. Her mind became clearer and she made another appointment with Brain Nicholls. She needed his assistance to set the wheels in motion.

'How's the house coming on?' were his first words when he saw her.

'The rooms I've cleaned look a lot better. There's a long way to go, but I hope to be able to move in very soon.'

'Is that wise, before all the work's done?' he queried.

'I think so. It'll save me money not having to pay for accommodation.'

'If you need any quotes for doing anything I may be able to help you there, as I know quite a few useful contacts,' he offered kindly.

'Thanks, I'll remember that. But today you can help me with something else.'

'No problem, what is it?'

'I want to set in motion divorce proceedings,' she said bluntly.

Brian looked taken aback by this; it was obviously not what he was expecting her to ask.

'Don't you want to consider it a bit longer,' he questioned.

'No. I've had years to consider what I wanted to do. Now I've made the break I want to get on with it,' Emily replied adamantly.

'Okay, I'll take a few details then.'

When he got to the question of money Emily stated quite clearly, 'I don't want anything off Howard. I told him so in the letter I left when I moved out.'

'Mrs Cartwright, if I might say so that is rather foolish on your part. After so many years of marriage you must be entitled to something from the relationship and marital home.'

'I don't want anything. I want a clean break. If I ask him for anything he'll make it a very nasty divorce. I know what he's like.' She gave a shaky laugh, 'I should do after all the years of living with him.'

'If that's the way you want it that's the way I'll sort the divorce out,' he sighed.

'Good.'

When he'd finished he suddenly said, 'Oh by the way I've just remembered, I've a message for you.'

Emily blanched, presuming it must be from Howard. 'A message?'

'A female rang for your telephone number.'

'Female! Are you sure about that?' she stammered.

'I took the call myself. I told her we couldn't give your details out, but if she cared to leave her name and number I would pass it on when I made contact with you. She said it was urgent. I was just going to do a letter to you explaining.'

'When did she phone?' Emily asked.

'Yesterday afternoon,' Brian reassured her.

Brian looked for the piece of paper. 'Here it is. Her name is Karen Whitehead.'

Emily had to think for a moment, the name didn't strike a bell immediately. It dawned on her — it was a friend she'd made at college a number of years ago. But then Karen had taken a job at another college and despite their promises one way and another they had lost contact.

What on earth could Karen want? She was even more amazed that she'd got Brian's phone number. Then when she thought sensibly about it, it was obvious she would have tried to ring her at Howard's house. It was out of character him to be so obliging and pass the number on. Emily knew he'd have had a motive for doing it and to his advantage. Howard never did anything out of the goodness of his heart.

There was nothing more she could do about Howard but she could make contact with Karen and find out what was so urgent she wanted to speak to her after such a long time.

7

Howard felt pleased with himself. He was certain Emily would see sense and be home shortly. It had been a good ploy of his to give the solicitor's number to Emily's friend, Karen. When they had worked at the same college they'd been very chummy. Emily was right in her assumption that there was an ulterior motive for him to give Karen the contact number so obligingly.

When the call had come through to Howard, he seized on it with both hands. Despite the curiosity in her tone of voice, he told her nothing of what had been going on. He'd leave that to Emily.

He felt sure that once Emily told her friend, Karen, what had been going on, she would try to persuade Emily to see sense and go back home to her husband. Howard had reasoned Karen would see him as the wronged party and think of him as a kind and caring person who didn't deserve this kind of treatment from his wife.

Not that he missed her companionship, he found that a constant source of irritation. It was worthwhile putting up with her constant chatter for her housekeeping skills. He'd had to go to a local launderette to get his washing done as he didn't know how to switch the washing machine on, never mind where to put the soap powder. He now wished he'd not insisted on such a technological machine when he built the house. If it had been a basic model he might have managed to cope with it.

He had soon run through the meals left prepared by Emily. He was convinced he could cook eggs in the microwave but never thought to take them out of their shells with the result that they exploded. He managed to burn the toast, when he decided to have baked beans on toast one evening and he had resorted to take-away meals. They were fine once in a while but they became boring.

Emily was impatient to contact Karen, her curiosity was getting the better of her, besides which, it would be nice to hear the familiar voice of a friend. She'd not realised until the message came how much she was missing the conversation of people from work.

She got straight through to Karen as she had to make the call from a phone box. The house phone was not connected, but she made a mental note of the importance of chasing that up. She had possessed a mobile phone thanks to Howard, but as usual it was the most modern and complicated that money could buy. Now she wished she'd not been so stubborn and left everything of his, as a phone would have been very useful.

In fact, the speed with which Karen answered made Emily suspect she'd been sat by the phone waiting.

'Hi Karen, Emily here,' she said cheerfully.

'Oh, thank goodness. I was praying you'd ring today.' Emily could hear a sound of desperation in the voice coming back to her.

'I only received the message from my solicitor's a short while ago,' she stated feeling the need to justify herself.

'Oh, yes, the thing is, I'm desperate,' Karen said in a slightly calmer voice.

'Desperate?' responded Emily, totally at a loss.

'Yes, I need to get away from here as quickly as possible and I've nowhere to go.'

'Sorry, I seem to be a bit slow on the uptake but I don't see how I can help you,' replied Emily.

'I thought you might have room for me to stay, otherwise I wouldn't have contacted you,' she pleaded.

Emily felt slightly put out that this was the only reason for the contact but she sensed the fear was genuine. 'It's a bit difficult you see as I'm no longer at home.'

'I did wonder, when Howard had to give me your solicitor's number, but please help me,' Karen sobbed, with no curiosity about what was happening in Emily's life.

'To tell you the truth I'm staying in an old house that really needs a lot of work on it, and I've only got one bedroom habitable.'

'I don't care what it's like, nothing could be as bad as here,' Karen once more pleaded.

'I don't know. It's not really fair on you if I said come here with the place in the state it is. There's not even any heating on,' replied Emily hesitantly running her fingers through her hair at the dilemma.

'I don't care, please let me come.' Then with total desperation in her voice she added, 'I don't know how I'll last any longer here. Please help me. I've no one else I can turn to.'

'Okay,' Emily replied in a resigned voice, 'Don't say I haven't warned you what a mess it is in.'

'There's just one more thing.'

Emily began to panic. What she had let herself in for and answered abruptly, 'Yes?'

'He's left me with no money whatsoever and he's got the car.'

Emily presumed by 'he' she meant her husband. 'Oh dear, I don't see how I can help you there.'

'I wondered if you could organise for a

train ticket and pay for it.' Emily could sense Karen's embarrassment at having to make this request.

'I suppose I could, but I'll have to look into it before I make any promises. I also need to see where you need to catch a train to in order to get to Hornsea.'

'Where?' Karen was the one to be puzzled now.

'Hornsea, which is on the East Coast!'

'Oh, I thought you were ringing from Bolton.'

'Does that make a difference?' Emily queried.

'No, none at all. It's probably for the best, as he'll more than likely presume I'll head back to Bolton.'

'Leave it with me and I'll call you back,' Emily promised.

'You'll make it soon, won't you?' The voice on the other end of the line beseeched her. 'I want to be away before he comes back otherwise he won't let me out of here.'

'I'll ring now and organise the ticket and see if I can pay for it by credit card. I'll ring you back in a few minutes.'

Emily got straight on to the task but at the same time was worried that she'd let herself in for a whole load of trouble. She soon found a train Karen could catch, through to

Hull and then change to Beverley. She phoned straight back as promised.

'I hope you can make it to the station by 3.30 p.m as there's a train to Hull and I've also paid for the connection to Beverley. Pick the tickets up at the ticket office. Sorry, I can't sort out how to get you to the station,' Emily told her.

'Don't worry I'll manage that. I'll be travelling light so it won't take me long to be out of here. What do I do at Beverley?'

'I'll be there to meet you when the train gets in.'

By the time Emily put the phone down she felt she'd been hit by a whirlwind. So much had happened, so quickly. She marched quickly back home and set off with her cleaning equipment to the bedroom she thought would take the least time to sort out.

At least she could make sure the room was cleaned and aired, if nothing else. She'd had the foresight to buy hot water bottles for herself in case of emergency and placed a couple of these in the bed and a casserole in the oven then set off on the journey to Beverley wondering in what state she would find Karen.

As the passengers from the train alighted, Emily looked them up and down expecting to see Karen. She couldn't see anybody remotely resembling her. She felt a slight tap on her shoulder and turned to see someone who resembled Karen but who had changed beyond belief. She found herself looking at a colourless face with deep sunken dark, haunted eyes. The hair was lank with obvious neglect to the roots as the bleached blonde was growing out. She looked anorexic and was clutching one small suitcase. Emily could see her eyes were beginning to swim with tears.

She felt so sorry for this sad and forlorn figure in front of her and put her arm around Karen's shoulders and left it there to offer comfort as she led her to the car park. Few words were said between them as this didn't seem an appropriate time. Emily was still dismayed at the change in Karen from the fashion conscious, self-assured person she'd always appeared to be, into this wreck.

Karen recovered herself enough to say, 'Thanks for all you've done. I picked the ticket up OK.'

'Good journey?' queried Emily, not asking more as she could sense Karen was hanging on to her last shred of control.

Once home she coaxed Karen to eat some of the casserole. Afterwards she could see she was too drained to be questioned any further. It would have to wait until morning — she would have to keep her own curiosity at bay in wanting to get to know more.

Karen managed to rouse herself just enough to show enthusiasm for the house, but that was it, no further conversation whatsoever from her. When Emily went to bed she heard muffled sobs coming from Karen's bedroom but had the foresight to realise this was a moment when Karen wanted to be on her own.

In the morning, as Karen stumbled into the kitchen, Emily noticed that she looked no better or refreshed for any sleep she had got. Her eyes were still smudged with dark shadows.

This person that Emily felt she did not know, sat in front of her like a zombie, spooning the cereals from one side of the bowl to the other. Emily knew that Karen was in need of some loving care in order to get back some of her original glow. She was slowly formulating a plan of what she could do with her own life but more importantly how she could do it with the help of the house.

Karen made a move to clear the dishes away but Emily laid a hand on her arm. 'There will be plenty of time for that. Now, I want to hear all about what has been happening to you.'

'Are you sure?' Karen queried with a slight hesitancy.

'I think I deserve some sort of explanation from you,' Emily replied, hoping it didn't sound too harsh.

'You do, and thanks once again. I don't know what I would have done without you.'

'Come on then, let's hear all about it,' she coaxed.

Karen's voice took on an unnatural calmness as she said, 'When we worked together I never liked to let on to you, or to anybody else for that matter, but my husband is a compulsive gambler. That's the reason he never held a job down for more than a few weeks, sometimes just days. The gambling always got the better of him and it came first.' Here she gave a harsh laugh. 'For the last eighteen months he's not even made the pretence of looking for a job. Instead, he's spent more time gambling away money he didn't have in the first place. Unfortunately, he's not had a run of good luck for months.'

Here she paused once more, this time to give a cynical laugh. 'What gambler does? But the more he's got into debt the more he's gambled in an attempt to get out of it. In turn, the loss of the money has made him bad tempered, so now he's turned to drink — a thing he's never done before. Then to crown it all, he managed to lose me my job, our only income.'

Now the hard reserve she'd put on broke as she sobbed, 'The mortgage hasn't been paid for months and the building society are going for a possession order on the house. We've not had any gas on for the last few weeks as we're in arrears with that. Thank goodness I had an electric oven installed although we've barely had money to buy food. The electricity will go off soon, that is also in arrears. I was frightened, really frightened of him, Emily. When he's drunk there is no controlling him. He's threatened me a few times and even gone as far as to say he'd shut my stupid mouth for good if I didn't stop nagging him. I was trying to talk some sense into him and save something of our life together. He's even held a knife to my throat when he's said this. I've been really scared because he's capable of doing me some real harm. He's ill, I know that and there's nothing I can do to help him. I don't know who can.' She suddenly stopped speaking as if she was deflated.

Emily had let her carry on speaking as long as she could to get it out of her system. Now the words had dried up Emily saw the tears pouring out.

'Oh, how terrible for you. I don't know what to say. How did he lose you your job?'

'He started coming into work,' Karen sobbed and Emily wondered what was so bad about that.

'Each time he came he got more abusive, and then the last time he burst into the kitchen where I was teaching and started knocking pots and pans off the worktops in his temper. Some of the things had hot stuff in them. It's a miracle nobody was seriously injured. Afterwards a few irate parents got in touch with the college management saying they would withdraw their son or daughter if college didn't make sure this didn't happen again. Despite my reassurances he wouldn't come into college again they didn't seem convinced and even though I wasn't actually sacked, I was told in no uncertain terms that they wanted my resignation. All those years I'd slogged at trying to better my career were lost.' Here she gave a deep sigh. 'A total waste of time and energy.'

Then it changed into a bitter laugh as she added, 'I never wanted to stay in teaching but I tried to make a good job of it. I'd always wanted us to save either to buy a small hotel or a restaurant where I could do the catering. I love being in a kitchen, it is the teaching side of it I can't stand.'

'But surely when you resigned at college you could have got another job somewhere else in catering, if not teaching it?'

'Oh I thought about it but how could I risk it with him going around like a loose cannon. He might have caused an accident where somebody was maimed, if not killed.'

Once more Karen cried in anguish, 'You realise I've no money to pay you, even for the ticket to get here? I'll move on as soon as I can once I get myself together and I'll pay you back.'

'Hey, don't be so hasty. Anyway, I've got a proposal to outline to you which could help us both. I wasn't going to say anything yet as I didn't think the time was right, but here goes. As you've probably realised this house is too big for me to live in on my own, besides which I need some income to run it. We're both in the same boat, I've resigned my post at college and to be honest with you I've no desire to go back into teaching. I've had enough of it. So what I thought I could do was turn this house into a sort of refuge home for worthwhile causes.'

'Like me?' Karen asked bitterly.

Emily gave a smile, 'Oh, I've other things planned for you.' For the first time Emily saw a flicker of interest on her friend's face.

'You have?' she queried.

'Yes. I don't propose to turn the rooms into self-contained units. I think the people who will want this kind of accommodation will still need companionship and home comforts. So what I propose is meals be prepared for them if they require them. This is where you come in. Would you like to be in charge of the catering?'

'Would I!' exclaimed Karen with a glimmer of her old self showing through in her expression of disbelief.

'Don't get too excited. I've a long way to go and the place has to be ready. I've to find the right sort of people who want to come and live here. But if it gets off the ground we can sort something out so you can keep your room and have some spending money. In the meantime it would be useful you being here just to help me and keep me company because it does get lonely with just my own company all the time.'

Karen jumped up and flung her arms around her friend. 'I always knew you were a good friend and when I rang you I felt sure I was doing the right thing. I'll never be able to do enough to thank you for this. I'll help you anyway I can. Just tell me what you want doing and I'll get on with it.'

'Hey, slow down, get settled in first. But if you cook me some tasty meals and get yourself better — that's enough to be going on with.'

For the first time in a long time Emily had a sense of satisfaction that she'd helped another person instead of pampering her spoilt and selfish husband.

8

Thankfully for them both, Karen's husband had made no contact. They only hoped so far he'd not managed to track her down, if indeed he'd even bothered looking.

Karen had fitted into her new life very easily and was more than willing to do anything Emily asked of her. Just being away from her husband seemed to be enough, to bring back some of her old vitality.

Emily was aware how rapidly she was running through her money just with the essential repairs to the house. It was Karen who suggested to her that now there were the two of them, maybe they could tackle some of the minor jobs together, thereby saving some money. Karen admitted that she'd had to learn the skill of decorating as well as other tasks around the house as her husband hadn't had any interest whatsoever in making their home nice. Emily was willing to agree to this suggestion; besides which, it would be fun.

★ ★ ★

Emily had put off clearing out the study on one pretext and another as she did have sense to realise this would be where any personal possessions belonging to her grandmother would be stored. She started sorting out what she hoped would be the less personal items and was pleased when Karen interrupted her to give her a reminder of her appointment with Brian Nicholls. This gave her the excuse she wanted to break off.

Emily had tried to convince Karen to see Brian Nicholls herself in order to sort out her own situation, but she'd flatly refused and wouldn't even discuss it with Emily. Her excuse was that to do anything so rash as to start divorce proceedings would only bring the wrath of her husband down on her head. She'd no doubt have to supply an address which would mean he would definitely know where to find her. All she wanted was peace in order to build her strength back up for a time when she couldn't put off tackling her husband any longer. She knew at the end of the day it would be inevitable.

Emily was going full steam ahead with her divorce proceedings, or at least as much as she could. Not that she was getting very far, much to her annoyance. Just as she'd expected, Howard was dragging his heels with the required responses that would allow things to move on.

During the course of her visits to him, Brian had discussed the grounds for divorce. He had declared unreasonable behaviour as the grounds they would file for the divorce. He kept on at her to review her attitude to the financial position, stating that as she'd always worked during the marriage and contributed to the pot of money then she would most certainly be entitled to a half share of everything.

Emily was resolute in her decision that she wanted nothing from the marriage. She wanted to do this project she had in mind, by herself. If she put any money in that came from the marriage then she'd feel beholden to Howard. As far as she was concerned he or his money had no part in any aspect of her life.

Brian put the best arguments forward he could; trying to persuade her she was being totally unfair to herself. A half share was no more than she deserved, most certainly after what she'd gone through and there was no logical reason to think of it as only Howard's money. But she was resolute.

Today she was here to see if Howard had signed and returned the petition on the basis she'd finally agreed with Brian. Once in his office she noted his disappointed expression. 'Nothing, I'm afraid,' responded Brian to her question how things were going.

'What happens now?' she asked impatient to get things moving.

'As he's out of the time limit to return the document it will go in the queue of the cases to be heard by the courts. I'm afraid it is now down to the speed of the courts, we are in their hands.'

'But I will be granted a divorce, won't I?' asked Emily with a hint of panic in her voice as this was so important to her.

'No worry on that score, you've got good grounds even if he tries to defend himself,' Brian tried to reassure her.

'How is the house going?' he asked trying to take her mind off the divorce.

She told him about Karen staying without giving anything away about her circumstances.

Then she outlined her plans for the house. Brian looked a bit dubious when he heard them, 'Are you sure you know what you are letting yourself in for?'

'Of course I do. At least as much as anybody can. I'm not a complete novice. I've certainly had to use my counselling skills on more than one occasion at College, in some very difficult circumstances. It gave me a lot of satisfaction being able to help people in need of advice. That's partly why I think this is an ideal solution for what to do with the house and for me also.'

'I must say I applaud you for the idea. I think you've probably hit on a winner although I have to say I don't think it will be very lucrative financially for you. Will you manage for money on the small amount you will earn? You do realise that house will cost a lot on upkeep?'

'Don't worry, I'll be fine,' she said with more confidence that she felt.

Income was a major source of concern to her as she knew she needed money. More so since she had revised her plans. Once she'd hit upon the idea of the residents she wanted to accommodate then she decided it would be prudent to convert the garage into a self contained unit for herself to live in. After all her years of tolerating Howard she was sure at times she would appreciate her own home to shut herself away in solitude. She'd enough common sense to realise a lot of the time would be spent in the main house and she wouldn't want it to be any other way.

Once back home she forced herself to go back into the study. The quicker it was done the better if she wanted to get going and start earning money.

Pulling open drawers, just as she'd anticipated, she found a bundle of photographs. She browsed through these and recognised pictures which she was sure were of her grandmother. Once she started looking through them she couldn't stop.

There was only one of her as a relatively old lady, but Emily sat looking at it a long time. What she saw was a tall, upright lady with a mass of unruly white hair wearing a floating skirt of bright colours and cotton top to match. Despite it being obvious from the style of clothes that she was already elderly, there was still something of a youthful air about her. The face looking back at Emily, as if staring straight into her eyes, was full of vitality. Emily picked one up that depicted Elena's youth and she could see how kind the passing of the years had been to her. Had she looked at herself in a mirror when she was the same age as her grandmother in the photo she would have seen the close resemblance to each other.

She put them down reluctantly, she knew she must get on with the job if it was ever to be finished. Turning to the main part of the desk she quickly sorted through. She pulled a small drawer open and her hand jumped back in alarm seeing the envelope it contained, as she could already see the words 'To my Granddaughter — Emily Cartwright'.

A letter addressed to her? Sense took over

as she remembered Brian saying her grand-mother had kept track of her and she obviously knew of her existence to have willed the house to her.

She wasn't sure what she should do with the letter — should she take it to Brian? The envelope was addressed to her so why shouldn't she open it?

It was strange to see her unknown grand-mother's writing on a piece of paper in front of her and the words 'Dear Emily,' on it.

If you are reading this letter then I will be dead and you will be in possession of the house.

No doubt at this moment you are sorting my desk out. You will have wondered, I am sure, why I left the house to you.

I want to explain myself then you may understand things a lot clearer.

I was an only child of Mildred and George Hartwell. I'd a happy childhood as my parents were very much in love with each other creating a caring environment for me to be brought up in.

I wouldn't say I was particularly close to one or the other of my parents as I loved them both. I never went short; there was always plenty of money for the little luxuries of life.

Sadly, when I was fourteen my father was knocked down by one of the motor cars we all had to get used to in our lives.

It was a cruel irony as he had survived the 1914–1918 war without any injury. Mother and I had thought ourselves very lucky to get him back unscathed.

It was a tremendous shock for both of us when he died from his injuries. Mother was beside herself with grief and shut me out of her life.

I went through a spell where I thought she was blaming me somehow for what had happened. I wasn't old enough to understand it was only part of her grief. My own life was equally devastated by the loss of my lovely kind and gentle father.

I soon learned it best to keep out of my mother's way when she was in one of her black moods. It therefore came as a great shock when eighteen months after my father's death she announced she was going to get married to Albert Robertson. Now you'll see where my surname, as you will know it, came from. It was through the church that they had met.

Albert insisted that I became known as his child, which seemed terrible to me, casting my memories of my beloved father to one side in that fashion. Actually he wasn't half as dreadful as I imagined he would be.

Albert was a widower and had one son about my age. His wife had died many years previously when the son was a young child. One of Albert's sisters had helped him bring up the boy. Looking back I think she rather resented the marriage and my mother.

Henry — that was my stepbrother's name, was a very attractive young man with an equally pleasant nature. By some twist of fate we seemed thrown together in each other's company as much to my surprise my mother had only eyes for Albert, just as she'd been with my father, but this time leaving me out of their affection. After the love between my mother and father I never thought she was capable of such love again, but it appears she was.

The next part of my story is difficult to tell to you and I am only glad I won't be around to see your reaction. Nobody but Albert, Henry, my mother and obviously I know the secret, but Henry and I became closer than stepbrother or sister. There I've said it and no doubt totally shocked you with this statement. But don't think too badly of me, it resulted from the circumstances although I know I have to also take some blame for what happened. But on the other hand if you do take after me you may be more liberal in your views than many people. You could well imagine what would have happened had this story got out when I was young. I'm sure I'd have been in a mental institution for the rest of my life. Here Albert and my mother were very protective of my secret shame and for that I thank them from the bottom of my heart.

So yes, we became lovers and your mother was the result of the union. Albert and my mother were appalled that I was pregnant and using very persuasive means found out who was the father of the baby.

I was quickly despatched to Preston to give birth then subsequently have the baby adopted. Even if I had managed to stay at home I would have only been able to keep the baby for six weeks then it would have been adopted, as that was the procedure in those days. There was no such thing as a single mum. So as far as they were concerned it was better for me to go away, have it adopted and nobody any the wiser.

This was against Henry's and my wishes, but in those days a young lady in that situation had no say in the matter and had to be thankful not to be put away in a home for the rest of her life.

I was very sad at the loss of the child — the lovely baby girl I had given birth to — your mother. By the time I arrived back home Henry had vanished. It was many years later I found out he had been vanquished to a life on the seas and none of us ever heard anything from him again. I often think about him and how he fared as he was such a lovely, gentle young man. Did he survive the harsh life of a sailor? Who knows? That will never be answered but I have never forgotten him and our love. I suppose today the way I felt after the birth and handing over of the baby would be described as depression, but at that time my mother and Albert thought I had gone a little mad. Thankfully, they did keep me at home and nursed me themselves to hide my illness. As I said earlier they had done everything to keep me out of a mental institution. I slowly recovered my senses but never regained enough confidence to enjoy the social circles as I should have in that age.

As mother and Albert grew older both kept poor health and I took it upon myself to nurse them, as I saw it as my punishment for my earlier sinful life. They hadn't deserted me in my time of need. By the time they both died, I found out to my shock and horror that all the money my father had left had been used to live on.

I can't leave you much inheritance, only the house. I've had to sell most things of value to supplement my pension. There are a couple of things I've left for you personally. If you look in the same drawer where you found this letter you will find a small secret compartment.

In there are two pieces of jewellery which I have been led to believe are valuable. They belonged to my mother. I tried my best to hang on to these so I could leave them to you.

Do as you please with them. Don't think because I kept them that you have to. I only wanted to leave them to you to sell, should you need to do so.

All I ask is that you lead a happier life than I have and you make the house full of fun and laughter as it deserves to be.

Don't think too badly of me after all I have revealed to you.

Your ever-loving grandmother — Elena.

By the time Emily had finished reading the letter she was sobbing her heart out for the sadness of this old lady and the very unhappy life she had led. The tears became mingled with tears of sadness for herself. She was glad Howard would never see this letter because it didn't bear thinking about how he would behave if he knew the contents.

She quickly found the secret compartment as described in the letter and opened it to reveal the jewellery. One piece was delightful — a pendant made of emeralds and diamonds which obviously were not imitation stones. The chain also had some diamonds and emeralds set in the links. It was beautiful and very delicate.

There was a brooch which appeared too ostentatious. It was twisted in an abstract shape and was very large. The diamonds were large, they looked like imitation stones but their perfect glow told Emily otherwise. She had enough sense to realise that it must be a valuable piece.

Nevertheless she made an instant decision that she would never part with the pendant, but the brooch was different altogether. She may need the money from that in order for her to do all she wanted.

★   ★   ★

She heard Karen's voice calling to her that tea was ready and put the jewellery back in its secret compartment, realising she must visit a larger town and get the jewellery valued then put in a safe deposit box.

She called back to Karen, 'Be with you in a minute.'

Then she said quietly as if her grandmother could hear, 'Thank you for all you've done, you don't know how much it means. I'll bring this house alive again in memory of you, I promise.'

9

Howard had been shocked to receive the divorce petition. He'd never suspected for a minute that Emily had so much courage for something so radical. He was furious and unsure what to do about it. For the first time in their marriage something was happening over which he had no control.

In some ways it had been quite pleasant not having her around the house, behaving like a scared mouse and always tiptoeing around, afraid to speak in case she upset him. If she'd shown any sign of an opinion of her own he'd not have found her half as interesting in their courting days. He got delight from his sadistic treatment of her. But as the marriage progressed this behaviour of hers began to irritate him, wishing he was married to somebody of more equal mind and ability. On the other hand she was an excellent housekeeper and he felt proud of how spick and span his home always looked. He'd have never have admitted it to her but he admired her holding down a full-time job and still carrying out all her wifely duties. She knew how to cook and he was already missing her delicious meals.

He was not going to make it easy for her if she was really determined on this course of action. He couldn't believe she was strong minded enough to carry out the course of action she was on and thought the solicitor had put her up to it. He still expected her to walk through the door at anytime begging and pleading with him to take her back. Of course, if she did that he wouldn't agree straight away. Why should he? She'd made these last few weeks difficult enough for him. His lovely house was loosing its sparkle and Howard couldn't stand things that didn't look perfect.

If she really persisted in this divorce, he wouldn't make that easy for her either. He would have to play it canny because, in actual fact, he recognised her generosity in not requesting half share of everything. He was sure this must be against her solicitor's advice. If he'd realised he'd have got away so easily with no settlement, had the right opportunity come along, he may well have divorced her years ago.

He decided he would not return the divorce petition straight away, he would show her he wasn't a pushover. If she still continued with the action then no doubt just prior to the court proceedings he would agree to settle out of court. He wasn't having his personal details aired in a court for anybody to hear and he didn't see why it should cost him more than necessary to get rid of the stupid bitch.

★　★　★

Meanwhile, Emily hadn't troubled herself unduly that Howard had not returned the petition to the court. She was well used to his petty, mean minded little ways and now felt very confident that the course of action she was taking was the right one. Had the house transferred some of her grandmother's strength of will to herself? She no longer felt afraid and intimidated by Howard. In reality this strength had always been there but had lain dormant due to the circumstances in which she had always found herself in.

Now she had more to worry her mind about than when she had first arrived. Her friend Karen, despite seeming to have more energy still often wept in the privacy of her own room at night. Emily had heard her crying during the day when she must obviously have thought there was nobody in hearing distance.

Although Karen made a pretence at eating adequate meals to build her strength up, most of the time it was obvious to Emily she simply moved the food around the plate from one side to the other, with her finally saying, 'I'm stuffed. I can't eat another bite.' Emily knew most of the meal went in the bin.

In Emily's opinion Karen seemed to have low self esteem, even having doubts whether she was capable of carrying out the catering for Emily. Whereas Emily knew she could carry out the task easily.

Emily had seen this kind of behaviour before in a work colleague and was pretty certain it was depression. She'd still a lot of work to do to get her own life back on an even keel and they both had the constant worry of a husband. Alan, would track Karen down and who knew what he'd get up to then. Emily gave a shudder at the thought. But Karen became obsessed that every time there was a knock on the door or the phone rang that it was him. She'd turn into a shaking wreck unable to move towards answering either. All colour would leave her face and she only returned to a modicum of normality when she realised it wasn't him.

How could she get Emily to the local doctors? When she thought about it, they both needed to go, in any case, to register themselves as patients.

Emily mentioned it to Karen as tactfully as

she could and suggested, 'Maybe it would be a good idea if we went along to the doctors to register then you could make an appointment for yourself to have a check up.'

She was sure Karen was on the point of refusing so she quickly went on, 'Because you are sleeping badly and look so pale, maybe you're just anaemic. I think that can make you feel pretty grotty.'

Karen conceded, glad her friend had not taken the matter any further.

'So do you think it would be worth a try on iron pills if the doctor agreed to that?' Emily persisted.

'You are probably right,' she answered with her usual apathy.

'I'll make an appointment for us to go along and register.' Emily was glad Karen seemed to have given in so easily but it was really due to lack of interest.

At the surgery Emily could see her friend looked genuinely afraid of seeing the doctor so she suggested, 'Look, do you want me to come in with you?'

'Yes, please,' Karen replied with relief.

As they walked into the doctor's room it was Emily's turn to blanch as she instantly recognised the dark hair over the eyebrow without even hearing the voice. The eyes looking at them both gave no hint of recognition which rather unbalanced and upset Emily. Nobody would ever think they'd met previously and held a conversation, although rather one sided and in odd circumstances.

When Karen had outlined the sleepless nights and excessive tiredness Emily felt she'd to butt in and mention some of the other symptoms. The doctor carried on and ignored Emily after the comments and instead asked Karen, 'Have you gone through any major trauma or stressful situation in your life recently?'

'Yes,' was the most Karen would divulge.

'Hmm, I think it would be a good idea to put you on a course of anti-depressants, they are non-addictive. Once you feel better you'll be able to stop taking them. They will help you get through the bad times.'

'Whatever you think,' Karen replied in a resigned voice, although Emily could see a slight glimmer of relief that he was trying to do something to help her.

Outside the surgery Emily said to her, 'That wasn't too bad was it?' Although if she'd been asked this herself she'd have had to say she felt a little shaky at the total lack of recognition from the doctor to herself. She just hoped she'd set her friend on the road to recovery.

It was time again to think of her own problems about money. She decided Leeds was probably the best place to take the jewellery for valuation and after enquiring around found out 'Terry's' was a very reliable firm. She had intended making a visit to Hull but never seemed to have got around to doing it. Now she had the excuse to go.

She browsed around the shops as she had time to spare, clinging tight hold of her bag, and she realised how deprived of fun shopping she had always been. Her shopping had been confined to the Co-op in Hornsea and a small indoor market attached to an amusement arcade.

She gently touched the fabrics and admired the new winter season's designs but despite the temptation, avoided buying herself anything as she knew she had to conserve her money. It wasn't as if she was in need of new clothes with her current lifestyle.

She did allow herself the indulgence of buying one or two small Christmas presents but it came as a shock to her to realise she'd not many to buy. As a present for Karen she chose a glittery top because she had brought so few clothes with her and Emily knew she had always been up to the minute in dress style.

She couldn't put it off any longer and went

to the jewellers, with slight trepidation in case she was making a total fool of herself and the stones were paste.

The pleasant young man admired the pieces in consultation with the senior colleague. The valuations, were a pleasant shock to Emily.

She asked, 'If I decide to sell, more particularly the brooch, do you buy such articles?'

'We only deal in new jewellery. What we could do was organise to buy them off you for other people but it would be better to send them to an auction at one of the larger houses in London. I'll write all the details down then you can phone them to make the initial contact. We've done that before for them so they know us.'

He saw her to the door and opened it and Emily walked out in a bemused state feeling she was in another world. Here she was, Emily Cartwright, talking about going to sell a very valuable piece of jewellery at a major auction house.

She headed back home with a sense of relief, knowing the next day she must put the items in a bank.

She was shocked and surprised to see a new car parked on the driveway that she didn't recognise. It wasn't Howard or any of his friends, so she only hoped it wasn't Karen's husband here to cause trouble, having left her on her own.

With trepidation she entered the hall to hear a voice she recognised. It was the doctor. Now a different panic took over as she rushed to where the voice was coming from thinking there was something amiss with Karen. She pulled up short with shock when she saw them both sitting having a cup of tea and chatting away quite happily. 'Oh, hello,' greeted Karen. 'Just in time for a cup of tea.'

'Thanks,' she said instead, feeling rather uncomfortable in her own home.

'Karen has been telling me the outlines of your proposals for this house. It sounds a splendid idea,' the doctor said.

Karen looked slightly sheepish as she asked, 'I hope you don't mind that I've mentioned it and I haven't spoken out of turn?'

'It's no secret,' Emily said rather more abruptly than she intended. 'We will have to promote it eventually if we are going to get any residents, so it doesn't matter.'

'Oh, good,' said Karen, looking pleased.

'So you approve, doctor,' she asked.

'Yes, most definitely, and please call me David.'

'I'm so glad you do,' she replied with a hint

of sarcasm. Then carried on in a normal tone of voice, 'My solicitor has some reservations about the effectiveness of the venture but I'm not out to make myself masses of money. I just want to see other people happy and give myself a contented feeling in the process. As long as I can keep body and soul together that's all that counts.'

'I applaud you for your approach.' Emily could sense this was said genuinely with no sarcastic overtures.

'Your grandmother would have approved,' he added.

Emily was taken aback because she couldn't remember having mentioned she was Elena Robertson's granddaughter when they met in the drive, and in the surgery he never even spoke to her. 'You knew her, didn't you? I remember you saying so when we met before.'

Now it was Karen's turn to look perplexed as she didn't know these two had met before. There had been no hint of recognition from either of them that time in the surgery.

'I did know her and as I said before a very fine old lady she was. I enjoyed my visits here and often stayed longer than I should chatting to her. She told me all about you. She was a very astute lady, and kept tabs on you whatever you were doing.'

Seeing Emily's dismayed face he added, 'Not in a nasty or nosy way. It meant so much to her to know she had a granddaughter. She was also a lonely old lady and at times I suspected very sad.' Here he paused for the words to sink in.

Emily asked rather hesitantly, 'She didn't suffer in the end, did she?'

'No, not at all, but I think we'll discuss that further another time. I have other calls to make. I am so pleased to see the tablets are agreeing with you, Karen, and you've no side effects. But if you need me you know where to find me.'

'Yes,' Emily stuttered, and added, 'Feel free to call on us anytime if you are in need of a cup of tea.' She felt foolish at having said this and could feel her face turning red.

'You're a dark horse,' challenged Karen as soon as he'd left. 'Not a word said that you knew him.'

'I didn't know him as such,' Emily blustered. She went on to explain. 'Not in the way you mean. On my first night here I hadn't the keys for the house, so I looked around outside. A voice asked me what I was doing. It was only when the moon came out that I saw his face, but he never introduced himself or said he was the doctor. I took him to be a nosy neighbour. I was as shocked as you are now when I saw him sat in the surgery.'

'You didn't say anything then,' accused Karen.

'There seemed no point. He'd made no indication he recognised me. And there again why should he?'

Emily could feel something very new happening to her. A slight feeling of jealousy that Karen obviously considered him a very nice chap and the feeling seemed mutual, the way David had been chatting to Karen when she arrived home.

He took it upon himself to call in regularly for a cup of tea and a chat with one or the other of them.

One day he rooted out Emily saying he had something to ask her. Emily felt her heart drop into her boots as she was certain he wanted to know more about Karen's background before he tried to take the relationship any further.

When he began with the words, 'I have a patient,' Emily gave a gasp of surprise. He asked with concern in his voice, 'Are you all right?'

'Er, yes, just a drop of tea went down the wrong way. I'm fine now. What were you saying?'

'I have this patient, Harry Fowler. He's in

his early eighties but still as spry as a man in his late sixties. At present he's in a residential home. His wife had to go into a nursing home when she became very ill and eventually they had to sell their own home, furniture and main possessions to fund the cost. She lingered a long time and when she died there was no money left for him. The do-gooders thought they should be in a home together. Once his wife had died he didn't need to be in a nursing home so they moved him to a residential home. It's no place for him; his mind is still too active. There's nothing wrong with him apart from what comes to us all — the ageing process. But he'll not last much longer if he's left to vegetate as he is at present in the home. Then I thought of your place here. It would be ideal as he doesn't want to rent anywhere, besides which, as I said before he's no furniture and to be honest it would be a lot of upkeep for a man of his age. I know this house is not ready yet but I am desperate to get him moved from that home and as soon as possible.

Emily felt filled with compassion. After a moment she said, 'Can you give us a week? The heating's just about finished so it'll be running by then, at his age it's important to keep warm. I'm sure we can get one of the bedrooms ready. The washbasins have been put in each of them.' Then another thought struck her. 'Is he capable of going upstairs? Because we haven't a lift'

'Probably better than me.' Here David laughed, it was the first time Emily had seen him do that. She decided he should do it more often as it softened the harshness of his features.

'I can see no problem then. Oh, but there is one vital question — does he want to come here?'

'I haven't asked him yet because I didn't want to disappoint him if you said no. But I've no worry on that score, he'll gladly accept.'

Emily was beginning to feel less confident and wondering what she was taking on. 'I hope he will be happy here with us.'

'He will. Take a look at what it's done to Karen.'

'Yes, of course,' replied Emily, feeling irritated he had to remind her of his apparent feelings for Karen.

'If I brought him along next Friday morning, will that suit?'

'It will be ready for him. Thanks for finding me my first resident. I appreciate it. Now that's one room gone.'

'It's a pleasure.'

10

Emily was in a frenzy getting the room ready for Harry. She was excited yet petrified because this was her first official resident. Karen was her friend, so it had been easy to take her in.

Doubts went through her mind. What if they took an instant dislike to each other? Would he really be as capable as David had made out? Despite the fact she wanted to make a good life for her residents, it wasn't her intention that it became a residential home for the elderly. She wasn't trained to be a care assistant.

What she wanted was the place to be a sort of permanent refuge for those in need, young and old alike, still able to tend to their own needs. Some may have traumas causing them anxiety and she wanted them to help each other.

This set off a new train of worry. What if any young residents could not deal with the elderly? Would various ages mix? It wasn't only different ages that wouldn't necessarily get on. Had the whole idea had been stupid? Karen took the more sensible approach.

'It'll be fine,' she said reassuringly. 'Look, David wouldn't have recommended you if he hadn't thought it were the right set-up for this chap, Harry. Trust me, I've seen how you deal with people and you seem to have an affinity with anybody from any age group or background.'

'You think so?' Emily asked, still with doubt in her voice.

'I know so,' replied Karen convincingly. 'Look at it this way; anything must be better than a residential home for Harry. It can be no pleasure for him sitting around all day. After all, they do say being around the young helps you keep young yourself. Anyway, you might end up with all old people here.'

'I do hope we get a mixture of age groups otherwise if we're not careful it could become recognised as an old people's home. What colour to paint his room? We want to make it bright and cheery, yet a gentleman from his generation must surely think some colours are only suitable for females.'

Karen chipped in, 'What about a pale green. That's supposed to be one of a restful colour yet it's not too drab or feminine.'

'Good idea and we will get curtains and bedding to tone in with that, but not a flower design.'

Emily, despite her reservations, was enjoying getting the room ready. If the money hadn't seemed to be going so quickly she would have enjoyed it even more. She was pleased when David called to see her.

'I've set in progress the organising for his fees to be paid directly to you,' he said to her.

Realising how lacking in business skills she must seem Emily exclaimed, 'I never asked you how he would find the money to pay if he had none left after paying all the nursing home fees for his wife.' It dawned on her that his fees for the residential home were obviously being paid for from somewhere.

'It's been sorted out with the help of his pension and income support. As he's getting his meals provided he'll just be given some spending money back.'

Emily felt contrite that she appeared to be taking all his money and voiced her concerns.

'Don't worry,' responded David, sensing her distress. 'He's more than happy with the arrangement. It's the same where he is now but as he sees it he's paying for something he's not happy with there. Already he's convinced he's going to be very happy here and he's even said to me he'd do without any spending money.'

'Oh, poor man, to feel like that. You must make sure he is left with enough money for himself otherwise however will he be able to feel he's leading as normal a life as possible in his circumstances?'

'His room — is it finished?'

'It is, just about, there are a few last minute touches required,' Emily said proudly. 'Would you like to see it?'

'Of course, why else do you think I'm here?' he replied laughing.

Emily was delighted with the overall effect that had been created. All the rooms were well proportioned. Although without en-suite facilities, she was having two bathrooms installed for the six bedrooms and there was a further toilet on the landing and another bathroom downstairs. She had created a small area in one alcove with an all-in-one unit of a sink, two burner stove, fridge and a storage cupboard. Although the meals would be prepared for those who wanted them, she felt this would give the residents a feeling of independence. They could make themselves a cup of tea or a snack in their room whenever they wanted. She had put in a bed, wardrobe, chest of drawers, small desk and a very comfortable armchair so he could sit and watch TV in the privacy of his room. Some of the downstairs living rooms had too much furniture in them so she was spreading it around the rooms and cutting down on expense. She was aware that Harry was bringing his own TV.

'Well done. This is ideal.'

Emily asked hesitantly, 'Do you think I've put him in enough furniture?'

'Plenty,' he reassured her.

He saw the small kitchen hidden away, 'What a brilliant idea. Will all the rooms have one of these fitted in them?'

'Yes.'

'Marvellous idea. I don't know where on earth you found them but they couldn't be better for accommodation like this.'

Emily added, 'I also intend to get the larger kitchen modernised and fitted out with a table in the middle — farmhouse style and apart from special occasions, we would all eat in there. It will be informal. The residents will be allowed in the small kitchen that exists now, for their own use if they want to prepare a larger meal than they can on the stove in their room. It will give them the opportunity to entertain their own guests without cutting them off from a normal lifestyle. There will be a sitting room for them if they want to relax along with others. I'm afraid Harry will have to manage the best he can until that work is completed. But I did warn you he was coming a bit sooner than I intended.'

'He'll not worry about anything like that. What about you, where do you get your privacy?'

'I don't really at the moment,' Emily admitted, and then she went into great detail explaining her plans for the garage, so as to make herself a small cottage.

David seemed to sense a slight hesitancy in her. 'You sound as if you're not too sure. It can't surely be the thought of living alone?'

'No, it's nothing like that. I've got to wait and see if there's any money left over for the work to be done. But that's my problem not yours.'

At this point Karen entered the hall and smiled sweetly at David. 'I didn't know you were here. Have you just arrived?'

'Actually I'm just leaving,' he explained.

'Tea?' Karen queried.

'No time, I'm afraid.'

'I'll see you out then' Karen said.

For the first time Emily felt annoyed with her friend that she'd butted into her business and conversation. There was too much for her to get on with to spend time brooding on it.

★ ★ ★

On Friday morning Emily had a shock when David's car drew up and the man who was supposed to be elderly got out. If David hadn't told her his true age she would never have thought of him in his eighties. He looked

114

like he was in his late sixties, or early seventies.

He was a tall, dignified, upright man like her father had been, but as soon as he spoke she knew he was of a much gentler character. He had a low kindly voice without the harshness of her father's.

With tears showing in his eyes he clutched hold of her hand. 'You don't know how much I appreciate you doing this for me. You've no need to fret; I won't be a burden to you. If you'll let me I would still like to pull my weight where I can to help you.'

'You're doing me a good turn coming here as I'm sure David has told you that you are our first resident. I only hope you can cope with all the disruption whilst the work gets finished. As for doing jobs, feel free, because that's the idea. I want you to treat this like your home, which of course it will be.'

'Come on; let's show you your room so you can get settled in.'

He was delighted with his room. He exclaimed, 'What lovely colour sense you have, my dear. You've made this room light, warm and homely. It reminds me very much of how Edna would have decorated a room.'

'Was that your wife?' queried Emily.

'No,' he replied with a closed expression.

Emily felt a fool that she'd made a blunder

so early on in the stage of them getting to know each other. Seeing her contrite look he said kindly, 'Don't worry, I don't mind you asking. It's all such a long time ago now and they're all dead, but me. When you've a few minutes to spare I'll explain it all to you.'

'Oh there's no need for that,' replied Emily, not wanting to intrude into what was obviously a very private part of his life.

'Of course there is, my dear. I want no secrets, if this is to be my home.'

After this induction into her new lifestyle she felt even more impatient to get the project completed.

Harry fitted in more easily than she could ever have hoped and he put many of his practical skills to good use. Emily was wary at first to let him help in case it over exerted him but when she asked David's opinion she had to review this idea.

David stated bluntly, 'It'll do him a world of good. That's what he needs. It's not work that will kill Harry but boredom and the feeling he's no good to anybody.'

'I've plenty I can find for him to do,' she said relieved.

She was not sure how to continue what she wanted to say next on the same subject because it was a bit more of a sensitive question, yet she wanted to know so she stammered, 'Er, what about pay?'

David looked blankly at her, 'Pay, what pay?'

'To Harry for the work he's doing.'

David gave a hearty laugh. 'He doesn't want to be paid. If I know Harry it'll be his way of thanking you for making him so happy. Call it a labour of love.'

'If you're sure, I feel a bit mean him doing things I'd have to pay other people to do.'

'He would be insulted if you tried to pay him. Believe me, best leave well alone.'

Harry had been there a week or two and was fully settled in when he and Emily were sitting together having a quiet coffee break when he said, 'If you remember, my dear, on my first day here I said I'd explain things about my past.'

Seeing her puzzled expression he carried on, 'I said I'd explain when I mentioned that Edna wasn't my wife. No, you see I was married to Martha, Edna's sister. When I met Martha I thought she was perfect. I fell for her apparent charm and looks. She was so desirable and appealed to me because she obviously needed somebody to take care of her. Edna, her sister was abroad. By the time she arrived back Martha and myself were married. It soon became apparent I'd made a grave mistake in my choice of wife. I'd been deceived by Martha; she was really spoilt and pampered and expected me to carry on treating her like that. She expected everyone to run after her every whim and she was a hypochondriac. If it wasn't one supposed illness, then it was another. Meanwhile there was Edna, a woman with a genuine medical condition, yet you'd never have known it. She'd been born with a heart defect, you see. In those days they couldn't do what they can do today to repair hearts. Not one word of complaint ever passed her lips. Whilst Martha was moaning and getting lazier and grew bigger as weight poured on to her, I fell deeply in love with Edna. I really learned what loving somebody was all about and there wasn't a damned thing I could do about it. I desperately wanted a family as I loved children. I'd always presumed that when I married I'd have a family, a large one. But Martha wasn't having any of it. She argued her body wasn't strong enough for bearing my children. Then she started to deny me my marital rights, saying she wasn't taking any chances on becoming pregnant.'

Seeing Emily's surprised face he laughed, 'That's shocked you hasn't it? One of my generation talking about such personal things. But I'll shock you even further. Edna and I became lovers. I knew she must never

118

have my child due to her poor health but she'd have even risked that to give me what I wanted. Divorce in those days wasn't easy and I suppose I was too weak to get out of my marriage. Besides, I knew if I left Martha she would then try emotional blackmail, no doubt creating some illness and saying she was about to die. It would have been worse with the woman I loved being her sister. You could imagine the gossip and I couldn't have done that to Martha, however she behaved towards me. So we carried on our lives as lovers, meeting whenever we could, which wasn't as often. Sadly, we didn't have long to enjoy our love as poor Edna's heart gave up. Even at her funeral I could only show my grief as her brother-in-law, not as her lover. I was left to cope with Martha as best I could. I muddled along letting my mind wander back to my memories to help me get through. As she became older Martha's illnesses became genuine, although I've to say none of us really believed her. Then as if to thwart me she lingered on and on. The rest you know, it cost us all we had in money to keep her in a nursing home. So you see at the end of all that I was left with exactly nothing.'

Emily stood up to put her arms around Harry's shoulder. 'I'm sorry.'

'Nay, it's not your fault, my dear. Don't be

sad for me, I've got a lot of good memories of my time with Edna. Taking me in here has renewed my confidence in the human race.'

'Thank you, Harry. You've helped me with that, as I was having doubts about what I was trying to do.'

'Never do that, you've made a real sanctuary here for those in need of it.'

The fact that this man had gone through so much yet held no bitterness gave Emily the much needed motivation to move forward with her own life.

Harry had got to know Emily and was beginning to appreciate what a nice person she was. He let out a silent sigh as he thought, 'If only I was forty years younger,' then gave himself a mental shake deciding he was a foolish old man with fanciful ideas.

11

Emily was so busy she'd not time to stop and brood on what had happened to her so far in her life. But last night, like so many nights recently, she'd had a terrible nightmare. It stayed with her all day with a feeling that she had really lived through it. In her dream she had lost the house, Howard had used cunning and guile to get it off her. As she was removed from the house forcibly, by a large, ugly man, she was kicking and screaming, 'It is my house. You can't do this to me. It was left to me by my grandmother. She wanted me to have it.' The ugly face just carried on leering at her, dragging her out of the house. Then Howard turned round to her and snarled, 'I can do anything I want with you. You're my wife, so shut up and do as you're told.'

She had screamed, 'I won't be your wife much longer.'

Then Howard would turn even more fiercely on her and shout, 'You're tied to me forever, so get that into your head.' Then he'd laugh and laugh with a terrifying sound. She had to stand and watch Karen, Harry and other residents she couldn't identify turned out despite their protests. Their belongings were flung from the windows. Personal possessions flew out of the windows with everybody having to duck to avoid being hit by it.

Then David would appear, pleading their cause to Howard who was watching it all with a smug expression then he laughed again when David begged on their behalf. David turned and walked away with his arm around Karen. Emily felt her heart was breaking both at losing her home and David's friendship.

When she woke she was bathed in sweat and it took her a few minutes to separate the dream from reality. Yet in the light of day it did appear a ridiculous dream, just as it really was. It still left a feeling of emptiness as if she had really lost everything precious to her.

She decided it was time to tackle the attics to put her mind on other things. She'd only cast a cursory glance up there and deduced there was nothing of real importance to sort out. A plan began to formulate in her mind. As she started to move around she noticed, for the first time some trunks. She removed dust sheets and pushed through things to reveal other pieces of furniture that would do very nicely for some of her refurbishing. She noted some that she would keep back to use for her own small dwelling, if and whenever it was completed.

It was time to part with the brooch. She'd still have the pendant left to keep but the sale of the brooch would certainly allow her to have her own small self contained unit.

If anybody had asked her, she would have said she was enjoying the companionship of Karen and Harry and also hoped she would of future residents. But she was beginning to realise once the house was full, she'd never have a quiet moment to herself. She supposed it was in her nature, but solitude seemed imperative to her. She liked to be able to choose the peace and quiet when she desired it and at other times, she would feel lonely and need companionship.

It was very strange to be in charge of her own destiny. Howard had always made decisions. If she'd ever put any of her thoughts or ideas forward, he'd say, 'Talk sense woman.'

In the end it was easier not to think of her own ideas or voice them. Now it was her choice to do something and if it didn't work she'd only herself to blame. It was a very new approach to life for her and unsettling at times.

Opening the first trunk she exclaimed in

delight at the gorgeous clothes. Judging by their tiny size she recognised they couldn't have belonged to her grandmother so presumed they had been her great-grandmother's. She held some up to herself but as she peered into a mirror, she'd found in the attic, it soon became obvious they were far too short for her. She must have inherited her grandmother's tall stature. She gently laid the clothes back in the trunk appreciating all the care that had gone into keeping them in their preserved condition.

As she was mulling over past events so Karen was sitting having a coffee and highlighting some of her concerns with Harry. Never before had she found it so easy to talk to a comparative stranger as she could Harry. She felt she'd known him years rather than weeks.

He'd seen her worried expression and said, 'Come on, out with it. What's troubling you today?'

Harry had already been given a good briefing from Karen about her life with Alan. Having had such an unhappy marriage himself he was full of understanding and compassion.

He tried to probe further. 'That husband of yours, has he tracked you down to living here? Is that what your problem is?'

'No, don't even suggest things like that or I'll panic.'

'Right. We've ascertained that's not causing you any trouble, so out with it then, what is worrying you? I know there is something.'

Karen did want to tell him but didn't really know where to start because to voice her concerns aloud sounded so pettish. David's visit again that morning had set thoughts in her mind. The excuse was that he'd called to check up on Harry. Karen knew it was really on one pretext or another and she was concerned where it was all going.

'It's David,' she said at last.

'David! He's a good doctor surely?' he replied, not comprehending at all what she was trying to say.

'There's no doubt about that, but it's all the calls he seems to be making here. It must be obvious to you that it's far more often than necessary.'

'I can't see what's wrong in a doctor being attentive.'

'But is that all it is?' Karen challenged.

'Of course, what else could it be?'

Karen replied quietly, feeling a bit stupid by putting her thoughts and fears into words. 'I'm concerned he fancies me.'

'Good gracious me, is that all?' he roared with laughter. 'When I was your age if a young and attractive woman had fancied me, I would have been very flattered. What is wrong in a young, handsome and unattached young man admiring you?'

'Yes, but it's not like that. I don't want him or any other man for that matter to fancy me. For the first time in my life I feel as if I am living my own life in my own way, making my own decisions and I am enjoying it. I don't want to be beholden to anyone even if it is some kind and caring person like David. I want to live my own life my way with no emotional ties.'

'I get the idea.'

Karen rushed on. 'I think Emily has feelings for him but doesn't realise it yet, so you can see why it is even more important that he doesn't give his attention to me. They'd make a lovely couple.'

'You know, I think you may be reading too much into it. From where I stand he's equally as attentive to both of you.'

'You really think so?'

'I do.'

'Thanks Harry, that has put my mind at ease.'

'I'm here anytime, my dear. I like to think I still have some use.'

'You have a lot. Look at all you've done around here.'

'I've got to admit I haven't been as happy as this in years.'

★   ★   ★

Emily had opened the second trunk. More clothes. Emily judged them to have been worn when her grandmother was a young woman. As she dipped lower down into the chest she exclaimed aloud. 'Now what have we here? What's this?' she whispered in a shocked voice as a figurine appeared. She looked at it more closely then gave a gasp. It couldn't be! She turned it over to look underneath and it confirmed her suspicions. It looked very like a Chelsea Comedia Dell'Arte figure. Having seen one recently on an antiques programme it had particularly stayed in her mind, more importantly because they were rare and valuable figures. 'It can't be,' she muttered once more in amazement. She was pretty certain it was genuine as it was so beautifully made. This was unbelievable! Analysing her grandmother's personality she could imagine the delight she must have had in leaving this extraordinary gift for her granddaughter to find in this manner.

Emily made the decision not to disclose her find for the moment. She had been laughed at and hurt too much in the past by Howard

127

by his sarcastic comments on her knowledge and love for antiques. Now she knew her interest was beginning to pay off. If she hadn't followed antiques programmes and studied books she'd have been none the wiser about the figurine. She could have tossed it to one side as worthless. Howard would not have appreciated the beauty never mind the value. She held it lovingly knowing if it was confirmed to be what she thought then it would have to be sold to fund her future.

She put it back safely in the trunk for the moment. As she came back down and into the hall she saw Karen passing through. 'Got a minute or two? I've something I want to say to you.'

Karen felt the old feeling of dread. All she could think was that Emily was jealous of her about David and was going to tell her to leave. This seemed to be confirmed as Emily said, 'Karen, I hope you don't mind me asking but have you any plans to leave here in the near future or hopes that one day marriage might be on the cards?'

She managed to stutter, despite feeling like bursting into tears, 'I want to stay here as long as you'll have me and no, I never want to get married again, whoever I might meet.'

'Don't be too rash on that score but I am glad to hear it, as I want to outline a plan I've come up with which would involve your being here long term.'

'Oh,' replied Karen, who was stunned and near to tears with relief that she hadn't to go.

'I don't know if you've ever been up to the attic?'

She was glad she could say, 'No,' and genuinely mean it, as she had never pried into the personal elements of Emily's life without being asked.

'Right, we'll go up later on and have a look at them. But this is my plan. As you know, I'm going to make the garage into my own little home.'

Hearing this Karen thought Emily had changed her mind and was now thinking of converting the attic instead, more so when she heard the words, 'As there is a lot of room up there I thought I could convert the attic into a self-contained flat.'

'That will be nice for you. Save you having to go outside to get to your part.'

'Not for me; for you,' Emily quickly jumped in.

'Me?' she asked astounded.

'Yes, you. I want you to feel you have some life of your own. You are much too young to be relegated to living in one room. When we are up and running properly we must sort your hours of work into a regular routine. We can't have you working all hours.'

'But you can't make a flat for me,' Karen said still in a state of shock.

'Why not?' Emily demanded.

'All the expense and in any case I've already got a room.'

'Look, Karen, the way I see it, if you ever want to leave to move on with your life, the next person I employ will want accommodation to be more than just a room. So why shouldn't you have the benefit yourself.' 'Well . . .'

'Good, that's settled then,' replied Emily, feeling pleased with herself.

Karen was just on the point of opening her mouth to try to explain to Emily that she had no romantic feelings for David when the door bell rang.

'I'll get it,' said Karen seeing the expression on Emily's face in case it was Howard.

Emily gave herself a mental shake thinking how stupid it was that at one moment she could feel the new self-assured person she had developed into then the thought that Howard could be on her doorstep turned her into a quivering mess. More so when there was no real reason for her to think Howard would visit.

Karen came back into the room alone. 'There's a lady at the door asking for you.'

'For me?' Emily asked astounded and

relieved that the knock was so innocent.

'That's right, asked for you by name she did.'

'I'd better see what she wants,' replied Emily, fear now replaced by curiosity.

What was it about? Was it one of Howard's ploys to get back at her? She just never knew with him he was capable of anything.

When she saw the pleasant motherly smile on the woman's face she knew instinctively that it couldn't be anything to do with Howard as he would never have associated himself with a person such as the lady at the door.

She was plump, well, fat really, not very tall with red, obviously dyed, coloured hair.

'Can I help you,' Emily asked wondering what was coming.

'I hope so, love. I couldn't come before because I knew I was going to be called by my son-in-law at a moment's notice. It's my eldest you see. She's forty. I told her it was far too old to have her first babby, but she wouldn't listen.'

Aware that she could be standing there quite some time having to listen to the monologue, Emily interrupted, 'Won't you come into the kitchen?'

It became apparent that this woman knew her way around the house, as she moved straight across the hall to the kitchen doorway. Emily had a momentary panic wondering who she had actually let into the house.

The friendly voice carried on, 'Now where was I, love?' But Emily never had chance to reply as the voice continued without pausing for breath. 'Oh, yes, telling about my eldest. The call came, it took longer than I thought, but you can never tell with your first, can you, love? Anyway off I toddled, all the way to a place outside Leeds to hold her hand.' Emily had to smother the laugh bubbling up in her at the thought of this squat figure toddling all the way to Leeds. 'She was real scared, it being her first. She'd needed to be, I can tell you, love. I've never known anyone have such a difficult time. Thought we was going to lose her and the babby, we did. Thanks be to God they both pulled through. I had to stay, she was that weak. How could I leave her in that state and my oldest as well? Always has a special pull does your first born, isn't that so, love?' Again she carried on giving Emily no chance to answer. 'Anyway, I've just got back and I said to Fred, that's my hubby, I must go and see the lady who's moved into what was Elena Robertson's house.'

Here, at last she paused for breath, before she asked, 'Here, have I seen you before? You look familiar.'

'No, we've never met before,' replied Emily more sharply than she intended but she was beginning to wonder when the tale would end and where it was leading.

The voice carried on as if she hadn't noticed anything amiss. 'Yes, well, told my Fred I did, so here I am, love. I used to clean a couple of half days for Miss Robertson, 'cause that's all she could afford. So I wondered when I could start for you and if you'd need me more often.'

Emily had to listen intently to the dialogue as it was said with a broad East Riding accent. She was really lost for words by the last request.

Sensing the hesitation the woman spoke again with disappointment in her voice. 'I understand, you don't want me to clean for you at all. One of those new independents are you love, the type who prefers to do it all for themselves?'

'No, not at all,' replied Emily, rather indignantly. Then she continued more calmly, 'Look, don't you think you had better tell me your name first before we discuss it?'

'Silly of me to forget that, but I felt that flummoxed at having to come here, I clean forgot to announce myself. Joan, Joan Young. If the old lady was still alive she'd tell you I could be trusted. I did for her for well over twenty years. She really needed more help as she got older but sadly her money was running out so I came less often. Here, if you found the place a bit dirty and dusty that wasn't my cleaning to blame. I only kept her main rooms clean for her in the end. When she passed away the solicitor told me I was no longer needed, but I pointed out to him that if he hoped to sell it then it should be kept clean. But he'd have none of it.'

Managing to get a word in, Emily said, 'Actually, I was going to advertise for someone to clean, so you could be the answer. How would you feel about working five half days, some days I might even need you for a full day.'

'Aye, I'm right made up at that. Just wait 'til I tell Fred. Start in the morning, shall I, love?'

'As it's Friday tomorrow, why not give yourself a day or two's rest now you're back and start on Monday? By the way you never said whether your eldest had a son or daughter.'

For the first time Joan laughed. 'I am doing it again, only telling half the tale. My Fred always says my tongue runs away with itself. She had a lass, a lovely little girl — Charlotte. As for having a rest I don't know about that. I've my own home to sort out. You know what men are like left on their own. But I'll see you first thing on Monday morning then, love.'

She heaved herself out of the chair with much puffing and panting. Emily was already questioning herself whether she'd be capable for cleaning, but it was too late now.

Once she'd gone Emily did sit brooding. Was Howard making a mess now she wasn't there? Her light hearted humour returned and she laughed out aloud at the thought of Howard managing on his own, much to the amazement of Karen and Harry who were just walking back in the room.

12

Emily was beginning to feel concerned that Brian, the solicitor, or herself had not heard from Howard. Unconcerned about his well-being, for she was long past that stage, she was wary over what he was plotting in revenge for her request for the divorce. She knew him to be sly and cunning. He hadn't answered the solicitor's letters and was capable of anything. With no correspondence, she had nothing to work on so it was impossible to come to any conclusion.

While she was thinking about Howard, he at the same time was thanking his stars about the call that had come just at the most opportune time. He'd been shocked when he heard the words, 'Long time, and no see. What are you up to at the moment?'

Howard exclaimed in delight, 'Amanda, what a surprise. It's lovely to hear from you again. To be honest I'm at a bit of a loose end.'

'Ah, still playing the dutiful husband,' she answered with a slight hint of contempt.

'No,' answered Howard indignantly.

'Oh, I see — playing the little wife up again are you?'

'No, not that either. She's gone and left me,' he stated, sounding sorry for himself.

There was a pause at the other end of the line, and then Amanda finally said, 'Well you have shocked me with that. I'd never have thought she had the guts to do it. Mind you, I know they always say the quiet ones are the worst. Why on earth didn't you give me a ring, I could have kept you occupied on your lonely evenings,' she cooed.

'I hadn't realised you had returned to England, otherwise rest assured, I would have contacted you.'

'For once the grapevine doesn't seem to have been working very effectively,' she said with a slight hint of query in her voice.

Howard admitted, 'I haven't been to a lot of the old haunts recently. I couldn't really face them and let on to them what Emily had done to me. It would have looked like losing face.'

'Oh, poor Howard, do you want me to come and ease the ruffled feathers,' she said in a sexy voice.

'Are you back living in your old flat?' he asked.

'I am.'

'I'll come there. I don't want anything to get back to Emily that she could use in her grounds for divorce. You know what the

Tomlins are like next door. They always liked Emily. I don't know if she's made contact with them, so I don't want to chance it. But look it's rather late now and I've had a hectic day. I'll come straight to your place after work tomorrow so get the champagne on ice,' he said in his usual take it for granted attitude.

'Will do,' replied Amanda cheerfully.

Despite telling Amanda he was tired, sleep eluded him that night as thoughts of Amanda came back to haunt him. Out of all the women he'd taken up with, whilst married to Emily, he had cared for Amanda the most. She was actually a very astute person and they shared the same sadistic sense of humour. He'd felt quite a loss in his life when she'd taken the post offered to her to go and work in another branch of the magazine in America. She'd hadn't said but he presumed she was back for good. There again she'd not said why she'd come back, because as he'd understood it the move to the US was supposed to be permanent as it was a substantial promotion. She had sublet her flat, so when he thought about it now, she must have always kept that door open for a return if she needed it. He was glad she was back. This was just what he needed to bring him out of his lethargy and get him out and about again on the social scene.

★ ★ ★

As promised Joan had turned up promptly at Emily's on the Monday. Despite her build she was agile and meticulous with her work but Emily did wish she didn't chatter all the time she was cleaning. She'd told Emily many tales in such a short time about her family, and distant relatives, that Emily was at a total loss who each one was and where they fitted in.

Emily soon appreciated that deep down she was a kindly soul and despite all the relatives she also seemed lonely and helped anyone in need.

She and Harry appeared to have taken to each other and at times would engage in personal conversations together to the exclusion of all the others.

Emily had noticed, one morning, it was rather more peaceful than usual with Joan around. In fact, Emily was rather enjoying it. There now seemed something lacking in the atmosphere. Her own mind was brooding on Howard's silence which had gone on far too long. Her mind was taken up with the events of her own life to consider there could be anything amiss with Joan and her lack of cheerfulness.

At some point in the morning she was aware that Joan was a long time cleaning

Harry's room and thought that she was going to have to make a comment on it. If she chatted to each resident whilst doing the rooms of all the residents she'd never get her work done in the allocated time. Emily couldn't afford to pay her so she could spend her time gossiping.

It came as a surprise when Joan had left and Harry approached Emily, 'Can you spare me a few minutes to discuss Joan.'

Emily gave an inward groan convinced that Harry was going to make a complaint about her persistent chattering. She was taken aback when he said, 'I don't think you noticed how down Joan was today. Not that I'm blaming you because you have enough problems of your own. But this morning, whilst cleaning my room, she broke down in tears and the whole tale came out.'

Emily felt terrible that she'd somehow or other not really thought this of Joan who always seemed so chatty and cheery that Emily had presumed her to be happy with no worries of her own.

'I'm sorry, Harry, that it happened whilst she was in your room,' Emily said, feeling contrite that Joan had felt the need to tell a resident of the house instead of the owner.

But Harry didn't look at all put out as he said, 'Oh no, I'm glad she did. It made me feel useful that I could listen to her woes and even still be capable of offering a few words of advice.'

'Is she happier now?' she asked.

'Sort of, but this is where you come in, my dear.'

'Oh,' replied Emily, not really sure how she would be able to help.

'Yes, I'll recount the tale as she told me then you'll understand.'

'Do you think you should tell me? Joan told you in confidence,' she questioned.

'No, she doesn't mind at all you knowing, although she doesn't want it made public knowledge. This was part of the advice that I offered, that I would discuss it with you on her behalf.'

'Okay. What has been going on?'

'It's her niece, Rachel, her sister's only child. Her sister's had a different life to Joan by all accounts. Her sister's husband has worked hard and been fortunate in achieving a good job so they've never been short of money. Their only daughter has lacked for nothing. She says she always felt the poor lass was lonely and lacked the love she so obviously craved. Joan's sister did confide in her that she had always wanted more children but for one reason and another it never happened. Joan's not sure about her sister's husband, she never took to him and she's pretty certain by how he's behaved he's never wanted any more. In fact, she's rather uncertain whether he actually wanted the one they've got, Rachel. According to Joan he could be very hard on the lass, so she's had a strict upbringing despite being spoilt. The father had a real old fashioned view on letting Rachel have any kind of relationship with a boy — even an innocent one. Joan's certain it was because of the lack of love and affection from her father, who by the way she adored, that when she finally developed a serious relationship it was with a chap much older than herself. She kept this hidden from her father. Joan only saw him a couple of times, once at the wedding — by that I mean Rachel's wedding, and briefly when she called at her sister's house on a quick visit when Rachel was there. She said she could see why the girl had fallen for him as he was a good looking bloke in a swarthy sort of way. Joan thought him arrogant and self-opinionated despite him trying very hard to appear friendly. He looks younger than his age so Rachel lied about it to her parents making him appear nearer her own age.'

'Heck,' Emily said wondering where the tale was going.

'You'd have thought he'd have known

better, being mature, but he was very crafty and got her in the family way. Joan was very surprised when he actually agreed to marry Rachel. Luckily, he'd already got a small house of his own, tiny and a bachelor pad but he said they could live there at first then he'd get something better in time. Of course, Joan's sister not being short of money, decided as it was their only child they'd have the full works for the wedding. It was funny, Joan had thought, that the father having objected to the marriage at first, stating it was for the wrong reason, then suddenly gave it his full approval and that was it. Joan attended the wedding. She only wished she could have given her own daughter such a good day. Apparently Rachel had looked radiant but Joan said the chap looked as if he wished he was anywhere else but there and was impatient to get it all over and done with.'

'I know the sort.'

'Then sadly Rachel lost the baby. Joan said it was one of those things and nobody's fault, but she was about five months pregnant when she lost it so it was a tremendous shock for them all. Joan's sister kept telling her how Rachel had refused her offer to come home to be looked after until she felt better but constantly looked sad and was forever bursting into tears. Anyway, for some reason the bloke wanted to move them to Scotland. He said he had a better job opportunity there. So there it was they were off to Scotland. Of course, Joan's sister was heartbroken that her only child was moving so far away; besides which if she got pregnant again she wanted to be near her in case she needed extra care.'

'Oh, poor girl,' Emily exclaimed.

'Time went by with little correspondence from Rachel until suddenly Joan received a letter from her begging her aunt's help. She says she can't possibly go home to her parent's house. Joan is so worried and can't for the life of her imagine what it can be that makes Rachel want to come to her not her parents.'

'I suppose you want to ask if Joan can have time off when she comes and she didn't like to ask me herself. After all, she's not worked here that long.'

'No, it's not that at all,' Harry quickly jumped in then went on to explain. 'No, she'd love to have her but she simply hasn't got the room to spare at the moment.'

'I thought she lived in a three bedroom house and there's only the two of them left.'

'That's true but you see their daughter and children are there at the moment,' he said, hesitantly.

'Couldn't Rachel just hang on a bit longer until they've gone back to their own home once their holiday is over at Joan's?'

'They're not on holiday, you see, my dear.'

'Oh,' Emily said rather shocked. 'You do seem to know many more personal details about Joan than I do. I thought she'd told me everything the way she kept chattering as she worked.'

'I know, for all she talks she's actually a private person. She has a real dilemma because it's obvious this girl, Rachel, needs help, but as Joan can't put her up and she refuses to go home Joan's at a loss what to do. Then I came up with a suggestion. What about here?'

'Here!' exclaimed Emily. She was going to say she couldn't just take anybody but stopped herself just in the nick of time.

'Yes, surely she's just the sort of resident you are looking for. Somebody who needs refuge like I did,' he questioned.

'Yes, of course. How right you are,' Emily admitted.

'You don't need to worry about money as Joan assures me she'll get income support or something like that to help her pay her way.'

'I do want you all to get on well together so if you don't mind I'll have a word with Karen. She doesn't need to know all the ins and outs but I want her to know what's going on and feel part of any decisions on residents.'

'You won't be long sorting it out, will you?' he asked anxiously. 'I think the girl's desperate to get away but the only way Joan can get in touch with her is for Joan to write, so that will probably take a few days.'

'I won't take long, I'll go and find Karen now. I think she's in her room, at least she was a little while ago,' she stated.

Karen was having a few moments on her own when Emily knocked on her door to ask, 'Can I come in?' A sense of unease always went through Karen when Emily spoke like this. She still wasn't convinced that something wouldn't happen to spoil her happiness here.

When Emily said, 'I just want to discuss details about a new resident we might have here, subject to your approval,' relief went through Karen.

Emily briefly outlined what Harry had told her but with more emphasis on the girl's need for accommodation.

Karen said without any hesitation, 'Of course she must come here. I couldn't think of a better place.'

'Thanks, that's what I thought.' Seeing a sign of tears had come to Karen's eyes she asked with concern, 'Is everything all right with you?'

'Yes, but it has just come to me how much I wanted children myself.'

'I didn't know.'

'I tried to keep the fact well hidden from everybody,' sighed Karen. 'I'd always thought when I married I'd have a large family.'

'Couldn't you have gone on a fertility programme?'

Karen gave a bitter laugh, 'It wasn't anything like that. I never had the chance to find out if I was fertile or not.'

Emily looked puzzled.

'You haven't a clue what I'm on about have you?'

'No, I haven't.'

'It was Alan who didn't want me to have children. There was only one person he cared about, that was himself. He made sure that I took my little pill each day. Stood over me to watch. He also took protection himself so as to be doubly certain. I was so desperate that I tried all kinds of measures. I tried not to swallow the pill hoping I could spit it out before he looked, but it dissolved in my mouth. Then there were the condoms to deal with. I tried to think of all kinds of ways of getting into the packets and damaging them without him knowing. Each time we had sex all I could do was hope and pray that some miracle would happen and the birth control wouldn't work. It was too much to hope for,' she sighed.

Emily felt so sorry for her because she'd been in the same position herself.

'I'm sorry but you should have told me when we worked together.'

'I couldn't. I felt so ashamed.' Then she gave a bitter laugh. 'Towards the end, when he was losing more and more money and getting drunk, he forgot to watch over me when I took the pill. Not that it mattered by then, as he never came near me. If he even accidentally touched me he would jump back with repulsion on his face. It's only since I've been here and had chance to stand back from it all that I realise it is probably as well that we didn't have children. What kind of father would they have had?'

'Any children would have had a caring mother which would have made up for his lack of love,' Emily said, trying to take some of the bitterness away.

'Maybe, but I wouldn't have wanted to inflict that kind of life on a child. I really do believe it has turned out for the best,' she said sadly.

* * *

Emily imparted the news to Harry that Karen was happy for Rachel to join them.

At the same time Emily was beginning to have self doubts and misgivings whether she was doing the right thing with the house because the residents she was getting had such horrific tales to tell.

She'd not reached a stage where she could recognise that the good she was doing others was also helping her to heal herself.

13

Emily was eager to break the good news to Joan and she thought it would help Joan to have her pick of the nicest room for her niece. There were only bits and pieces to be finished in the main house, then that would be complete. All she needed after that were the residents to fill it. She'd decided not to make any rash decisions about advertising. Already without any effort two residents had arrived. She decided personal recommendation was the best way as she only wanted genuine people who would see it as a good home to help them out of their current predicament and give them a pleasant place to live in. For the people who were not in need of that kind of sanctuary, there were plenty of other places that catered for them.

She had finally taken the jeweller's advice on selling the brooch through an auction house and made contact with one. She had been pleasantly surprised how easy and painless it all was. All she had to do was send the, now insured, brooch to them and sign an agreement for the item to be entered in the next auction. At last she was delighted to find it had exceeded her dreams, making so many more things possible. A slight feeling of sadness went through her that it had actually been sold, but not for a sentimental reason and she was sure the old lady would have approved of what she was going to do with the money. When she'd converted the garage she'd have a nice little home of her own.

The plans had been drawn up and approved with a lounge/dining room and a compact kitchen downstairs. Upstairs the designs had allowed for a large main bedroom across the front of the garage where she'd have views over to the main house and a smaller bedroom to the rear with a small bathroom.

As she concentrated her mind on Joan she heard the key in the back door announcing the arrival of Joan.

As soon she saw Joan's face she could see she was looking expectantly at her. Trying to put Joan's mind at ease and bring back the usual cheery expression on her face she said, 'Rachel can join us as soon as she can get here.'

Once the words were out instead of a smile lighting up Joan's face, to Emily's amazement, she burst into tears.

'Hey, come on, she'll be all right once she's here. We'll take her under our wing,' Emily said hoping the words were reassuring to Joan.

'It's not that,' she sobbed.

'Come on, let's go and sit in the lounge where we'll be more comfortable.'

Between sobs Joan muttered, 'They say it comes in threes, that's true enough.'

'What's happened now,' Emily asked quietly.

'It's my Fred.'

'I didn't know he was ill,' replied Emily, jumping to conclusions.

'He's not; he's been made redundant. He's sixty-one next month. What chance has he got of getting another job?' she said in despair.

'Surely there will be something that would suit him?'

Instead of cheering Joan up these words brought a fresh bout of tears. 'It's not just that, but it seems like the last straw on top of everything else. I can't cope anymore, I'm too old to have to sort out everybody else's problems as well as my own.'

Emily remained silent as she knew better than to interrupt Joan once she was in full flow.

'I was a fool when I was young, a flighty piece. I see I've surprised you,' she said as she saw Emily's shocked expression.

'I've not always looked like this. I was quite attractive when I was young and so slim you wouldn't believe. Being one of five made me as I was, trying to get attention which always seemed to be lacking. My older sister always had airs and graces even in those days. I only had one sister, all the rest were lads. I think I set out to shock everyone with my behaviour and to prove I could pull the lads as well as my sister. I must have seemed like a dirty slut in comparison to her.'

'No, I don't believe you there. You are being too harsh on yourself. Your memory must be playing tricks on how you remember it.'

'Ah, there's nothing wrong with my memory of those days. We had to share a room being just the two girls and I shocked her no end. I used to leave my clothes everywhere including my dirty washing which in those days included sanitary rags.' Seeing Emily's bemused expression she went on to explain, 'No, in them days it wasn't easy to get disposable sanitary towels so we used to use rags then had to wash them out. How she stood it I don't really know. Yet she's still friends with me, always has been.'

'They do say blood is thicker than water,' Emily said kindly.

'When I was seventeen I started courting. I

thought I was being clever as my sister hadn't even got a boyfriend. Then I took it a step further and let him have his own way with me. I felt so smug that I'd got one up on her. I'm sure you've heard the rest of it before. I ended up unmarried and pregnant. But there was no question of not getting married in those days if I wanted to keep the babby. Not that it was much of a wedding — not even a proper wedding dress. It was then that I woke up and realised that it wasn't what I wanted out of life. I didn't want to be married and tied down with a child as I wasn't much more than a child myself. I don't even know if I was ever in love with Fred. I think it was the novelty that he fancied me. He was an only child you see and his mum had spoilt him something rotten. His mother didn't believe a lad should help, that was woman's work in her eyes. I think he was really looking for a mother figure in me who could provide his sexual enjoyment. When my sister married she did so to somebody who had ambition. But Fred had no aspirations to achieve anything. He's been at the same firm most of his life, apart from when he did his national service. Not that I'm saying there's owt wrong with that. He's still doing the same job he started on. All our marriage I seem to have had to cope with the repercussions of strikes and short time leaving me with little money to feed our family. We'd just seem to be getting on our feet when another strike or short time would come and send us back where we'd been.'

'I didn't realise,' Emily said.

'My sister's been ever so good to me, which I don't deserve from her. That's why I want to help her now. She'd pass me on clothes of hers which were best quality. Sometimes I'm sure she'd only worn them once and I don't think she gave them to me because she no longer wanted or needed them. I think it was just kindness. She'd always slip me some money when she knew times were really bad. It's Fred who is the problem. When we got married we were very lucky to get a brand new council house. We still live in the same place. We were even offered the opportunity to buy our council house really cheap but Fred wouldn't. Said whilst we rented it we weren't responsible for the repairs. All our marriage we've done nothing. I bet I can count the number of holidays we've had on one hand.'

By now Emily was feeling contrite that she'd had bad thoughts about this woman because of her constant chatter. Now she could understand why. Never having anything herself she was obviously trying to make up for it by taking notice of what was going on in other people's lives.

Joan carried on, 'Now I've got my youngest back home with her children. That's one thing I can say about Fred, he's never hit me. In fact I've never seen him get angry. That's his failing; he's too contented. Now Alison's husband is a bad lot. I never wanted her to marry him in the first place. But you know what they're like when they are young and think themselves in love.'

Emily knew that feeling and instantly felt sympathy for Joan's daughter. Howard might not have hit her but he'd certainly used mental abuse, which to Emily was just as bad.

Joan's voice brought her back from her own thoughts. 'Anyway, they got married. Not that we'd much money to spare for the wedding. She didn't need to wed which surprised me no end. Even so, there was no talking her out of the marriage. As with all these blokes, he didn't show his true colours until after the wedding. By the time she'd really seen what he was like she was pregnant with her first. I begged her to leave him then. It wasn't hard to see what was going on as he didn't trouble to make sure he hit her where the marks didn't show. She used to come and visit us and would be black and blue with the injuries. I think she was just on the point of leaving when she found out she was pregnant with her second. She'd not wanted another and I don't blame her. He must have sensed she was going to leave and got her pregnant on purpose. Although she'll never admit it I'm pretty certain she thinks the same. It came as a real shock to her to be pregnant again. He was supposed to be looking after the birth control. She was a fool to trust him with that. Anyway once she'd got two children she stuck with it as long as she could but she's finally conceded we were right. So she's back home with us, her and her children as she's nowhere else to go.'

'Yes, Harry did mention they were with you but I'd mistakenly thought they were on holiday.'

'She had to leave him. I don't think her body would have stood many more broken bones. Besides, I never told a soul before, but she's tried twice, without success thanks be to God, to take her own life. I think it was more a cry for help as she loves her children to bits and would never intentionally leave them, particularly for him to look after. But it really put the wind up me the last time as I was frightened she'd have another go and succeed. I was amazed after that how easily she gave in and agreed to come and live with us until such time as she got her life sorted out. So that's our daughter, then on top of that there's Rachel, with Fred's redundancy making the third thing. It wouldn't be as bad if our daughter and grandchildren weren't back with us but with them to feed as well, I don't know what will happen.'

A plan had slowly been formulating in Emily's mind as Joan recounted her story. 'I've had a thought,' Emily said. 'It may be a silly idea but is Fred any good at gardening?'

'It's the only interest I've ever known him have. We've only a tiny garden but he's made it beautiful. Forever out in it doing something or other.'

'What I was wondering, and as I said I don't know how it would work, but I've not had time to do anything about this garden yet. As you can see it is neglected, but I'm sure with a bit of attention it could be brought back to its former beauty.'

'Aye, Miss Robertson could only afford a young chap to come half a day a week. All he did was mow the lawns and not a lot else. He'd no appreciation of it. Money was his only concern.'

'Yes, so I was wondering, do you think Fred would fancy a job gardening here or at least until something else comes along to suit him better.'

Joan was astounded. 'He'd be in his

seventh heaven looking after this garden. I don't have to ask him to know what his answer will be,' enthused Joan further.

'Look, don't get too excited yet because I really don't know how it will work out as I've already said. It's only once the place is full and running can I see how the finances will work out, and only then will I know if I can think long term. It'll have to be temporary to start with and I'm afraid I'll only be able to pay the going rate which I don't think is excessive for a gardener. You might not be able to manage on that money,' Emily cautioned.

'We will, with my little bit as well. Then Alison might find herself a part time job,' she replied excitedly.

'That's settled then. You'd better send him to see me then I can sort it out in more detail with him, that's presuming it is what he wants.'

'You know, the more I see you do, then the more you remind me of Elena Robertson. It's a strange thing that, because you would never have met her, being dead when you bought the house.'

'It's not quite as strange as you think,' admitted Emily. 'You see Elena Robertson was my grandmother.'

'Well I never,' said Joan, in a shocked voice.

'You're right that I'd never met her. Sadly

she was dead by the time I knew of her existence. I didn't know a thing about her until I got the solicitor's letter.'

All the while Joan had been trying to sort her thoughts out and now burst out, 'But you can't be her granddaughter. She was a single woman and had no children.'

'She had my mother, but because she was an unmarried woman she wasn't allowed to keep the baby and it was adopted. I didn't know any of this myself until, as I say, the solicitor told me about her and the fact that she'd left me this house in her will. I feel it a great honour to be related to her from all the good things I've heard about her.'

'Well, you could knock me down with a feather. Who would have thought it, that she'd had a baby? She really was a lovely lady. Couldn't do enough for anybody and she thought more about other people than herself.'

'She didn't suffer at the end did she? I asked the doctor and he said no but I wasn't sure if he only said that because he knew it was what I wanted to hear.'

'Why bless me, no. It was a great shock to us all as she wasn't ailing. Just went to sleep one night and that was it. I suppose the way most of us would wish to go, peacefully.'

'I'm so glad about that,' admitted Emily.

'No wonder I thought I knew you the first time we met. You're like your grandmother, both in looks and the way you conduct yourself. A very determined lady she was, just like you.'

'I won't say I'm determined, at least I haven't always been, but I am trying to be more so now.'

Although Emily had told Joan about the relationship with the old lady, there was no way she was going to divulge the contents of Elena's personal letter to her. That was a secret that she'd carry to her own grave without telling another soul.

'I'd best get on with my work now, love,' Joan said once more her cheerful self.

Emily was pleased that Joan's face now had a happier expression than it had before. She had also learned a lesson herself, how easy it was to take people at face value. Looking at Joan she'd have thought she hadn't a care in the world.

★   ★   ★

Emily wasn't sure what was happening to her own body as she seemed to have a tiredness that never went however much sleep she got. She wasn't unduly concerned but decided to pay David a professional visit.

Over the last few weeks his frosty approach towards her had melted and when she entered the surgery he seemed delighted to see her. 'Now what can I do for you? Which of the residents needs something from me?'

'It's none of them, it's me,' Emily explained.

'Oh,' he replied looking startled and worried.

'Yes, I think I must be lacking some vitamin or other because nowadays I feel tired whatever I do. Everything is such an effort, not like me at all.'

'How are you sleeping?'

'Surprisingly well to say I'm tired all day.'

'I'll organise blood tests to put our minds at rest that it's nothing major but I think what you really need is a break from here. Look how hard you've been working on the house without a stop. On top of that there is the trauma of leaving your husband. Whatever you think it has an effect on the body. It's not always physical effort that brings on tiredness like this. It can also be mental fatigue.'

'How did you know I'd left my husband?' Emily snapped, rather taken aback.

'Sorry, wasn't I supposed to know? Karen mentioned it. I hope she wasn't speaking out of turn.'

'No, it doesn't matter. Sorry I reacted like

that. I suppose you would say that it is some of the mental effect of it all,' she replied, more calmly.

'I would. See the receptionist to book the blood tests then get yourself away for a break from it all.'

'Aye, aye, sir,' laughed Emily.

But David's face didn't break into a smile. 'I mean it, if you don't you could end up really poorly.'

'Okay, point taken. I will try to sort something out. It's actually quite a good time now as the main house is finished and they're ready to start on my place. They don't need me around for the starting process.'

'Good,' was all he answered.

Emily pondered on a break away. It was all right saying she'd have a break but she'd never been on holiday on her own before. She quickly decided she didn't want to go abroad. It came to her that although she'd seen Blackpool and Morecambe on the west coast plenty of times, she'd never seen Scarborough on the east coast. The more she thought about it the more the thought attracted her. It was just far enough away to leave all the work behind, yet if there was an emergency she could soon be back home. As she thought about this she mused how nice it was to say home — my home.

14

Once she'd made up her mind to go to Scarborough, Emily was on her way in no time. She'd never bothered to get herself another mobile phone, after leaving hers with Howard. For some reason she enjoyed not being available. She promised Karen that once she knew where she was staying, she'd give her a ring with a contact number which she prayed she wouldn't need. She also made Karen promise not to reveal the number to anybody else.

When she reached Scarborough she was in a dilemma as to where to stay, as there were so many places yet many had 'No Vacancies' displayed. She'd not bothered to book in advance. Her grandparents, her father's parents, used to enthuse about a hotel called Norlands. It was as good a place to start as any.

She headed to North beach where she was told to look for Peasholm Park as the hotel was situated nearby. Emily was a great believer in fate and wasn't surprised at the availability of a room. It was delightful with ensuite facilities and a view over the park. She was told dinner commenced at seven. It being five o'clock she decided to have a quick walk around the park then have the pleasure of dressing herself up for dinner. Something she'd not had the opportunity to do of late. It was a small park with an attractive lake which was lit up at night.

Whilst she was eating her enjoyable evening meal she did feel a tinge of loneliness. It wasn't Howard she wished was sitting with her but David. The realisation came as a shock to her and she gave herself a mental shake realising how foolish these thoughts were.

Knowing this was supposed to be a holiday and rest cure she decided to go back to her room after dinner, watch the television, which in itself would be a luxury, then have an early night with a book.

She enjoyed the treat of a lie-in before rushing down to breakfast. She had no sooner sat in the dining room than a voice she recognised said from behind her, 'May I join you?'

Turning around she saw it was David, and thought her eyes as well as her mind must be playing tricks on her. He couldn't be here; he was at work in Hornsea. 'Er, yes,' was all she managed to stammer.

She managed to gather her wits together

enough to ask, 'What are you doing here?'

'I'd a few days leave due to me so I thought I might as well spend them here.'

'Are you staying in this hotel?' she asked still dismayed.

'I am.'

'Well, what a coincidence,' she stated.

'It is indeed,' smiled David.

In fact, it had been Karen and Harry behind the scenes that had sent him on his way to Scarborough and this hotel.

After Karen had a little chat with Harry, she started to observe David with unblinkered eyes and saw it was for Emily that he reserved his special smile.

Emily had told them both, when she returned from the surgery, that it was David's advice that she needed a break from everything. The pair of them had got their heads together, and thought they had been given the ideal opportunity to do a spot of match making.

Once Karen had received the call from Emily telling her where she was staying, she got straight on to David to say, 'I'm just ringing you, David, to confirm Emily has gone away for a short break as recommended by you.'

'Good, good. Where has she gone?' he tried to ask innocently.

'She's gone to Scarborough and is staying at the Norlands Hotel.'

'Norlands, right, yes.'

'Yes, Norlands, that's it. She said it was quiet and pleasant and she was surprised it wasn't full up at this time of year.'

'Oh, so they still had vacancies?'

Once he said this Karen knew he had taken the bait and quickly said, 'Must rush now, David. I've a lot to get on with.'

Once off the phone she turned to Harry who was listening to one side of the conversation. The pair of them looked very pleased with themselves and gave a small self-satisfied laugh.

Whilst they were congratulating themselves, David was rushing to see one of his partners in the practice. 'I've a few days' holiday owing to me, Mac. Do you think you could manage without me from tomorrow as I've decided to take them now?'

'That's a bit sudden,' he queried.

'I know it's short notice but I would really appreciate it if you could. You know how it is; when you get the sudden feeling you want a break.'

'I know, no need to tell me. I've felt that often enough myself. Off you go and enjoy yourself, I'll cope here fine.'

David heaved a silent sigh of relief that

he'd sorted himself out so easily. He arrived late evening and missed Emily at dinner but he got up early and sat in the foyer, out of view, determined to catch her at breakfast. It had worked and he was now sitting opposite Emily. He suddenly felt tongue tied.

Emily plucked up courage to ask, 'What are you doing today?' as David started to ask, 'Have you anything planned today?'

They broke off what they were saying and started to giggle like a pair of school children playing truant.

'Nothing planned, that's the same question I was asking you.'

'I've nothing planned either.'

'Have you ever been to Scarborough before?' David enquired.

'No,' she admitted.

'I have. Would you allow me to be your escort for the day?'

Emily paused before she answered, 'Well, if you're sure you haven't something else you'd rather be doing.'

'No, not a thing because as I said before I've nothing planned.'

Finally it struck Emily that he'd not said what he was doing staying here so she asked him, 'How come you are staying here?'

'Oh, I had a few days' leave due and thought it was as good a time as any to take them. The parents used to come here so I thought I'd give it a try.'

'What a coincidence our both being here at the same time then,' exclaimed Emily.

'Now about today,' David continued. 'Anything special you fancy doing?'

Somehow or other during the conversation they'd eaten their breakfast without either of them really noticing. So David said, 'Are you ready?'

'Yes.'

'Let's head into Scarborough and then see how the fancy takes us.'

On the sea front Emily exclaimed at the sight of the amusement arcades. 'My father rarely let me go on them when we went to Blackpool. He said they were an utter waste of money.'

'Come on,' he said, grabbing hold of her hand and dragging her into the nearest one. He got her a bag of two pence pieces and she moved from one machine to another like a young girl let loose for the first time. She soon got hooked on the ones where she had to nudge the coins over the edge with another coin.

Next she spied the parachute ride on the small pleasure park and turned to David with questioning eyes.

'I'm game if you are,' he said knowing

instinctively what she meant.

They had a fantastic view over the bay as they circled around at a steady pace.

'I think the boats are fascinating, don't you?' enquired David, as he looked down at them.

'M'mm, do you fancy seeing if we can have a ride on one when we've finished this ride?' Emily asked with a cheeky grin.

'Okay, but don't come looking for a doctor to tend you if you feel sea sick,' he laughed.

Never in her whole life had she had such a good time and the feeling of relaxation that she could behave just as she wanted without being told off by either father or husband.

There was no sea sickness for the pair of them as they went on a cruise around the coast line. They saw it from a different perspective than driving around it. David placed his arm gently around her shoulders.

As they walked on the jetty a delicious smell of onions frying wafted to Emily. 'I could just murder a hot dog. It's the sea air to blame for giving me an appetite.'

'Just what the doctor ordered,' laughed David.

By the time they'd returned to the hotel they were both exhausted, starving and ready for a bath after being on the beach for much of the afternoon.

When they parted for the night Emily was half hoping that he'd give her a goodnight kiss. Yet the other half was petrified how she'd react if he did. She'd no need to have worried because in actual fact he just said, 'I can't remember when I've enjoyed myself so much. Thank you for a great day, Emily. Let's try to make tomorrow the same.'

'Yes, please,' said Emily feeling thrilled that he wanted her companionship the next day as well. She never questioned herself about the fact that he seemed so available and had no plans of his own.

Another glorious day dawned. David suggested with a kindness that made Emily realise how much it had been missing in Howard, 'I know what you women are like. Let's go around the shops this morning then I hear there's a good afternoon concert at the Spa Theatre. How's that sound to you?'

'Excellent, but are you sure about the shops?'

'I'm well trained. I've a sister who used to drag me around with her when Mum asked me to take care of her.'

'Is she younger than you?'

'Yes.'

'Is she your only sister?'

David laughed, 'No, I'm one of ten.'

'No! You must be having me on.'

171

'It's true.'

It soon became obvious he was used to shopping whatever the reason, as he went through the rails of clothing in the womens-wear shops and held items up that he said would suit Emily. One particular bright top he was really keen for her to get after trying it on, saying it suited her perfectly.

'I've still to be a bit careful with the money 'til I see how things pan out and, in any case, I don't desperately need a new top,' she explained.

'No, I intended it as my present to you.'

'I couldn't possibly let you buy me it.'

'Give me one good reason why not?' he asked.

Emily couldn't think of a valid reason so she had to concede defeat.

She wasn't sure what she thought the concert would be when she had agreed to go, but it exceded all her expectations. Although the orchestra played some serious classical music, they also had some light hearted moments playing well known popular music. The conductor was a comedian into the bargain. At one point a female singer came on stage that Emily had to acknowledge had a wonderful voice. As the concert finished she became aware that David was holding her hand. She'd been that enthralled with the music that she'd not even noticed.

'I don't need to ask if you enjoyed that. Your face speaks for itself.'

'I'm so glad you suggested it, David.'

'We'll have to do it again.'

Emily felt a flutter of delight that he'd made reference to the possibility of future outings and this wasn't a one off.

The following day they became a little more sedate by having a drive up the coast to Whitby and walking around the quaint resort, including climbing the many steps to see the whale bones. They'd informed the hotel that they wouldn't be in for dinner, as they'd both had the desire to sample the fish and chips of Whitby. Emily had told David about Friar Tucks in Bradford and after eating the ones in the small cafe they had found, she informed David that they were still not up to the same standard.

David looked at her and said, 'Maybe one day we could go there together.'

Emily was becoming more and more certain that he was attracted to her and not Karen and she felt pleased, yet shivers of apprehension went through her at the same time.

Having arrived in separate cars they took their leave of each other on the last day to make their own way home. David had to be back for surgery by four o'clock so was in a rush to get back and primed about what had been going on whilst he was away.

As he said goodbye Emily could hardly believe this was the same person that she had had so much light hearted fun with over the last few days. He was back to a much more formal doctor-patient relationship. Not even a peck on the cheek was forthcoming.

David didn't want to appear like this but he was in a dilemma within himself. He didn't know how to handle the situation. Behaving like this he felt he was on safe ground. He so much wanted to take Emily in his arms and declare his love for her.

Emily was also suffering feelings very new to her, certainly very different to how she'd felt with Howard, even at the very beginning of their relationship. At the same time she felt wary remembering the front Howard had put on when she first knew him in order to entice her into the relationship. She knew David wasn't like that but a shadow of doubt wouldn't go away as hard as she tried.

When she arrived back home it became apparent that Karen was waiting impatiently for her to come in and she burst out, 'You had a visitor yesterday, said he would come back today at tea time.'

'Who was it?' asked Emily sharper than she intended.

'Howard.'

'Oh, no, what does he want?' moaned Emily as a chill of fear went through her.

After such a lovely time away it was the last thing she'd thought about. She knew there was little point in running away and not being there when he arrived. He could be very persistent and would wait until he saw her, however long it took.

Seeing Karen's look of panic she quickly reassured her. 'Don't worry. I'll deal with him,' she said this with more confidence than she felt.

'Do you want me to stay with you?' enquired Karen kindly.

'No that would do no good with Howard, only incite him to anger. That would make him much worse to deal with.' Then seeing Karen looked really worried she smiled at her. 'But thanks for the offer. I'll be okay.'

Karen was troubled. She'd gathered from the small things that Emily had let slip that he could be very persuasive and capable of using ruthless means to get what he wanted. She didn't want Emily to give all this up and go back home after all the hard work. It wasn't just for selfish reasons but the thought she could possibly be homeless did worry her tremendously. In reality she was actually thinking about Emily, how much more she had become her own person in this environment and instinctively knew Howard was no good for her.

Despite Emily putting on a brave face she was actually quaking inside waiting for Howard to arrive. She braced herself to stand firm against him. As soon as he walked into the hall, without Emily even inviting him in, he glanced around and stated, 'I thought you said this place was near derelict?'

'What I actually said was it was in need of loving care which is a totally different thing.'

'It means the same thing to me.'

'It would do,' Emily dared to say.

He glared at her but carried on, 'I thought you said there was no money left to you?'

'There wasn't.'

'Pull the other one. How you have managed to give it all the *loving care* it needed to restore it?' he asked in a snide tone of voice.

Having to think quickly on her feet because there was no way she was going to tell Howard the whole truth she said, 'I was lucky, I found a brooch my grandmother had left me so I sold it to pay for the work.'

He didn't reply to that but carried on looking at her suspiciously. It wasn't the whole truth but in the circumstances it was justified.

'Might as well have a look round whilst I'm here,' he said, moving towards the first door.

'I don't think there is much point, do you?' she said, as she moved to bar his way in. Emily had amazed herself that she had summoned the willpower to defy him so openly.

'Something to hide?' he was quick to ask.

'No, not at all, but this is my life so it's of no importance to you.'

'I'm still your husband,' he replied sulkily.

'Hopefully not for much longer,' Emily snapped back.

'I've taken time off work to come here especially to see you and give you one last chance to come back home,' he said petulantly.

'This is my home.'

'Don't be silly, Emily, this old place can never compare to what I built you.'

'Yes, you're right there.'

Howard misunderstood this and persisted further. As the conversation went on the old familiar feeling of being browbeaten by him was returning to Emily and she could feel herself weakening and was afraid if he stayed much longer she'd give in against her intentions.

'I'm not coming back to you,' she replied with a great strength of will.

'We'll see about that,' he snarled. 'Let's see how you manage when I get half of all this, which I see as my right as your husband.'

The words inflamed Emily at the thought he wanted to get his grubby hands on what was rightfully hers. She remembered her refusal to touch half of what was his so if it came down to it then it would be tit for tat.

'You'll not get a penny of it.' Then she had an inspiration and continued sounding brave as she quaked inside about the reaction of what she was about to say. 'After all, what will your friends think when I air in court all your sordid little affairs and the fact that you can't father a child. Then there's the fact I've not taken anything off you. I could make you sell your precious house to give me half share!'

She was aware she'd hit a raw nerve, as she had intended, when she saw his face blanch. He moved as if to hit her but backed off and shouted instead, 'All right, I'll sign your damned divorce papers. You're not worth a second thought. After all, you're only the daughter of a bastard. What a laugh, your father bragging about what good stock you came from. He took me in good and proper. Just the kind of trick one of your kind would get up to. Well I'm not being party to your sordid little tricks.'

Emily was opening her mouth to reply at the injustice of all he was saying but instead all there was to be heard was the sound of the front door slamming and it reverberated through the house as he took his hasty departure.

Emily flopped on to the bottom step as her legs turned to jelly. She never knew she had it in her to defy him in such a manner and only wished she'd found the strength years ago.

Hearing the bang Karen came rushing into the hall. 'Are you all right?' she asked with genuine concern in her voice.

'Fine,' she said still shaking.

She saw Karen looking at her dubiously.

'Yes, I really am. I don't think we'll be seeing him again.' Then, the full implications sinking in, she added, 'I think this calls for a celebration,' and burst into a slightly hysterical laugh.

Howard, as he drove home, was also planning his own celebration. He was going to be free of Emily and so easily. He'd felt by giving her one last chance to come to her senses he'd appeased his own conscience. On the journey there he had actually been afraid she would go back to him. When he'd seen how well she was doing he did feel a genuine anger and wanted part of it but then sense had come to him just in time to save him doing something he might have regretted. He'd decided to let her have it all, it was a small cost to pay to be rid of her. His mind seemed totally oblivious that she had been very generous with him in not making any demands from the marriage.

He was getting used to his set-up with Amanda. Once he'd signed the divorce papers he could persuade her to move in full-time with him. He'd soon realised she was a useless cook and housekeeper, but she'd an excellent brain that worked in much the same way as his with the same ruthlessness. Even the thought of her in bed was enough to bring about an arousal. There she was putty in his hands, willing to comply with all his requests and deriving as much enjoyment from sex as he did. He decided they could soon rectify the small housekeeping problem by getting a daily that could do the cleaning for them and also a bit of cooking. It would be worth it to sit in the evening and have a meaningful conversation with somebody with whom he could pit his wits against, instead of a mouse meekly giving into him. He never gave a thought to the fact that had he treated Emily more like he did Amanda and let her develop at her own pace he would have found her a caring and intelligent person. At no time had he treated her tenderly or taught her the art of pleasurable love making. To Emily it was an act to be endured. He had to acknowledge he'd admired Emily more than he ever had in his life before when she threw her challenge at him. He felt sorry that she'd not shown that same fiery temper whilst they had been together, it would have made for an interesting relationship.

15

Although David was still calling on the pretext of checking up on Harry and Karen and even Emily herself, at the same time his attitude was once more very much that of doctor and patient. He was very distant to them all and never mentioned the days in Scarborough, which puzzled Karen and Harry. They were sure their little ploy had worked; particularly once Emily had recounted details of her trip, including her time with David and how relaxed and kind he had been.

Karen had thought that Emily might not have let on that she'd seen David there. So what had gone wrong? Emily hadn't given them the slightest hint that anything had been amiss. Besides which, she'd had a cheerful enough expression on her face when she arrived home. Surely she wouldn't have if David and she had been in some sort of disagreement before parting.

Emily hadn't too much time to brood on David's behaviour as her own small cottage was nearing completion and she was busy sorting through the furniture stores in the attic. That reminded her that she'd never done any more about the figurine. Partly because it was very pretty and whatever it was worth it had been part of her grandmother's life. But the other reason was she'd been made to look a fool so often by Howard that she still had a phobia thinking she may be wrong, and then other people would treat her with the same contempt, just like Howard always did.

She'd obviously had to tell Brian of the possible find because of probate and he'd encouraged her to get it valued. He'd recommended a trip to York, a good selling centre for such things particularly with the American tourists.

Emily felt she needed somebody to support her on this venture so decided to ask Harry if he would go with her.

'I'd love that,' he exclaimed. Then he looked sad as he went on, 'I used to manage odd trips to York. Yes. It holds some good memories for me.'

'I'm sorry, I didn't know. I wasn't trying to upset you,' replied Emily full of understanding what he meant.

'Good gracious me, it's all a long time ago now. Besides, I'll be going with a pretty girl on my arm again,' he said once more his cheerful self.

Karen felt rather put out that she'd not

been invited to go along with them on the trip. Emily didn't want her to feel left out but considered Harry of an age that wouldn't think her foolish if she'd got it all wrong. Besides that, he wasn't a gossip; he could keep things very close to his chest, which was what Emily wanted. Karen, without intending it, was rather good at letting the cat out of the bag where Emily's personal life was concerned.

Harry had not lost any of his memory of York as he directed her around the outskirts to where it was possible to park. He suggested he would like to treat her before they started on their trek around York centre.

Emily quickly protested, 'You can't do that.'

'Why not? I've nobody else to spend my money on. Besides, you'll give me pleasure and happy memories to escort a young lady for lunch once again.'

Emily said no more and let him take her arm as he led the way to where he wanted, to 'Betty's Cafe' which Emily had already heard much about. Despite it being early for lunch there was already a queue for tables. Harry insisted to the waitress that they had one on the ground floor near a window so they could look out of it. She had Welsh Rabbit which was the best she'd ever tasted then Harry insisted that she have one of the beautiful cakes, despite the protests about her figure. She had one shaped like a butterfly with a delicious custard cream filling in a puff pastry.

'Delicious,' she said when she had finished.

'I knew you'd like it. All the ladies like it here.'

Emily laughed, 'You sound experienced in the ladies department.'

'Not really, but I know you women, can't resist cakes like us men.'

'Oh, yes,' she laughed, looking at his plate where he'd just eaten the same as Emily herself. Harry laughed when he caught her eye.

Outside Betty's, Harry suggested where there were a few antique shops. Having decided which shop she would like to try first, a young female assistant said, 'Mr Smythe has just nipped out, but should be back in a few minutes if you want to hang on.'

'We'll wait. I presume it's all right if we have a browse around?'

'Of course,' replied the girl pleasantly.

Emily nudged Harry. 'Look at the price of that,' she whispered in his ear.

Harry just nodded in agreement.

The more she looked around the more she

realised that many of the items were selling for what appeared to be high prices. She only hoped they paid the vendor equally good a price. A voice suddenly spoke behind her. Emily looked around to see a short, very plump man standing there. Somehow the name had conjured up the idea of a tall, upright, rather pompous figure. Instead he spoke with a broad East Riding accent. 'I believe you've something you want me to look at?'

'Yes, this figure,' she said as she moved to the counter and carefully started to take it out of all the protective wrapping she had put on it.

'H'mm it's very nice, very nice indeed. I presume you do know what you have here?' he said holding the figure up to the light.

Pleased that she had obviously been correct she said with confidence, 'I do.'

'Are you just looking for a valuation for insurance or do you want to sell it?' he enquired.

'Sell it, please.'

'Right, give me a few minutes to make some phone calls to see what I can do.'

She starting to feel very excited now it was confirmed to be what she'd hoped.

The amount he offered was in excess of what she'd researched herself. 'Thank you for the offer. I would like to think about it. I presume the offer will hold good all day.'

'Yes,' he replied looking rather bemused that she hadn't accepted instantly.

'I agree with you, Emily. Think on it before you make a decision,' Harry chimed in.

'Your father's right. I wouldn't want you to go home and think badly of me wondering if I've robbed you. I've been in this game too many years and have a good reputation to keep.'

Emily saw the funny side of Harry being called her father but kept her face poker straight. 'Thank you for all your help.'

Once they were out of the shop she said in an excited voice, 'Thank you, Father, for your help.'

'Anytime you need it, Emily,' he said, with a tinge of sadness on his face, not laughing at the joke.

Deciding not to mention Mr Smythe's error any further she continued, with obvious delight in her voice, 'Actually, it was a very good offer, but I could see he really wanted it, so I decided it would do him no harm to sweat on it for a bit. I bet when he made his phone calls he found a buyer, all he needs to do is pass it on and make his profit within days.'

'There's more dealers down here,' Harry pointed.

'Oh they won't be necessary. I made my mind up about the minimum I'd sell it for and he's well exceeded that with his offer. Let's go and have a coffee then we'll go back and sell it.' Emily even amazed herself how calmly she was behaving.

When they entered the antique shop once again Emily was pretty certain she'd been right in saying Mr Smythe had a buyer lined up. He rushed up to her and stuttered, 'Good, you've come back.'

'Is that really your best offer?' she asked, with tongue in cheek.

'Well . . . I'll go up another five hundred. I'll never be rich doing deals like this.'

Playing him at his own game Emily replied, 'I know, it's terrible pushing such a hard bargain.'

The deal was done and being such a large amount of money Mr Smythe rang his bank to transfer the funds to Emily's account. Having the bank's assurance that all was in order and the funds available and transferred immediately to her account, she left the shop feeling satisfied with the outcome.

Outside the shop Harry asked, 'Where did you learn such bargaining skills?'

'I've never done anything like that before in my life,' she said astounded at her own nerve, yet she felt pleased that she'd managed to squeeze some extra money out of Mr Smythe.

'However you did it, well done. Keep it up,' laughed Harry.

As she was no longer carrying the valuable item around she asked Harry, 'Would you mind if we had a little look around? I've never been here before and don't know when I'll get chance again.'

'No, not at all, it's just what the doctor ordered.' Once the words were out he knew he'd put his foot in it by mentioning the word doctor as her face instantly lost its smile. He took hold of her arm and said, 'Come on, let me show you the Shambles.'

It seemed one exclamation of delight after another as she saw the impressive City of York. Having noticed views of the very large building that she'd heard so much about, particularly when it was on the news that it had been struck by lightening and damaged with fire, she pointed as she asked Harry, 'I presume that is the Minster?'

'It is and I was saving that for last. You do want to see it, don't you?'

'Yes please.'

As they entered the building a sense of calmness came over Emily. It was a long time since she'd been in a church. Howard had scoffed at all forms of religion. Now she said to Harry, 'I want to go and say a prayer.'

'I'll join you, my dear. I like coming here. It gives a sense of peace to me.'

'I know just what you mean, I felt it as we walked around,' she agreed.

Once she started to pray so many of her troubles seemed to pour out of her, as if she was brimming over with the need to tell the events of her life. She finally finished with the Lord's Prayer and stood up. Her legs nearly collapsed as they had pins and needles with the length of time she'd knelt on them. She felt infinitely better getting so much off her chest talking to God.

Harry looked at her with concern as he asked, 'Are you all right, my dear?'

'I'm fine, Harry. In fact a lot better than I've felt for a long time. That did me the world of good.'

Feeling contented within herself and instinctively sensing how much Harry had enjoyed his day out she suggested, 'Look, that pub is advertising meals. Let's eat there. It's on me.'

His face lit up with obvious delight and she vowed to herself that when she could spare the time and where it was appropriate, she'd take him with her on outings. He'd become very precious to her, far more than just one of her residents. Despite never having had any children of his own, here was Harry with two females who looked up to him as a surrogate father. Harry was aware of the deep affection the two girls had for him and he was happy. In fact, the last time he'd had such happiness was when he'd the relationship with Edna. Not that he'd any wrong ideas about the pair of women who respected him now. They were more like the granddaughters he'd never had.

A few days later, Emily was delighted when she received a call from Brian to say he'd received the divorce papers, signed by Howard, so all should run smoothly. Knowing this was going to be settled she wanted to explain one or two things to Karen and Joan because she felt she'd left them in the dark, particularly when they had been so open with her about their own situations. She wanted to feel she'd cleared it out of her system and could leave that part of her life behind her.

She wished Karen would stop having the look of panic on her face every time she said she wanted a word with her. This time, when she said she wanted to talk to Joan as well, Karen looked petrified. Before she started to say what she'd planned she laid her hand on Karen's. 'Don't look so worried. I've no plans to tell you anything that will upset your life here. What I wanted was to talk to the pair of you about my own life, or should I say my past life now.'

Karen's expression changed to one of puzzlement but Joan quickly comprehended and said kindly, 'There's no need, lass, to explain anything. That part of your life has gone and anyway it's none of our concern.'

'There is every need, Joan. I want to tell you or maybe I should say need to tell you, so I can put a final close on that chapter of my life.'

'Fair enough, if that's what you want then we're listening.'

Emily turned to Karen, 'We called ourselves best friends all those years ago but how could we have been? I knew so little of your life or you of mine. I didn't tell you the whole truth about my life, never suspecting that you were doing the same over yours. There was many a time I wanted to tell you but I felt so ashamed feeling it was somehow my fault, which I now realise it wasn't.'

Karen interrupted her, 'I know just what you mean. I was far too embarrassed to tell anybody about how I was suffering. I felt a failure.'

'Well you've had the courtesy of telling me all about yours so now it's my turn to share mine with you.' Here she paused and took a deep breath before starting on the tale. 'When

I was courted by Howard, he was very attentive towards me, yet for some reason I always felt uneasy in his company.' She went on to explain the details of how her father had forced her into marrying Howard. 'Once married,' she continued, 'it turned out that Howard saw me as a breeding machine and the little woman who would spend her time at home keeping house. My career meant nothing to him. Children didn't come along, as you're already aware. I took all kinds of abuse from him, over this. He even accused me of deceiving him by using birth control, when I wasn't.' Here she looked at Karen. 'Rather the reverse to your situation. You see why I understood so easily?'

'It seems you've suffered for the same reason in a different way,' Karen admitted.

'I didn't become pregnant. Howard became obsessed, each month checking my most fertile time of the month. He was convinced I was to blame; after all, how could it be his fault? He was perfect. As he saw it there couldn't possibly be anything wrong with him so he sent me along to the doctors for tests. Everything came back giving me the all clear with no reason to explain why I wasn't becoming pregnant. Yet Howard still blamed me, he said it must be something they'd missed. After sending me back numerous times to the doctors he was finally assured I was fertile. He was convinced enough to go for tests himself. It turned out he was sterile due to mumps he had as a child. He was furious with all the medical profession, said they were all a set of idiots.'

'You poor thing,' Joan interrupted.

Emily carried on, 'Then the affairs started. He didn't even bother to hide them. He admitted he was very careless where birth control was concerned; hoping he'd get one of the women pregnant so as to show everybody it was my fault after all. Thankfully he left me alone then, because with his carelessness I was afraid he'd catch something horrible and pass it on to me. He took it as an insult to his masculinity that he couldn't give a woman a child. The more frustrated he got, the more he took sadistic pleasure out on me as some sort of punishment. Sadly my grandmother will never know how she enabled me to get away from that nightmare situation.'

'I never realised,' mumbled Karen.

'I didn't want you to know, or anybody else for that matter, and made sure nobody did. It doesn't matter now because it is all in the past.'

Both Karen and Joan looked contrite, because they'd commented to each other how lucky Emily was. Now they knew her life had been no better than theirs, they felt they'd misjudged the situation. They were only glad her grandmother had given her the opportunity to get out of it, and in turn she'd given each of them a chance for a new life.

Joan thought how much happier Fred was in his new gardening job. Already she could see a change in the garden, but it wasn't just a change in the garden but a change in him. She'd thought him too old to alter but he was much happier in his working life and he'd become much more attentive towards her. Suddenly he'd ambitions for them to enjoy life and was already saving up to take her on a holiday abroad. Yes, Joan acknowledged she'd a lot to thank Emily for.

'Do you know,' Emily stated and Joan focused her mind back to the present, 'I feel as if a weight has been lifted from my shoulders by telling you all this. I can look forward to my new life here with you all.'

Yet, for some reason she still felt a twinge of sadness. She knew that was to do with the fact David was back on his old footing with her, not showing any signs of affection. She wasn't like Karen in saying a man would never feature in her life again. She'd enough sense to understand that all men were not like Howard.

16

Emily was getting pleasure she'd never had before, sorting her new home out. In York she'd noticed fine wallpapers in Laura Ashley, ideal to match the period of furniture she would be putting in. She was determined that would be her first stop when she went shopping.

Howard had scoffed often enough at patterned wallpaper. For him, his home had to be plain walls with the minimum of furniture in each room. All that had to be ultra modern with the kitchen filled with stainless steel.

She wanted more warmth in her new home and picked a paper with varying shades of yellow for the lounge and hall, which had a faintly etched design on it, and chose some thick rich red fabric to add extra warmth to the room. She had one extravagance — a mirror she fell instantly in love with whilst making her purchases. It was frameless, but was etched in a beautiful design.

She chose a traditional floral paper for the bedroom with matching curtains — making it a feminine room — something she'd never been allowed before.

The bathroom paper of Dutch scenes on a white background was totally radical for her and she settled on the purple/lilac shade.

To help Emily cut down on expenses Karen put her decorating skills to good use with Emily working as her assistant. Emily raided the big house for much of the furniture she needed. Howard would never have approved of her lounge as she had put in various items making it fuller than he liked to see a room, yet in her opinion it was still done tastefully and looked very attractive.

Emily walked around the house admiring her handiwork and touching each piece of furniture. She was glad she had splashed out on her extravagant mirror. It was hung above the beautiful fireplace. Howard had never seen the point in having a focal feature to a room but Emily was glad she'd let her own ideas run free and had felt no constraints. She looked at the fireplace with mahogany surround and inset tiles with flowers sweeping up either side of the cast iron grate with recessed fire grate. Despite so much fancying an open fire, it would be impractical. Instead she had got a very realistic compromise in a gas flame effect fire. She'd been thankful that gas had actually been laid to the main house. It appeared it was one of the things her great grandparents had insisted on when gas lighting became fashionable.

On one of the walls in the lounge she had hung a photograph of her grandmother which Emily had chosen and had framed to suit the room. She had also brought her grandmother's desk from the main house into her lounge. It sat below her picture and Emily thought it an apt memorial to her grandmother.

Much to Emily's disappointment, many of the other pieces of furniture had been too large for the tiny cottage, so she'd mainly brought the smaller items across to the new home. She'd had to get herself a dining table and chairs as the one in the house was far too large, besides which it was needed there. She had great fun attending auctions to find what she wanted and fulfilled one of her yearnings, never satisfied before. This was the perfect opportunity to ask Harry to accompany her again. She valued his knowledge and advice.

As she looked around and saw the items she remembered the great fun they'd had studying and bidding at auction. The door bell rang and Joan stood there. 'I thought I'd let you know my niece has just arrived.'

It had been agreed that Rachel would make her own way to the house; as both Fred and

Joan worked there they'd be there to greet her.

When Emily entered the hall she was amazed to see Rachel standing dejectedly where Joan had obviously left her. Despite it being a cold day for the time of year, she only had a dog-eared cardigan over her thin dress. In her hands she clutched a carrier bag which seemed to be the only thing she had with her. She looked like a scared rabbit as she stood looking forlorn.

'Come on, let's go into the kitchen. It's warmer there. Put the kettle on please, Joan. Nothing like a good cup of tea after a long journey,' stated Emily boldly, taking control of the situation.

'Thank you,' the young woman replied timidly.

Emily knew from Joan that Rachel was in her early twenties but she looked a young teenager.

Once they were seated Emily asked kindly, 'Are you having the bulk of your luggage sent on?'

She saw Rachel looking embarrassed and Emily wished she hadn't asked. 'This is it,' Rachel replied, as she pointed to the carrier bag.

'Oh, right,' Emily replied, not quite sure what to say as it was her turn to feel embarrassed.

Joan jumped in seeing Emily's expression. 'I told you she was married to a bad one.' The young woman said nothing but seemed to hang her head in shame.

Tea was made and Emily indicated to Joan to come and join them. Joan could no longer keep her impatience at bay as she asked, 'Come on, tell us the proper tale. I know what you said in the letter but it can't be all of it.'

Emily tried to protest, 'Joan, let her get settled in first,' but Rachel butted in saying, 'Please, if you don't mind, I would rather get it over and done with and tell you all about it now. Then maybe I can start to put it all behind me for good.'

'Okay, I'll leave you two alone then you can say what you want in private,' Emily said as she made to stand up.

'Please, will you stay? I'd like you to hear it all as well as Auntie Joan,' she begged Emily.

'Come on, lass. You get it out of your system,' said Joan kindly, laying her hand on her niece's for reassurance.

'Does Mrs Cartwright know about my marriage, how it came about and the move to Scotland?'

'Aye, she does, lass.'

Emily quickly said, 'Call me Emily. We don't go in for formality here,' and for the first time it struck her how different this was to her behaviour at college.

'I'll go back as far as the miscarriage then.'

Joan interrupted, 'I know, me and Fred was real upset to hear about it.'

'You'd no need to be. I know it was terrible and I was heartbroken but at the same time I soon realised it was probably best. We'd not been married a week before Michael started to treat me badly.'

As Rachel saw Joan's shocked expression she quickly reassured her, 'I don't mean he hit me. No, nothing like that, but it was as bad. As his house was too far away for me to travel to my job, and I don't drive, I gave up working. Not that it was much; just factory work and having no skills and being pregnant there seemed little point in applying for another job. But I can't explain the loneliness in that little house. In no time at all I had it sorted from the mess and jumble it was when I moved in. I cleaned every day, just for something to keep me occupied. The shops were a trek away but I would go, even for one thing, just to pass some time.'

'You could have always come to see me, why didn't you make contact?' Joan asked.

'I felt too ashamed and no money for bus fare. You see after only a week of marriage Michael took to not bothering coming home

201

many an evening and sometimes not at night. It was on one of those occasions that the miscarriage happened. He'd not bothered to get a phone installed in the house as he said he had his mobile so it was a waste of money. I begged for a phone and in the end he did promise to get it organised but like most of his promises, nothing happened.'

Joan said gently, 'I wish you had found the courage to write before.'

'I started to bleed and have terrible stomach pains but not having a phone I lay all night in agony, afraid to move. Finally, in the morning Michael rushed in for a shower and change of clothes. I begged him to phone for an ambulance and for him to stay with me. All he did was make the call, but then left me on my own again saying he'd no time to spare to stay with me.'

'How cruel,' Joan exclaimed, with tears in her eyes.

'I don't think he'd have been much comfort if he had stayed. In any case, the ambulance soon arrived and they couldn't have been any kinder looking after me. They were stunned that my husband had left me on my own. They did all they could for me at the hospital, but they did say if I'd been taken there sooner who knows — they might have been able to save the baby. Not once did

Michael visit me. He did manage to pick me up to take me home, but then all he said was that it was probably for the best, as he'd never really wanted a baby.'

Now it was Emily's turn to express her shock. 'And I thought Howard was cruel with words.'

'All I could do was cry. Mum wanted to come and stay to look after me but he said I couldn't have her there. He didn't want her nosing around and I'd no energy left to argue. It was taking me all my time just to manage to get through each day. Then he dropped the bombshell that we were moving to Scotland. I tried to protest that I should have some say in such a radical decision but he was very good at browbeating me and getting his own way. He said that he'd get me a nice house, better than the one we had, but instead, he installed us in a shambles miles away from anywhere.'

'How could he?' Joan said in a loud voice showing her obvious anger.

'I pleaded and begged with him to come home each evening but it made no difference. I was convinced by then that a woman was the cause of his staying out all the time. When he did come home it always ended in an argument. His excuse for staying out was always the same, that he had been drinking with his friends and he was too drunk to drive home. He reckoned there wasn't any other woman and he barely gave me any money. Again, each time I needed some I'd have to plead and beg. I suggested I got a job — which actually he didn't object to, but then he'd no need to. It was impossible for me to get one because all the jobs that were available, were too far away for me to travel to each day, particularly with not having transport.'

Here she suddenly stopped as if to catch her breath then continued, 'I forgot to say he'd got me pregnant before we wed, yet not once had he touched me since the wedding.'

'He'd no need to with having other women,' Joan interrupted angrily.

'Yes, that's what I thought. But let me explain, Auntie Joan, and you'll see it's not like that at all.'

Emily was slowly beginning to develop her own idea of events but kept her own counsel and waited. She didn't want to make a fool of herself by jumping to the wrong conclusion.

Again Joan interrupted Rachel, 'He didn't hit you did he?'

'No,' Rachel replied, not looking put out that her aunt had already asked this question and kept interrupting. Emily supposed she was used to her being like this.

'No, he didn't hit me,' Rachel repeated, as if she wished it had been that. 'He just yelled at me and threw things around as he told me the truth.'

Now she was sobbing as she spoke and Joan comforted her, 'Nay, don't take on so. It's best to get it all in the open.'

Rachel carried on as if her Aunt had not spoken. 'You see, he told me he was gay.'

Joan's mouth opened and shut with no words coming out. If it hadn't been such a terrible situation Emily would have had to laugh at Joan being lost for words. But Emily wasn't as shocked herself, these words confirmed what she had been beginning to suspect.

'Apparently, Michael and his partner had a massive fall-out just before he met me. Michael was having self-doubts about whether he was really meant to be gay and that was what prompted him to ask me out. I think that was what also prompted him to have sex with me. I have to admit, for his age, he did seem rather inexperienced. He's probably a far better lover with a bloke. Of course, he'd not intended for me to get pregnant. He probably forgot that it was even possible. For some reason, the better side of his nature prompted him to do the right thing by me. But after our wedding he met his old partner and they made up. I suppose much of the rest you can now work out. That's where he was each night.'

'It still does not explain the move to Scotland,' Emily exclaimed, puzzled.

'Ah, Simon, that's his partner, got moved there with his job. We had to move so Michael could be near him. Simon even got Michael a job at his firm. I just couldn't stay under the same roof as him any longer once I knew the truth. It made me feel sick to even look at them. As I said before, he kept me short of money. He was obviously spending it all on his other life.' Now she gave a hysterical laugh. 'He left me that short I'd to pinch the electricity money to afford to get here. He won't half be cross when he finds it missing.'

'Oh, you poor dear why didn't you say something before now? I'd have sent you something,' her aunt said.

'Because you've enough on your hands with Alison back home and you've been more than kind sorting it out for me to move here. I got myself in the mess so it is up to me to get myself out of it.'

'Why didn't you tell your Mum and Dad? I'm sure they would have understood and helped you. Knowing your Dad he'd have gone all the way to Scotland to pick you up,' Joan persisted.

'Dad was furious at me for getting pregnant and told me I had made my bed so I had to lie in it. He had made it plain there was no going back to them.'

'I'm sure he'd have relented. It was probably said in the heat of the moment,' Joan said.

'I wasn't risking it.' She had now turned to Emily. 'Sorry, I forgot to say when we met, thanks for letting me come here.'

'No problem. I don't know if your aunt explained but it is for reasons like this I have set this place up.'

'A shame more people don't get organised like this then. I consider myself one of the lucky ones having this chance to get away and make a fresh start.'

Emily wasn't sure she'd call her lucky, not in comparison to herself. At least she'd had the wherewithal to leave Howard. This poor girl still didn't really know how her life would shape up. At least recounting the tale seemed to have helped, her cheeks now had a hint of colour to them.

'I think it's time we showed you the room your aunt has chosen for you,' said Emily kindly. 'If you don't like her choice I'll let you look at the other vacant rooms.'

One look at the peacefully decorated room and Rachel burst into sobs. 'It's beautiful. I don't know how I'll ever repay you.'

'Just unpack your things and settle in. There's nothing to repay me for. This is the whole point of the place. Have a rest now, as Karen hasn't even started preparing dinner yet, so you've plenty of time. I'll give you a call when it's ready and then you'll meet Karen and Harry who also live here.'

Looking apologetic Rachel said, 'I don't have much appetite at the moment. No need to cook anything for me.'

'There's every need,' said Emily, sharply. 'Karen's food is delicious, it would tempt anybody to eat. And if you're worried about meeting Karen and Harry then don't be. Nobody here is without their own story of tragedy.'

Emily put Harry and Karen very briefly in the picture without giving too much away. That was for Rachel to tell if she ever wanted to.

★   ★   ★

Rachel soon fitted into the household, far easier than Emily imagined, and it seemed as if she had always been there. Without being asked she took to helping her aunt with the work. Emily didn't interfere with this, it was probably her way of helping herself to feel better. Besides which, it seemed as if she felt beholden to Emily for what she'd done for her and was forever looking for ways to make some payment.

Karen had soon worked out that Rachel had very little clothing with her, as she'd seen her rush to the bathroom for her morning wash with the same cardigan on she'd arrived in, worn over her threadbare nightwear.

Looking quite innocent one morning Karen said, 'I've been having a sort out of my things, seems I've a dressing gown too many and some other odds and ends of clothing. I wondered if they would be any good for you, Rachel, as we're of a similar size.'

Seeing Rachel's hesitancy she went on, 'Of course, if you don't want them I can send them to the charity shop.'

'Oh, in that case I'll save you the trouble of having to take them. I'll take the things off your hands — thanks,' replied Rachel.

Emily wasn't certain where the spare dressing gown had sprung from as she knew Karen hadn't many things when she arrived, but she was grateful for Karen's generosity and kindness. Knowing she also lacked a decent coat, Emily sorted one out for her, but she couldn't use the same tactic as Karen to give her it. She'd see straight through the ploy, so she decided it was probably best if she just offered it as a gift. Rachel did hesitate about taking it and Emily was aware she was hesitating to accept.

In the end she said, 'It's most kind of you, I don't have a coat.' Then she gave a small giggle, 'Of course, you know that.'

★ ★ ★

Having been so busy with all the problems that kept cropping up Emily had not once given a thought to her old job of lecturing. If anybody had asked her if she missed it she could have honestly replied, 'Do you know, I've never given it a thought.'

She knew without a shadow of doubt she'd made the best choice of her life so far, moving here and taking care of the people as she was.

17

Emily gave a jump of joy as she read the letter. She'd been granted her decree nisi. Now at last she was nearly free of Howard. She'd only have to wait six weeks then the divorce would be absolute.

When she told Karen her good news, Karen turned to her and asked with concern in her voice, 'Has it upset you, the letter telling you that?'

'Not at all,' Emily replied in amazement.

Karen looked at her with a strange expression as if she didn't believe what she was saying.

Emily seeing the look quickly tried to reassure her, 'No, I'm telling you the truth. I feel, for the very first time in my life, as if I've been set free. Now I can live my life as myself. So much so that tonight you can cook something very special, do you hear? I think this calls for a celebration and I want everybody to join me.'

Emily was certain Karen still didn't understand her euphoria. The more she saw of Karen and her moods, the more convinced Emily was that she was still a very mixed up person. She was still petrified of her husband, Alan, in case he turned up to cause trouble; for some strange reason she had not stopped loving him and had an inner hope that she could turn the clock back and be in a happy married life again. Emily knew only too well that life wasn't like that, things didn't always work out as we wanted them to. It was obvious no miracle would come along for Karen.

Emily had gone through a lot leaving Howard and knew that until Karen got Alan fully out of her system she was stuck in limbo and would find it difficult to move forward.

Knowing that Karen was having these tremendous struggles with herself it came as no surprise when she asked Emily, 'I think I would like to go to church on Sunday. I know I won't find the answers there, but it might help me clear my head and find some peace.' Then she hesitated before asking, 'I don't think I've got the courage to go by myself — would you come with me to give me some support?'

'Of, course, if you put it like that,' Emily reassured her, trying to sound as if it was no problem. But once Emily was back on her own she reflected about her own experiences of church so far.

Emily's parents hadn't been church folk

and never bothered to take her along as a child. When a neighbour of theirs, who went to the local church regularly, asked Emily's mother, 'Would you like me to take Emily along to church on Sunday and get her into the habit?' her mother agreed willingly, glad one duty was taken out of her hands.

Emily was furious, even at that young age, when her mother told her what she'd organised on her behalf and challenged, 'Why do I have to go when you don't?'

Her mum was flustered with this comment as she wasn't very good at coping with antagonism. 'I did go when I was a girl, but it's just one of those things — we don't now. We seem to be busy with one thing and another on Sundays.'

'So how come I'll have time to go?' demanded Emily.

'You're older now and don't need entertaining on a Sunday and it's time you went along to get your own thoughts about religion. You're old enough to understand what is going on.'

'Thanks very much, Mum.' With that Emily stamped out of the room in a childish temper. She was fuming. Into the bargain old Mrs Cotrill, who was going to take her, was a fuddy duddy.

Despite being a timid woman against her

husband, Iris could be strong with her daughter in her own beliefs, if not her husband's, and was determined Emily should have the opportunity of religious education.

Emily soon decided it was more like a comedy than going to church when she went on her first Sunday. She couldn't believe the hats the women wore and to shock Mrs Cotrill she said to her, 'Blimey, do they think they're going to Ascot?'

Mrs Cotrill looked most put out. 'In the house of the Lord, headgear should be worn by women.'

As she was only eleven at the time Emily hadn't a hat on and said hopefully, 'I'd better go back home then this week and give it a miss as I haven't brought a hat with me.'

'It doesn't matter for a young lass, but when you're a grown up and come to church, remember the hat,' she told Emily condescendingly.

Being only a young child the adults talked in front of her as if she couldn't understand or hear what they were saying when they gossiped after church.

'Did you see Mrs so and so's hat last week?'

'Yes, terrible wasn't it?'

'I think Mavis is putting on weight. In fact she's got quite plump now.'

'I know, not as trim a figure as us and her being younger into the bargain.'

So the cattiness went on with Emily watching in both amusement and disgust and decided that if this was what religion was about they could keep it.

They had to sing dreary hymns that she'd never heard before. All she could do was open and shut her mouth and hoped she looked like she was singing. Then there was all the kneeling to say prayers. She'd have sworn her knees had never been the same since.

As the vicar stood up at the pulpit to read the sermon Emily really believed this would be the moment of interest. He went on and on, his voice getting higher and higher as he seemed to be getting angrier and angrier, as Emily sat open mouthed not having a clue what it was about. Her head kept dropping forward with boredom, only for her to feel a sharp dig in the ribs and Mrs Cotrill glaring at her and mouthing, 'Pay attention.'

When she arrived home she tried to describe to her mother the terrible experience she had been through. 'It'll do you good. It might instil some discipline into you,' she told her, in a no-nonsense tone of voice.

She'd suffered a few more Sundays and then much to Emily's relief Mrs Cotrill was taken ill. Emily was fully aware it was unchristian of her to cheer when she heard the news, but it was such a relief to know there would be no more church attendance in the near future. Once she was better Mrs Cotrill packed up and moved to live with her sister, so that was the last her mother mentioned about her attending church.

The next time she went to church was for her own wedding. When Howard and she went to see the vicar she soon appreciated that the vicar held more modern opinions on the approach to church attendance. Although he was initially a little reluctant to perform the marriage ceremony in his church as neither went and didn't appear to be of a religious nature. He couldn't understand why a registry office would not suffice. Howard soon talked his way around him by stating that when they had children he'd make sure they attended every Sunday. This seemed to pacify the vicar enough and he agreed to marry them in his church, provided they attended three sessions for the reading of the banns.

That time on the Sunday attendance the service still didn't interest Emily, but she did consider the sermon less tedious. She wasn't sure if there was actually an improvement in the sermon or her own maturity and understanding helped.

Now what had she gone and done but promised Karen she would go to church with her next Sunday? She knew it was her own fault that she had been backed into a corner with no opportunity to find a good excuse to get out of it. She remembered her visit to York Minster and the peace it had brought her. Something of a rebellion went on inside her as she prepared herself on the Sunday morning for the ordeal ahead. There was no hat on her head; in any case she didn't even own one to put on.

It came as a shock, when they entered the church, to find nobody with a hat on. Instead bright, cheery faces greeted them. 'A pleasure to see you here. It's a family service — here's the service sheet for you to follow.'

Then another voice asked, 'Are you on holiday or have you moved into the neighbourhood recently?'

'Oh, moved here,' stammered Emily, taken aback at so much friendliness.

'Where to dear?' another voice chimed in.

When she told them the first lady who had spoken said, 'That's Elena Robertson's old house. She was a grand old lady, did a lot for the church in helping with the fund raising.'

Then she looked keenly at Emily. 'Are you a relative of hers?'

'Yes,' replied Emily, not feeling the need to

enlighten her further.

'I thought so, you look very like her. Anyway you'd best find yourself a seat as the service is due to start, but it's lovely to see you here.' Then she quickly added, 'And your friend, of course.'

Poor Karen, she'd been pushed into the background when it had really been her idea to attend.

The service moved so quickly it left Emily bemused. She'd no time to look at the service sheet to see what was coming next. When the hymns started she expected the loud peals of the organ, instead a guitar started playing a modern tune. Children joined in the sermon. Instead of sitting bored Emily sat mesmerized as she listened. Something inside her happened and she once more felt calm take over and an uplift of her emotions.

When the service had finished Karen turned to ask, 'All right for you?'

'Yes, thanks,' she replied, still looking bemused.

Karen had a more relaxed look about her than Emily had seen before. Once again, as they left the church, various people spoke to them. One of the ladies, who had spoken to them before, said, 'There's coffee and biscuits provided in the church hall if you'd like to come along and join us.'

Emily looked at Karen questioningly, 'Do you want to go?'

'Yes, please.'

They'd agreed that from then on the Sunday lunch would be in the evening thereby freeing up Karen from her cooking to attend church. As soon as they entered the church hall a gentleman came across to join them. 'Just go to the hatch over there for your tea or coffee and help yourself to a biscuit.'

Once they were seated others joined them at the table and she'd never seen Karen as animated as she chatted back to them, far different to her usual reserved manner. Emily made a silent promise to herself that she'd come to church each Sunday with Karen, as long as she needed her to, if this was the effect it had on her.

She gave a slight jump as a voice to her right said, 'It's Songs of Praise next Sunday. I hope you and your friend will join us and that you've got a good singing voice as we sing lots of hymns during that service.'

'I don't know about a good voice, but I'll try my best to join in,' she replied back cheerfully.

The vicar came over to them to welcome them both into his church and made his introductions. He'd obviously been primed that she was a relative of Elena Robertson, as

Emily could sense he would have loved to ask outright what relative. He'd already stated early on in the conversation, 'Funny, Elena never mentioned she had any relatives. I always thought she was the last one of the line.'

Emily tried to brush it off by saying, 'Well, it just goes to show, none of us fully know about another person's life.'

He took no offence at this. Instead he changed tack and asked, 'I hope you will be joining us here again.'

Before Emily could answer, Karen, who had stayed quiet, suddenly jumped in, and Emily noticed her face was flushed with excitement. 'We will, thank you Reverend for such a beautiful service. It's done me a world of good.'

Emily could see the Vicar — or Bill as he'd told them to call him — was rather taken aback by this statement. He asked, 'Would it be all right if I called to see all of you at your home. I've heard so much from the doctor — David — about what you are doing.'

'Yes, of course, feel free to come along any time, as there's usually one or other of us around.'

'Thanks, I will. I'll take my leave now, I'd better circulate.'

That was Emily's initiation in going back to

church. Life was settling down for her. Even David had once more relaxed his steely reserve with her and had actually enjoyed a laugh once or twice recently.

Karen looked better for her regular attendance at church and for the first time in her life Emily felt she was also benefiting from religion. Bill had become another frequent visitor, often staying and having a coffee and chat with whoever was around. Although they all welcomed him into the house, so far none of the others had attended the church.

As Emily entered the house, after a trip to the market, Karen called to her, 'Bill called this afternoon.'

'Good, that would have been company for you,' replied Emily, aware that everybody else had been busy with one or other task either for themselves or for Emily.

'It was good to see him but actually he called to see you for a private chat.'

'To see me?' Emily asked, curiously. 'I'd better give him a ring then,' she said impatiently.

'No,' said Karen stopping Emily in her tracks. 'He'd to attend some meeting tonight and tomorrow was a busy day so he said he'd call tomorrow night about seven, at your cottage. If he doesn't hear from you he'll take it to be okay and come along at that time.'

'No problem, that's fine. I'll see him then,' replied Emily. It had rather whetted her curiosity to know who he wanted to tell her about. By now she was convinced that was the reason he wanted to see her.

She found out she wasn't wrong, because as soon as they'd got the pleasantries out of the way he said, 'One of my regular parishioners is in hospital. You won't have seen her at church as she's not been too well for a while. She's had a bad heart for years but the medics usually have it under control. She's an independent lady and has been doing far too much recently. She lives on her own you see and has a large garden to upkeep. She's not said but I think she's run through any money she had a while ago and she disposed of her part-time gardener's services and has been trying to look after the garden herself. The doctor says that's what has brought on this exceptionally bad angina attack. I think she even panicked herself as she thought it was a massive heart attack. She's been told she'd done no further damage to her heart, which is a small miracle but it was a warning for her to slow down and she has got to stop the gardening.'

'So where do I fit in? I hope you don't want me to become a gardener,' she laughed.

'Would you go and visit her at hospital?'

'Of course, is that all?' she asked, feeling a little disappointed it wasn't possibly going to be a new resident.

'Silly me, my wife is forever saying that I never get to the point of the tale. You know what they are like when they have always been so independent.' Emily had to gather her wits about her as he was jumping around with the story, and she felt at a loss now as to just who was independent. But it soon became clear as he continued. 'It's not only the garden that's too much for her, but the house as well. She's also dismissed her cleaner. So I thought of here, particularly after I have seen how happily everyone has settled in.'

'Yes, but they all wanted to come here. Does this lady want to come? By the way you've not even told me her name.'

'Here I am again going on and forgetting the essentials. Her name is Ida, Ida Sloan. That's why I wanted you to go and see her. You see, I've not directly mentioned the idea to her but I have hinted. I thought the feminine touch might be best.'

'I don't know about that,' said Emily smiling. She could see Bill was looking unsure of himself, so quickly went on to clarify her reply, as she'd noticed before he could be a bit slow when making a joke about something. 'I only meant the feminine touch might not be best. Of course I'll go and see her. I don't think I have anything urgent to do tomorrow so I'll go along then. That's as long as nothing comes along that needs my immediate attention.'

'Oh, thanks Emily.'

'Don't get your hopes up too much,' Emily warned. 'If she really doesn't want to come here then there's not a lot I can do.'

'I do hope she agrees. I just know she would be happy here.'

For once Emily had slight misgivings about what she was doing. She'd set the place up for people if they willingly wanted to live there. She didn't want elderly people to feel as if they were being pushed into a place which they thought was only a posh name for a residential home in another guise. The fact the woman had a bad heart worried her. She'd no nursing skills nor did she profess to have any. Anybody joining her in the house really needed to be fit and well, thereby making them independent. Anybody could be taken ill at any time but was she being fair to the other residents thinking about taking in an ailing resident? This was one time she wished she had a partner she could confide in and seek advice.

18

Emily soon began to wish she'd not agreed to Bill's request to go and visit the hospital. The more she thought about it the more she decided to take this old lady into the house would be a disaster.

As she walked down the hospital corridor, she could barely concentrate on finding the ward; her thoughts were so taken up with the woman she was visiting. Then the words, 'school marmish' sprung into her head as a picture of what she thought she would be like. This set off another train of thought about one of her own school mistresses, Miss Crossley. When she moved to the high school she had been dismayed to recognise the teacher of history to be the woman she'd often seen at the house opposite theirs, with an even more elderly lady — her mother presumably.

It was really the yapping dog that had made her take notice of them at all. Her own mother had kept on stating she would like a dog like that, but in white. Not being up on breeds of dogs Emily wasn't sure what it was, it just seemed an annoying, noisy pest. It was a poodle. Her father had been adamant that there was going to be no dog in their house. Her mother had tried to say in her timid way, 'But poodles don't shed hairs, so there will be no mess if we have one.'

Her father had been quick to point out it would cost money in food and kennels when they went away. Besides which, it would need taking for walks and he was sure the novelty would soon wear off so it would be left to him. Emily hadn't been bothered either way. If anything she had agreed with her father that they did seem more trouble than they were worth. Now Emily gave a small laugh at imagining how her father would have looked taking a small white dog with a pom pom tail for a walk. He'd have been a laughing stock in that village.

If she had ever wanted a dog of her own she would have been more interested in abandoned dogs of the 'who-knew-what' variety. She had gone through a phase when she wanted to save one of these poor creatures, but however much she had begged and pleaded with her father he still replied, 'No, I'm not having a dog in this house,' and her mother didn't even bother to back her up because it wouldn't be the poodle she wanted.

By now she'd reached the ward entrance

but still wasn't quite sure how she would be able to identify Miss Sloan, as she hadn't really a clue how to recognise her.

Seeing a young nurse coming out of a door she called out, 'Could you help me? I am looking for Miss Sloan.' When she saw the puzzled expression on the nurse's face, for a terrible moment she thought she was in the wrong place, but then had sense to add, 'Ida Sloan.'

Emily saw comprehension dawn on the girl's face as she said, 'Oh, Ida, this way please.'

After walking a good two thirds of the way down the ward the girl stopped and pointed to a bed stating, 'There's Ida,' as if Emily should know her.

When Emily looked across at Ida she couldn't say she actually looked like a school teacher as she sat up in bed. She looked more like a female version of her father. This made Emily even more wary as she stated, 'Hello, Miss Sloan. I'm Emily Cartwright.'

'Oh yes, Bill mentioned you. Please, call me Ida, Miss Sloan is far too formal,' she replied in a very friendly voice.

This took the wind out of Emily's sails as it wasn't what she'd expected at all. 'Right, yes, Ida it is. I was just going to say Reverend Salter told me all about you.'

'Yes, Bill. He's a good sort.'

'I hope you are feeling better,' Emily stated, not sure what to say to make conversation. When she looked at the old lady propped up against the snowy white pillows she didn't look particularly ill.

'Yes, my silly heart gave me quite a scare. It was my own fault really. You'd think after all these years of it being not very good, I'd have had more sense. But no, I go and overdo things and end up in here. I feel fine now. I don't really know why I am still here, but they will insist I've to stay a bit longer. They won't give me the all clear to go home however much I beg them. Dread to think what my garden must look like now and I don't know how I'll get it back up to scratch.'

Emily saw a slight look of what could only be described as fear on the old lady's face and understood how she obviously had reservations how she would cope. It was too early on in the relationship to say anything about it so she carried on, 'It's very pleasant in here. They've obviously made an effort to get away from the clinical feeling of a hospital by adding splashes of colour and even having duvets on the beds.'

'Yes, I can't complain, they've been very good to me.' She changed the subject, 'Tell me, am I right in thinking you've moved into

228

Elena Robertson's place?'

'Yes, that's correct. It's a lovely old house.'

'It's a bit run down if I remember correctly. I did visit Elena there once or twice.'

'It was but after a lot of work it's all coming together now.'

'That's good to hear. Are you related to Elena? I can see a resemblance there.'

'Oh, yes, actually I am,' Emily admitted, hoping she did not probe any further.

'Thought so,' replied Ida, looking pleased with herself. Emily felt relief go through her as she then continued, 'I got on well with Elena. She was a lovely old lady.'

Here Emily wanted to give a giggle at the absurdity of this comment as the lady in front of her was elderly herself. She had already decided, prior to the visit, that at their first meeting it would be prudent not to put her proposal to Ida. She would use more subtle tactics by putting the notion into Ida's head and let her know how she was using the house and the fact that there were still vacancies for more residents.

Emily said, 'These old houses take some looking after on your own. Do you live in a large house?'

'Aye, it's a fair size. It is not just the house but the garden as well. How are you coping with yours?'

Emily felt pleased with herself that the bait had been taken but kept her smile well hidden as she replied tactfully, 'I don't actually live in the main house.'

'You don't?' Ida asked, puzzled.

'No, I've had the garage converted into a little cottage for myself.'

'That must be nice and cosy. But I thought you said you had modernised the main house?'

'I have,' replied Emily, still determined to give only the minimum answer to each question, so it didn't appear she was being over willing to give her a lot of information about the house.

'You can't have just left it empty?' asked Ida, getting more curious.

'Oh no, people live in it.'

'Oh I see. You've let it out. Is it a holiday let place or a long term let?' asked Ida, certain she understood.

'Neither.' She felt she had to go into further detail and enlighten Ida with the purpose of the house. 'No, I've made it into a home for people in need of a sort of refuge for one reason or another.'

'Unusual,' was all Ida said.

But Emily went on enlightening her a little more. 'I suppose it is. Each has their own room with a mini kitchen but we have a cook who prepares meals so we can eat together like one big family if we want to.'

Ida couldn't hold her curiosity to know more as she asked, 'I suppose it is only young people that you have there? Like a commune kind of thing is it?'

'No not at all. It is for people of all ages. I've got an elderly gentleman of eighty living there and he's still fit and well. Then there's a friend of mine, slightly older than me, she's the one doing the cooking and also there's a younger girl, the niece of my cleaner, Joan. I'd say it is independent living as everybody can come and go as they wish, have friends in and lead the life they want to. At the same time they also have companionship if they require it. It is just a bit less lonely than living in a house or flat on their own.'

Ida now changed the subject as she asked, 'Do you mean Joan who used to clean for Elena?'

'I do.'

'I would have liked her to clean for me if I'd had the money. Very thorough she was as I remember it.'

'She is.'

'M'mm, sounds quite interesting.'

'It keeps me occupied and I'm enjoying every minute of running it.' Emily left it at that as she felt she'd said enough on this first visit to plant the seed of an idea in Ida's mind.

After a little more general chat Emily said, 'I'll have to go now, but I'll call again to visit before you leave to go home.'

'Please do. When you get to my age there are not many left to come and visit.'

If Ida could have seen Emily's face as she walked out of the ward she'd have seen a self-satisfied smile.

★   ★   ★

Although nothing had been settled about Ida coming to live with them, Emily was pretty certain she would in the end and thought it was only fair to warn Harry, Rachel and Karen. Knowing Ida was of similar age to Harry, Emily had imagined he'd been delighted to have her company in the house. Instead he showed a slight hesitancy as he asked, 'Do you really think she will fit in as a spinster? She might be a bit too prim and proper for here.'

'Harry, I'm surprised at you,' Emily laughed, but she saw Harry looked genuinely concerned.

'Sorry, Harry, I shouldn't have said that. No, actually when Bill asked me to go along and visit her I had my own reservations. Since

I've met her and had a chat I think she'll fit in fine. I'm sure she'd soon adapt to our way of life here.'

When Emily asked the rest of them their opinion they hadn't much to say on the subject, not even Karen. She seemed to be having one of her bad days and wasn't really bothered, nor was Rachel as she was still so pleased that Emily had taken her in that she'd willingly agree to anything.

On her next visit to see Ida, Emily at least felt she wasn't doing anything to disturb the peace of the house if she pressed forward with getting Ida interested in joining them. She was pretty certain Harry would get over his uncertainty once he got to know Ida and hopefully they would become friends.

Ida didn't look as cheerful as the other day when Emily approached her bed. She asked her with concern in her voice, 'Aren't you feeling too well today, Ida?'

'I feel fine, just fed up with myself. Do you know they've had the nerve to say I've got to go on a home visit before they will consider letting me out of here.'

'What do you mean by that?' asked Emily, not really sure what it involved and the implications.

'I have to go with someone from here and they will test me to see if I can make myself a cup of tea and a light meal. They look at other things, like can I get out of bed okay, and, of course, get washed.'

'But you can do those things can't you?'

'I should hope so. But it does somehow feel like climbing a mountain when I sit here brooding on it.'

Ida wasn't in bed but sat in an easy chair next to the bed and much to Emily's surprise was already dressed as if ready.

'When do you go?' Emily queried, wondering if she was due to go that afternoon.

'Tomorrow, hopefully, that's if they have somebody available to go with me.'

'Right, I'll come again to see how you got on. But I'm sure you have nothing to worry about. After all, it wasn't your faculties that were affected, only your heart playing up.'

'I know that, but look you don't want to be wasting your time visiting an old body like me. I'm sure you lead a very busy life.'

'I don't mind in the least coming.' Emily stopped herself before adding that she had nothing better to do. That would have sounded hurtful.

'If you don't mind me asking,' Ida continued, 'how are the residents chosen to come and live in your place?'

Emily gave a small laugh. 'I think it's more the other way around. They've chosen to come and live there themselves.'

Seeing Ida's startled expression she went on to explain. 'I've not advertised or anything yet to get residents and in fact, don't intend to. I want people to come by word of mouth. Karen is a friend and she rang me to ask to come and stay, not knowing I now had the house. David, the doctor, told me about Harry and Joan about her niece, Angela. I've not been in a rush to get anybody else because the work wasn't finished until now. I've still two rooms to let, then Karen's going to decorate the attic flat herself and move in there now it's been converted so it'll free up another room.'

Seeing Ida was listening with keen interest she carried on, 'All the rooms, even though I say so myself, are very attractive and tastefully done out giving a light, peaceful feeling. They have furniture in but if anybody wants to bring along any of their own they are more than welcome. As I said before, all the rooms are self-contained, apart from the bathroom, but there are more than adequate facilities. We all eat in the kitchen, although there is a dining room, but that's mainly for special occasions. There's also a general purpose sitting room if people want more company. It's not a bit like a residential home, you're free to come and go as you want, have friends in and Harry even likes to do work around the house. Rachel's got into the habit of helping her aunt clean to keep her occupied until she sorts out what to do with her life. So you see, it's more like a family but if people want they can still have their own privacy.'

'I see,' Ida said quietly. Then she asked, 'I presume Harry has a lot of money to pay for himself seeing he must be a pensioner like me.'

'Not at all, he's got his pension then some social security benefit to help him.'

'Ah, that's interesting,' was all she added before changing the subject.

Emily was still worried whether Ida's health was really up to going home. The fact the hospital were insisting on a home visit didn't sound too good. So she made a decision to call on David on her way home and get his opinion.

She arrived at the end of surgery and the receptionist said he would be able to see her.

'Hello, what can I do for you?' he said, when he looked up and saw Emily. He quickly added, 'Come and sit down.'

'I've actually called concerning a person Bill Slater told me about. He thought my place might be a good idea for her. She's in hospital at the moment having suffered an angina attack.'

'What's the problem?' David asked with interest.

'I was wondering if she was really well enough to come to live with us.'

'What's her name?'

'Ida Sloan.'

He thought for a moment then said, 'She's not one of mine, but I'll have a word with my colleagues and find out what I can for you. You do realise because of patient confidentiality I might not be able to tell you very much.'

Emily had never given this a thought, as she had been glad of the excuse to call in and see David. 'Look I don't want to get you into any trouble. Forget I asked.'

'No, don't worry. I'll call around to see you tomorrow and let you know what I've found out.'

Emily seemed to be walking on air as she went out to her car. He'd been so friendly again; his reserve was slowly breaking down.

★   ★   ★

Karen commented the next morning, when Emily came down that she was dressed up and asked, 'Are you off out somewhere special today?'

'No. I want to be in because David is

calling to see me about Ida, but I don't know what time.'

Emily never noticed the knowing look that passed between Karen and Harry.

As the day moved on and there was no sign of David she became despondent, then she told herself not to be so silly. He was a doctor and a busy one. He'd arrive when he had time.

She jumped when he said from behind her, 'Emily.' He looked contrite as he saw her shocked expression. 'Sorry, I didn't mean to make you jump. I thought you'd heard me come in.'

'No, I was miles away.'

'I liked the tune you were humming,' he added.

Emily felt her face flush red in its old childish manner that she thought she'd outgrown.

'About Ida,' he continued. 'I don't think you've a lot to concern yourself about if she does come to live here. The only thing I would say is that she would be better with a ground floor room if possible.'

'I don't know about that, I'll have to give it some thought.'

'As long as she sticks to her medication and doesn't go mad doing things to exert her heart her angina should stay under control.'

'Thanks David, that is very useful. I hope it didn't cause you problems finding out.'

'None at all,' he laughed. 'It's been my pleasure.'

He stayed where he was, hesitating as if he'd something to say. He stuttered, 'Er, have you been to the restaurant at the far end of the shops, the one with the glass front?'

Emily laughed. 'I haven't been to any restaurants since I came here.'

'Well, we had better rectify that. Would you like to go with me for a meal there?'

'Would I? I'd love to, just tell me when. I'll be ready.'

'Would Saturday suit you? I'm not on duty then.'

'Let me just look at my diary,' she said laughing. She saw his face drop and quickly answered him, 'Only kidding, I've nothing booked in it at all.'

'Oh right, I'll collect you at 7.30?'

'Yes please.'

With that he turned heel and was nearly out of the door as he said over his shoulder, 'See you then.'

Emily couldn't really fathom him out. He could be so friendly one minute then the next abrupt. Maybe going out on Saturday would solve the problem.

When she told Harry and Karen about the

proposed meal one would have thought it was them who had been invited, they became so excited for her.

Karen even went as far as to say, 'I think this calls for a new outfit. You've not bought anything since I've been here.'

Emily was getting carried away with euphoria and quickly agreed by saying, 'You've suggested it, Karen, so you'd better come along with me to pick something. How about going to Beverley tomorrow?'

'Oh, great.'

★   ★   ★

Emily didn't trawl around many shops in Beverley, she headed straight for Monsoon. She was sure she would find something suitable in that shop, it being one of her favourites.

Karen had always had good clothes sense, but since coming to join Emily she seemed to have lost interest. She'd never bothered to have her hair bleached again and it had grown out to reveal a salt and pepper colour. As soon as she saw the wonderful clothes her face became animated, more than Emily had seen for a long time.

Emily picked out a few items to try on and was delighted to see Karen clutching some hangers with skirts and tops on them. 'I think I'll try these on. Might as well, whilst you're trying on things,' Karen said, showing more interest in anything than she had since Emily had first renewed their friendship.

They were like a pair of giggling schoolgirls as they tried the outfits on in the fitting rooms and paraded in front of each other for an opinion. After getting Karen's confirmation she finally settled for a dress of chiffon, in varying shades of a plum colour, with an inner lining the same colour. The skirt flowed out at the bottom whilst the rest of the dress hugged her trim figure. She studied her reflection in the mirror and was pleased with what she saw.

Karen had picked a bargain floral skirt and a plain t-shirt to match.

'Now I think I'll get some shoes,' exclaimed Emily, enjoying the feeling of splashing out on herself for a change instead of the house.

They found an expensive leather shop with shoes and handbags to match. Emily looked at Karen questioningly. 'Shall we?'

'Why not, it costs nothing to look.'

There was a sale on and Emily found a lovely pair but with a heel slightly higher than she'd worn for a long time. Being on her feet all day at college she'd got into the habit of comfort rather than style. She had to admit, despite their elegance, they were also very comfortable. 'I only hope I can walk properly in them,' she said to Karen after she'd told her they looked perfect.

Another thought struck her. 'They won't make me taller than David?'

'No, they won't. Stop fussing and get them,' she laughed.

As Emily paid for them the assistant said, 'We've a handbag that matches these in the sale if Madam would like to see it?'

'Why not?' Then said, 'I'll take it,' after seeing it matched the shoes perfectly.

★   ★   ★

As Emily got ready Karen came in and offered to do her makeup for her. Although Emily wasn't bad at doing her face, Karen used to be excellent at making up her own. Now she barely wore any makeup.

'Please,' Emily replied to the question. 'Make me look my best, if that's possible,' she laughed.

Her stomach had the tremors as if this was the first proper date she'd been on. She supposed it wasn't as daft as it seemed when she thought about how she'd met Howard on a blind date. Something about their relationship had never seemed like dating.

For once David arrived exactly on time. He stood like a teenager, moving from one foot to the other.

Emily had never seen him dressed up like this and he'd even managed to tame his unruly hair. He really did look handsome.

'You look lovely,' he said when he saw her.

'You don't look so bad yourself.'

The waitress showed them to a table in a quiet spot at the back of the room.

Emily said to David, 'I'm glad they didn't put us in the window, I'd have felt too much in view.'

'I asked for a table here. That's the only trouble being a doctor in a place of this size, so many people know me and it's embarrassing when they come up to me on an evening off and give a detailed description of their ailments. I thought hidden away here nobody would recognise me.'

Emily laughed. 'That doesn't really happen?'

'It does. I've had some embarrassing moments, I can tell you.'

They became so deep in conversation that Emily was only just aware that the food was good. With reluctance they took their leave, being the last people in the restaurant.

When they arrived back at Emily's house she asked, 'Would you like to come in for a coffee?' She wasn't sure if he'd go back to his reserved self, but he was delighted with this request.

They spent some time chatting and as he left he took her in his arms and gently kissed her on the lips. Not with an intense passion but enough to start the fires burning in her.

She had pleasant dreams that night but only hoped when David woke to the cold light of day he didn't go back to the reserved person he could be with her. Although his last words to her had been, 'We must do this again, and very soon,' implied he shouldn't change, but who knew?

19

As promised Emily went back to see Ida once she knew she would have had her home visit. Ida's face lit up as Emily walked down the ward. Emily thought, 'Poor dear, I bet hardly anybody else has been to see her.'

'You're looking well today, Ida,' she said as she arrived at the bed.

'I am. I feel like new after all this rest.' Her smile disappeared and a hint of sadness replaced it.

'How did the home visit go?' Emily asked, suspecting it could be something to do with that.

'Oh, well you know,' she replied, noncommittal.

Emily laughed, 'You sound just like one of my students. No I don't know so that is why I am asking you, Ida.'

'Sorry. To be honest it was a lot harder than I had imagined. I'm not sure that they think I'm fit enough to cope totally on my own. I'm all right pottering around the house but when it comes to the heavier tasks then that's a different matter.'

'Yes, but you did have a very bad angina

attack and it takes a lot of recovery to get over something like that,' Emily said calmly, trying to put her mind at rest.

'It has set me thinking. I realised the other day that if I sold the old house I would have a little bit of money. Not a fortune but more than enough for my small needs. You get a lot of time to sit and think in here,' she said by way of an explanation before carrying on. 'So I was wondering, do you think I could rent one of your rooms?'

Emily had imagined Ida would have needed a lot more persuading before she came round to this way of thinking. Now she hesitated as she answered, 'If you are sure that is what you really want. It's a big step you know.'

Ida looked determined but at the same time slightly disappointed at Emily's reluctance to say she could move in. She replied, 'I am sure,' in a very positive voice.

'I see,' replied Emily, still not saying a lot.

At the lack of a positive response from Emily, Ida asked with disappointment in her voice, 'Am I too late, have all the rooms been taken now?'

'No,' Emily admitted, 'there are still some vacant. But how will you cope with the stairs? I was wondering if you'd manage going up and down to your room all the time.'

'Haven't you any ground floor rooms?' Ida asked hopefully.

'No, if I had I would have offered you one straight away.'

'Then I'll have to manage the stairs,' replied Ida, with a hint of pleading in her voice.

Now it was Emily's turn to feel contrite as she seemed to be putting obstacles in the way of a person who would make a perfect resident.

'Look, I'll tell you what,' she said making an instant decision. 'There are plenty of rooms on the ground floor, some not even in use, so I'll see if I can organise something for you.' Then Emily laughed, 'I must have known as I had a ground floor bathroom installed.'

'Thank you. To think you'll really go to all this trouble for me. You don't know how much it all means,' Ida replied, with an obvious expression of relief in her voice and a glint of tears in her eyes.

Emily knew she'd made more work for herself, just as she thought it was easing off, but it was worth it to see a person look so much brighter, as if a massive weight had been lifted off her shoulders.

'As I will be getting the room ready from scratch, you can let me know if there are any items of furniture from your house you want putting in it,' Emily suggested.

'I'd like my own bed from home. After sleeping on this one here I don't think I ever want to sleep on a strange one again,' Ida laughed.

'That's fine by me, because that is the one thing I haven't got, a spare bed. But if you think of anything else just let me know.'

On the way home Emily settled on the study as she had somehow never felt really at ease in there. Besides which, she had now got the desk in her own home. Nobody else seemed to use that room and surprisingly for a study, it was a large room with French doors leading to the rear patio and garden. Yes, she felt pleased with her choice despite the fact it was a bit dark and drab but they could soon alter that.

She quickly outlined her plans to Karen, as she would need her assistance in getting it ready. As Emily made a move to get on with the work Karen called out, 'Not so quick.' Without saying any more she turned around to look at the kitchen door. 'Oh, Harry, just in time.'

Emily looked at Karen questioningly; what was going on?

'We're ready and waiting for you to tell us about your meal out with David, as you haven't said a word about it,' Karen said once Harry was seated.

'It was fine,' smiled Emily, keeping them in suspense.

'We know that, it's been obvious by the expression on your face ever since, hasn't it Harry?'

'It has that. I don't think he could have prescribed any better medicine himself.'

'So come on, we want more details.'

'The food was good and we had a pleasant table out of the limelight,' Emily replied prevaricating.

'Yes, and what else?' asked Karen, getting impatient.

'Yes, well, then he came in for a coffee and he did give me a goodnight kiss,' admitted Emily, hoping to satisfy their curiosity.

'Great, so when are you going out together again?' asked Karen, looking very pleased.

'Oh, I don't know about that, but at least he did say we'd do it again quite soon.'

'Now keep him on the boil this time, seeing as you've moved this far forward,' Karen advised.

'Yes, well can you get on the boil yourself and help me with the study,' laughed Emily, taking it all in good humour.

They settled on pale peach walls which they knew would be restful but not too feminine, as Emily felt Ida wouldn't be keen on that. The curtains and carpet that were in already would blend and save some expense as Emily hadn't expected to be making this into a guest room. Some of the furniture that she had left in would suffice, depending on what else Ida decided to bring along with her. She was lucky to get the plumber to fit the kitchen unit in between jobs so by the time she drew up in the car with Ida all the work was completed.

On the journey Emily could sense a slight trepidation in the old woman and thought she was probably wondering what she was doing leaving her own home to move into a new place. She was very quiet as if in deep thought which Emily found slightly unnerving.

Once the car was stopped Emily turned to Ida to reassure her, 'You'll be fine. In no time you'll feel you've always been here. Your room looks a treat and has doors opening out on to the back garden. I've put a couple of chairs and a table on the patio outside so you can enjoy the garden whenever you feel like it and if the weather is fine.'

'You're so kind,' Ida replied, with tears in her eyes.

Trying to diffuse the situation a bit Emily said, 'Let's go and meet everybody and show you your room. Better to see it than sit here describing it.'

Emily knew she'd made a good choice with the room when she saw Ida's genuine delight. Yet she knew if Ida had seen it a few days ago she'd never have believed the transformation. Now it was all light and cheery.

'I'll leave you to get yourself sorted out. When you are ready come along to the kitchen and I'll have a pot of tea. You'll find tea seems to be on the go most of the time here and the kitchen is the heart of the place.'

'Thanks, that's most kind. I could do with one. I won't be long.'

'No rush, just in your own time,' Emily replied kindly.

By the time Ida entered the kitchen Karen was there doing some food preparation.

Karen was introduced to Ida and Emily was amazed at her rather cool welcome. She had not been like this with Harry or Rachel. Besides which, she'd not shown any qualms about Ida joining them. It had been Harry who had done that.

Trying to break the ice Emily said, 'Karen's just in the process of moving into a small flat I've had made for her in the attic.'

'That sounds grand,' replied Ida warmly, but Karen carried on with her cooking as if they hadn't spoken to her.

Emily felt annoyed with her because she'd spent a lot of time and effort turning the attic rooms into a flat. She had been a good friend to her and didn't deserve this attitude with her residents.

They had used three of the four attic rooms for the conversion. Emily had thought it prudent to keep one part as an attic then for storage. There was always something bulky to store including the suitcases.

The flat had its own front door with the lounge in the centre, a door off one side into a bedroom with a lounge on the other side. There was also a small, compact kitchen and another door off the lobby into the bathroom.

Like the rest of the house, despite being attics, the ceilings were still high giving a feeling of spaciousness. Emily had let Karen have her own choice in decoration and a good rummage through the attics to use the furniture she wanted.

Emily admired Karen's design skills and she had used one of the trunks as a coffee table with an attractive cover on top. There were an oddment of easy chairs and Karen selected throws from remnants of fabric found in the attics for them. Although it wasn't overcrowded it wasn't Howard's idea of minimalist, but it was warm and homely.

With this present attitude Emily was beginning to wonder if she had got it wrong and Karen didn't want to move into the flat. She wasn't under a compulsion to use it in the evenings. She could sit in the general sitting room if she wished. Maybe Karen was frightened at the thought of loneliness.

Before Emily could talk to her Harry entered the kitchen and Karen rushed to take his arm. He was very pale and looked as if he was going to drop to the floor.

Emily quickly pulled a chair across to him. 'Here, sit down. Is there anything I can get you?' she asked with concern in her voice.

'No, there's nothing. I'm fine now. But I am forgetting my manners. You must be Miss Sloan, pleased to meet you, my dear. I'm Harry.'

'Call me Ida, please. I'm pleased to meet you. You haven't a bad heart as well, have you?' she queried.

'No, fit as a fiddle,' laughed Harry. He wasn't going to let on, but this meeting had really knocked him for six. When he'd walked into the kitchen he'd thought for a moment he'd seen Edna sat there. The likeness was remarkable.

But then as the woman had turned to face him he realised her features were sharper than Edna's had been. Even so, it had briefly brought back some painful memories to him, no wonder he'd felt so faint with the shock.

Over the last few weeks, he'd felt happy and relaxed that a lot of the memories that had haunted him after all these years had receded. He wasn't sure how he was going to cope seeing this face everyday, it would give him so many reminders. On top of that, despite the haughty appearance, she'd been just as friendly as Edna.

He tried to act as normally as possible as he said to Ida, 'I hope you settle in here as well as I have. I know it was the best decision I'd made for a long time, coming here. It's taken years off my age being around these young lasses.'

Emily giggled, 'Not quite so young.'

'Aye, but still young enough to be my granddaughter,' he laughed back.

Trying to be friendly, Ida asked Harry, 'Have you any family?'

'No, sadly not,' and she saw the shutters come down in his eyes and knew it was still obviously a painful subject, and left well alone.

'My room is delightful,' she said changing the subject.

'I know. Emily let me have a peek. It's a delightful house altogether. It has such a good feeling about it. Karen's moving into her own little place. Have you heard about that?'

'Yes, it sounds delightful.'

'You've only Rachel to meet, but she's gone to her aunt's to see her cousin today.' Then he laughed, 'And I mustn't forget Joan.'

Ida chirped in, 'I did know Elena Robertson through the church and I had called here several times, so I have met Joan before.' She added, 'I presume it is the same Joan, the cleaner, you're talking about.'

Still laughing Harry carried on, 'It is. So you'll know what you're letting yourself in for?'

'I do, she's a case, but a kindly soul.'

He said more seriously, 'She has a heart of gold. She would do anything for anybody. But I suspect she's not had an easy life of it herself.'

Emily hadn't broken Joan's confidence by telling Harry what she'd told her of her life. So it came as a shock to see a man who was astute enough to understand deeper emotions. Howard had never been capable of that.

Karen was stirring the sauce harder than she needed to. She felt indignant. Harry had become her father figure, her confidant. Now this intruder had come, somebody his own age and he was already talking to her like she was an old buddy. She could see they were capable of sitting hours on end reminiscing about the past. Her nose was well and truly pushed out of joint and she didn't like it.

Unlike Emily, Karen harboured bitterness about what had happened in her life and felt she deserved happiness now. Anything she felt was coming in the way of that happiness she resented. Blinkered by her resentment she failed to notice Ida, like Harry, had a caring nature, and never having any family of her own would be more than willing to take Karen under her wing as an adoptive granddaughter. Karen had made her mind up that because Ida was a spinster she would be frustrated and even at her age was out to snare any man who showed her the slightest attention.

Emily could feel the tension emanating from Karen. It hadn't been Karen who had bothered her regarding getting on with Ida, it had been Harry. Yet here they were, getting along fine, whilst Karen had barely managed to say a civil word to Ida. She only hoped Rachel would accept Ida more easily.

Emily was beginning to learn that whatever age people were it wasn't all plain sailing for them to settle in with each other. To think she had thought students were difficult. She gave a sigh of exasperation at them all and decided to leave them to it as she sought refuge in her little cottage.

20

Emily was really puzzled by Karen's attitude with Ida which was continuing to cause an atmosphere. There was no excuse for it, whatever Karen had suffered in the past.

Harry was equally mystified because Ida was such a nice person. It had been far easier her joining them that he'd imagined. He had to acknowledge that her reminding him so much of Edna had helped. He still couldn't fathom Karen at all. Ida had barely had a chance to say two words to her, never mind upset her.

Emily was determined she wasn't having any ill feeling in the house. She didn't like the atmosphere and she'd lived too much of her own life in such a manner. When she found the appropriate opportunity she tackled Karen about it. 'How are you finding Ida?' she queried.

'All right,' replied Karen, noncommittally.

'She's a very pleasant person.'

'I suppose so,' she replied, more like a sulky teenager than a grown woman.

Emily felt it best to take the bull by the horns and asked outright, 'What is it that you don't like about her?'

'Nothing,' replied Karen, still not being drawn out on the subject.

'Well, I would never have known, the way you have been treating her.'

'I don't treat her in any way,' she snapped back, slightly losing control.

'No, you're right there. You can't say a civil word to her let alone have a conversation.'

'I'm busy a lot of the time,' she said excusing her behaviour.

'Look, Karen, I don't know what it is, but I do not want this atmosphere to continue. For this project to work we all need to get along well, and most importantly, we should set an example by being more than just residents ourselves here.'

Karen was beginning to experience the familiar feeling of panic inside her. Would Emily be so annoyed there was the possibility she was going to tell her to pack her bags and go? She wished now she hadn't made it as apparent that she resented Ida. Now she made a blustering effort to explain her reason for her attitude towards the new resident. 'She's come here and has taken over Harry. He's barely had time to speak to me. All he can do is chat to her,' she said petulantly, more like a small child than a grown woman.

'Karen, that's nonsense. Ida also spends a

lot of her time chatting to Joan, when she's here cleaning. They've so much in common with the pair of them knowing my grandmother. She can't be chatting to Harry all of the time.'

'Well it feels it.'

'I think you've got an over-active imagination. Harry's friendly with us all.'

'I'm sorry then. I will try harder to get on with her,' mumbled Karen.

For the time being Emily had to be satisfied with that and could only hope things would settle down, because she had grown fond of Ida herself. She sensed Harry was getting more than fond of her but had no intention of telling Karen that. She only hoped he wasn't going to be hurt once more in his life; he was far too old for that.

There was nothing really tragic in Ida's past, so she talked quite willingly and openly about her past life with Emily and Harry and anybody else if they were in the room. Her father had died when she was a young girl, so her mother and she had a close relationship. Ida admitted quite freely she'd never been that interested in marriage and said maybe she'd never met the right man. Apparently she had wanted to be a school teacher, which was probably the reason that Emily mistook her to have been one, as she looked the part.

There was no money to pay for her training, and Ida had been trained in shorthand and typing instead. She had them all laughing as she recounted some of the jobs she had undertaken. She had worked at an undertakers when young and despite the seriousness of the job the younger staff would have various escapades. She also worked as a cinema usherette and was quite a film buff. It was a surprise for them to hear such tales from this person who appeared so prim whereas she had led an interesting life despite her spinsterhood and lack of family.

After working and studying for most of her spare time she had passed exams and found a job in a typing pool. She had to admit, after some of the rather unusual jobs she had done, she'd found it all rather mundane.

She explained, 'All the other girls were besotted with one man or another at the company, so when the chance of promotion came along, I got it. I've always thought it was because, even then, they saw me as a spinster and thought any training they gave me wouldn't be wasted. I became Mr Goodyear's personal secretary at a very young age.'

Ida went on to describe Mr Goodyear, she had obviously thought a lot of him and Emily suspected she may have had a soft spot for him, far more than just a secretary-boss relationship. As things turned out he was a happily married man with two young daughters. She had stayed in the job until Mr Goodyear retired when she decided it was time to stop work. Her mother was getting on in years and not in good health so the decision was made for her.

Emily thought, 'Poor dear, what a quiet life she has led,' but she was soon to revise this idea as Ida told of things she and her mother had got up to. Emily had considered herself very fortunate to have gone abroad at her young age but Ida had travelled abroad long before Emily and her family started.

Ida and her mother hadn't missed any opportunity that had come along to have fun. They had been on remarkable cruises and met some impressive people. Emily had been surprised to find that Ida could drive and had done so in the latter part of the last war, as an ambulance driver.

As she explained, 'I had a car until a couple of years ago. I wasn't using it much and it was costing me more than I could really afford, so I decided it was time I went back to shank's pony. There are more than enough drivers on the road and then of course, there was my heart playing up.'

To hear she'd had flying lessons many years

before and actually enjoyed piloting a plane was a real surprise; in fact, her life seemed to have been more interesting than anybody Emily knew.

Emily wasn't grumbling about her own life, although dull, and the years ahead looked as if they would be interesting. Her divorce had been declared absolute and she was free of Howard. She was so pleased that she was a 'free' woman that she had a small celebration.

Bill's wife, Pat, admired all she had done to the house after Emily offered her a tour around. Emily was proud to show her and felt Pat was a good person to know as she was seeking more residents.

She was pleased that David seemed to take special interest in her being a single woman again. He'd continued calling at the house often, at times still blustering that it was on the pretext of seeing one of the residents. They had been out a couple of times. He was still a little cool with her but he never put his harsh reserve up again.

Harry and Karen had congratulated each other, during the party, when they saw Emily and David together. Karen felt happier than she'd done for a while because Harry had sat and chatted with her as he used to do before Ida came on the scene.

Karen had misgivings about her initial

attitude towards Ida. She hadn't meant to be nasty and accepted that it was jealousy. Before Ida had come Harry had been so close to her, like a father. He didn't ignore her when Ida was there but all his attention seemed to be on Ida and what she had to say.

Despite her age Ida seemed to have an air about her that attracted people to her. Karen had always wished she could be like that. It was nothing to do with looks but some inner vitality. People swarmed around her like bees to a honey pot. Rachel talked to her more than she had ever talked to Karen, despite the age difference. When Rachel had arrived Karen was hoping she'd make a real friend of her. She knew she had a good friend in Emily but a lot of Emily's time was taken up with the house and David. She'd wanted somebody of her own and Harry had been the substitute.

Then there was Joan, she and Ida had something in common, them both knowing Emily's grandmother.

Harry was far more concerned about Karen than she appreciated. Time he spent with Ida was also spent in airing these concerns and the pair of them would sit putting their heads together thinking of possible remedies that could help her. They were aware she had such an intense feeling of loneliness and hurt that she would be bitter and resentful.

It was very difficult when she had no interest in men and the pair of them considered themselves too old to take her out and about with themselves.

In fact, had they asked her, she could have agreed to accompany them because that was just what she craved, the companionship of loco parentis parents.

★ ★ ★

Emily was walking through Hornsea when she felt a tap on her shoulder. She almost dropped her shopping bags. She turned to see David grinning at her, 'You could have given me a heart attack,' she snapped at him.

Instead of apologising he just laughed and said, 'You couldn't have fallen into a safer pair of arms.'

'What are you doing here?' she finally asked, when the laughter had subsided.

'I was trying to find you.'

'No seriously.'

'Yes, really that was what I was doing,' he replied.

'How did you know where to look?'

'I rang to see if you were in as I wanted to come for a chat. Karen said you'd just nipped to the shops. I thought as it was such a lovely day I'd walk around then I might bump into you on the way, and I have.'

'So what did you want to see me for?' she asked full of curiosity.

Now his face took on a serious expression. 'It's a very delicate matter and not for discussion in the street.'

'Right. Are you coming back to my place now?' she rambled.

Usually, when he wanted to talk privately it was about a possible future resident, but to say it in that way also implied it could be more personal to him.

★   ★   ★

Once settled in the privacy of her own sitting room with a cup of coffee, Emily said, 'Come on then, spill the beans, you'd better tell me what you were coming to say.'

'Yes. It's rather a difficult one and I've pondered long and hard if I was asking too much of you.'

Emily was still none the wiser by these words and getting more puzzled by the minute, she asked, 'Are you by any chance talking about a patient of yours?'

'Yes, didn't I say?'

'No, you didn't. Don't you think it would be better if you just spit out what you want to ask me then we both know where we are?'

'Okay. I'll start again. I have a patient, a young lady.'

Here Emily interrupted once more, 'I'm glad it's another young person as I don't think I could put up with any more sulks from Karen if it was another patient of Harry's or Ida's age.'

'Still playing up is she?'

'Better than she was after our chat. But I'm sorry, I interrupted you, please carry on.'

'Yes, well this patient is just seventeen years old, and I suppose it's the usual story. She's pregnant and the lad doesn't want to know and is denying it's his.'

'But there is no problem or stigma in being a single mum these days,' she asked puzzled.

'Usually not, no, but you haven't met her parents. Her mother was forty five when she had her and I think the father was over fifty and they doted on her. With elderly parents themselves they are old-fashioned in their ways. When they heard of their daughter's pregnancy, they stormed straight around to me and insisted she be put in a home for unmarried mothers and the baby adopted.'

'Do those places still exist?' asked Emily, appalled at the parent's attitude.

'Not to my knowledge. Nowadays people

do as they want, because as you pointed out there's no stigma attached to a young girl being pregnant.'

'I know you must have told the parents this so how did they react then?'

'They were stone deaf to my words. They really are unbelievable. If you saw them you would think they came straight out of a Victorian novel.'

'Can't the girl make them see sense?'

'To be honest I think they take even less notice of her than me. They really do expect her to do as she is told.'

'So what happens now?'

'Ah, well, you see me and my big mouth. I sort of mentioned I knew of a house that might just possibly have a room available for her and it could be the answer to their problem.'

'Oh you did, did you?' Emily said not sure if she felt pleased or angry with him.

'I never expected them to be as pleased as they were. To be honest I think they mistook what kind of house I meant. They agreed there and then without finding out any more details, that she was 'entered' in this home — as they put it.'

'But, she's pregnant,' exclaimed Emily. 'In truth I hadn't quite considered such a resident joining us.'

Then seeing David's concerned look she added, 'No don't get me wrong. I don't disapprove of the girl being pregnant. It's more myself that I'm thinking about and whether I'm capable enough to give her the help she obviously needs. What happens if she goes into labour here, for example?'

'Don't worry; I've done lots of thinking myself. I do still think it would be a good thing for her. I also forgot to mention she is independent in that she works and intends to do so for as long as she can. She's got a good job for her age and although she's not worked long enough to be eligible for maternity rights they have said if she wasn't off work too long they'll keep her job vacant for her. Nowadays if it's a straightforward birth there is no reason why she can't go back to work quickly, as long as she gets her child care sorted out.'

'I see. Well, that leaves me with no real argument why she shouldn't come here,' she admitted rather grudgingly.

'The poor girl is in a terrible state about her parent's attitude and most of all about having to have the baby adopted. She wants to keep it. In the end I decided the support you would be able to offer her here would far outweigh the other implications of her being pregnant,' he said sheepishly.

'I don't know. What am I letting myself in for if I agree? You knew I wouldn't refuse when you put it like this,' she said, with a smile in her eyes.

'It might even be good for Karen,' he challenged.

'All right, don't say any more otherwise I might change my mind.'

'Her name is Angela Bowen. Don't expect her parents to visit her though, will you? They've made it quite clear they won't and don't want any further contact with her, at least until after the baby has been adopted.' Then he laughed. 'Anyway, it will give me a good excuse to call here more often.'

'Do you need an excuse?' she laughed.

'Well, you know what the gossips are like, with me being single. The poor dears are longing to pair me off. I've told you all there is for now. I must rush as it is nearly time for surgery. But thanks, once again.'

As they both stood he took her in his arms and gave her the first intimate kiss she'd had from him. On all the outings he'd given her a quick kiss when he left her, but now Emily could feel his passion.

He dragged himself away reluctantly, but feeling that, at last, he had plucked up the courage to kiss her in that personal way and she had not put up any resistance.

'I really must go now,' he said.

'I know. See you soon then,' she sighed, wondering how much longer they could carry on in this manner denying their affection for each other.

21

David was brought up in Bradford on one of the poorer housing estates of the city. He was one of a large family, so large that the council had converted a pair of semi detached houses into one large house for them all.

His parents were staunch Catholics and despite the era, his father wouldn't hear of using birth control. His mother had been pregnant at very regular intervals during her child bearing years. Sadly she'd had six miscarriages on the way but she still had ten surviving children. Once he was old enough to understand about the miscarriages David was convinced that nature had its own way of birth control, although not very effective.

By the time he was born some of his siblings had already grown up and left home. There was a five year gap between his brother Jimmy and David. This often convinced him that his mother had thought Jimmy would be her last to be born and had a shock when David came along followed closely by his sister Gail. They were so close in age they would join forces when the others got at them. Gail was the one person David felt he had affinity with in the whole family. From the moment he became aware of life he felt he was different to all his brothers and sisters.

They had a poor standard of living with his father a labourer on building sites, not a lucrative job at the best of times and work dependent on the weather. It was nearly impossible to live on the money from the state.

By the time David came along, the eldest two still living at home had full time work, so for once in her marriage his mother had more money coming in and less money worries. Presuming Jimmy would be the last child his mother had got rid of all the baby clothes, pram and other things a baby needed.

David grew up better fed and clothed than his brother and sisters and his mother was adept at rummaging through piles of clothing at charity shops and jumble sales in order to get items in good condition.

At school, David had learned how to read and he never had his nose out of a book. It was as if he was trying to quench his thirst in learning and knowledge. By the time he was eight he had probably read more books than the rest of the family put together. His father often said to his mother, 'This one can't be one of mine. Are you sure they gave you our babby at the hospital?'

His mother would laugh and answer, 'I'm sure, isn't he the spitting image of your Pa?'

'Aye he is,' his father would have to admit. But this likeness still never put him off saying it again and again because his father was at a loss to understand David.

All the others had played together, had gangs of friends and the house was never empty. David enjoyed his own company and his father never saw him with a friend, a fact he found mystifying. If David wanted companionship he sought it from his sister, Gail.

Gail was easy going and had no problem with her brother tagging along with her and her friends, particularly once he proved himself more than capable at tending many of the wounds they might sustain whilst playing.

It soon became a family joke. 'Just send them to David, he'll get them patched up.'

He'd stand on the kitchen stool to reach into the top cupboard and from there he'd take disinfectant, bandages, lint and anything else he thought relevant to the particular wound.

He would clean the wound, apply a first aid dressing and tell the 'patient' to come back and see him in four or five days and he'd take the dressing off. It was amazing how dutifully they'd come back. David would sit back with a contented little smile on his face.

The whole family had to attend church every Sunday. It was no good any of them faking an unknown illness to avoid going. Their mother quickly saw through their guise and would say, 'Fine, if you're so ill that you can't attend church then you stay in bed all day. There will be no getting up for Sunday roast and no TV.'

It was amazing how many miraculous recoveries were made, as it was preferable to go through the tedium of the service than miss their favourite meal of the week.

David had the disadvantage of following on from so many brothers and sisters who had attended the same school prior to him, that a reputation had already been set. The teachers expected from David what the rest had given to their school work — the minimum of effort. They had soon to revise their opinion when they found he got on with his work diligently. He was a good little worker with an agile mind.

The eldest of the family had attended a Catholic secondary modern school, then as the school system changed the others automatically moved on to a Catholic comprehensive school.

At eleven, when David made his bold statement one day during Sunday lunch, 'I'm going to take the entrance examination for Bradford Grammar School and try to get a grant to attend,' an astounded silence fell on the group at the table.

His father was the first to break the silence as he roared with laughter, 'He's having us on. Nice one, David.'

David carried on looking solemn faced as he said, 'I mean it, I'm not joking.'

Now his father's laughter changed to anger and he bellowed, 'Over my dead body. I'll have no son of mine not properly educated.'

Still David persisted, this was so important to him. 'But that's just what I will get at Bradford Grammar. I will get a good education and a chance to go to University.'

'Hark at him,' his father sneered. 'He must think I'm Rothschild.'

'No, Dad, please listen. There are grants and such things available and that's what I'm going to try to get.'

'And what about the religious side of the education, answer me that?'

David wasn't going to drop the bombshell that he didn't want to be a Catholic any longer. There was time enough for that in the future when it came to his confirmation, so he said meekly, 'I'll still go to church on a Sunday and I've learned a lot of it already.'

His mother, who had kept quiet and very

rarely interfered in her husband's authority now said, 'Let him go, Father. He'll more than likely not be there that long in any case. As I've heard it, they work them very hard, so he'll no doubt not keep up with them and have to move on to the Comprehensive school.'

It had always amazed David how his mother referred to her husband as father, in fact, he didn't think he'd ever heard her actually call him by his name. But now he was peeved that she'd partly stuck up for him but not with any confidence in his abilities. It suddenly struck him how much under his father's thumb his mother was.

Now he heard his father answer, 'Oh, I suppose so. I can't be doing with all this unrest. Go and take the blessed exam, but don't come back here crying when you fail.'

David saw a gleam of satisfaction in his mother's eyes and realised she was on his side, but had enough tact not to challenge his father outright. She had her own way of dealing with his father.

Determined to prove his father wrong he passed the entrance exam with ease and was awarded a grant on the basis of his results. His next hurdle was the school uniform. He had visions of the usual secondhand clothes being sorted out for him to wear. When his mother told him they were going to get his uniform he had no interest. To his amazement they took the bus into the town centre and walked up Ivegate to the school uniform shop. It was even more of a shock when his mother said, in her best Sunday voice, with pride in it, 'My son requires a full uniform for Bradford Grammar School.'

David stood with his mother, mouth wide open in shock. His mother gave him a sharp push in the back. 'Come on, you will need to try the things on.'

He felt so proud when he stood fully kitted out in the shop ready for inspection by his mother.

'Right, young man, we'll take it all. Are you sure there is nothing else he'll need?' she asked the shop assistant.

'P.E. kit,' he suggested politely.

'Sort one out for him, please.'

When David saw his mother hand over the cash to pay, his eyes nearly popped out of his head in surprise. He'd never seen so much money in his life.

As he stood in the kitchen on the Sunday evening, prior to starting school the next day, with all his uniform on so all the family could inspect him he saw a look of pride in both of his parents' eyes. An elder brother, who still lived at home, handed him a package.

'What is it?' he asked, unused to getting presents except on birthdays and Christmas.

'Open it and see,' one of them shouted and a lot of laughter went with those words.

He ripped the packaging off to reveal a brand new leather school satchel. 'For me?' he exclaimed in a state of shock.

'I don't know anybody else in need of one, do you folks?' his brother asked. Then he went on, 'It's from all of us, we all chipped in to buy it for you.'

David didn't let his family down. He worked hard and got to University to study what he desired so much — medicine. Working so hard he made few friends but he got his wish and was accepted into medical school with ease. It was immediately apparent to the interviewing panel that it was his deepest desire to be a doctor.

By the time he went to university there were only his sister and himself at home, but he was still aware it was a strain on his mother and father to fund him during his studying, as it would be years before he was earning a decent salary. He no longer suffered taunts from his father; although at times he did still look at him puzzled wondering where the brains had come from.

Gail had continued on to the comprehensive in the footsteps of her siblings, had achieved good results in the 'O' levels and was forecast to do equally as well in the 'A's. She'd stated she wanted to be a teacher.

He knew the pair of them were an enigma to their parents as none of the others had ever had any notion of studying and the other lads in the family had followed their father into the building trade whilst the girls had trained as shop assistants.

Again he felt proud of his mother as she stated, 'Now you have all nearly fled the nest I've too much time on my hands. I've heard the local catalogue company are recruiting in the packaging department. I'll try and get set on there, that will help the money situation. You go ahead, lad, and train to be a doctor. Fancy me being able to say my son is a 'doctor'. I never thought I'd be so proud.'

His father laughed. 'Oh, away with you, you silly woman,' he said, seeing his wife with tears running down her cheeks. But David could see the pride shining in his father's eyes.

He started medical school and he knew it was eyes down and constant studying for him. Many who started the same time as him thought it was a game being there and didn't take their studies seriously. But David knew he'd no option but to work hard, he couldn't let his parents down. He couldn't afford to fail any exams and didn't. He was well aware of the laughs and comments because he didn't bother with the girls. He knew a few even went as far as to question his sexuality.

His elective year came closer and he did any part-time work he could get in his free time. He had chosen to go to Australia and he saved to get the money together.

He had no idea which direction he wanted to take in medicine, but when he came back from Australia he knew for sure. He had worked with the flying doctor for most of his time there and had enjoyed every minute of his experience. Flying wasn't his favourite thing but he did want to be a G.P. He was aware he would have to work on his communication skills because he wasn't capable of talking with ease to people but he'd learn.

Once he had finished his entire training programme he found locum work for various G.P.s and completed the further training required. He was taken on in a practice, not as a partner but employed and he worked there diligently, saving every penny he could afford. When the opportunity came along to buy into the practice at Hornsea he had some money behind him.

He loved his work and knew he'd made the

right decision in his choice of career. He rented a house when he first went to Hornsea then he managed to buy himself a pleasant little home of his own. It was his very first house. It didn't feel like a home with its meagre furnishings and very male orientated appearance but it was a base. He'd been too busy making sure his partnership was working rather than putting any effort into it. He did have a daily, who was the total opposite to Emily's Joan. She barely said a word but she did keep the place clean. She insisted on calling him Doctor David, she felt he was too an important a person to warrant the name David from her.

Now he was in a dilemma. If it had been a medical problem he'd have known how to cure it. But he didn't know how to deal with a heart problem called love. When he'd first seen Emily snooping around Elena Robertson's house he'd felt annoyed with her and thought her an irritation, if anything a scatter-brained woman. That was the reason he'd not acknowledged her when she'd brought Karen along to the surgery. He'd taken easily to Karen because for some unexplained reason she'd reminded him of his sister, Gail.

Much to his disappointment he very rarely saw Gail, as once she was qualified to be a teacher and had taught a couple of years, she studied a course — 'English as a Foreign Language' — and now taught in the sunny Costa Del Sol in Spain.

Gail had never been inclined towards marriage either. He knew they both puzzled their parents, as all the rest of their children had left school, met a good Catholic young woman and married. They carried on going to church and had children. Their life was going to work if they were in employment then going to the pub or local club on a weekend. Because David didn't live that kind of life they thought he was a snob. On one family occasion he'd heard a loud voice say on his entry to the room, 'Who have we here? Oh it's Doctor David.' It hadn't been said kindly and had hurt him deeply.

David never admitted it out aloud to Gail but he often thought it was seeing his mother old before her time, after bearing so many children and constantly working, that had made him take a different view about marriage. He had always been determined he'd have something to offer a wife so she wouldn't just be a slave.

He knew Gail felt the same and wanted a different life to the rest of the family. David had eventually denounced his Catholic upbringing and if he ever attended church then it was Church of England. He had a strong suspicion Gail no longer attended church although she'd never said so outrightly.

Gail was more experienced than he was in the partnership side of things as she had had a couple of lovers. Both relationships had fizzled to nothing and now, despite being in her late thirties, she still didn't seem bothered about marriage and a family.

It was dawning on David that he might have left it too late to have both the wife and family he desired. If he was lucky it might just be the wife. Then out of the blue this person called Emily had come into his life.

But he felt more naïve than a teenager and was uncertain how to go about courting a woman. He knew he had confused Emily with his friendly approach one minute and his coolness the next, but he couldn't help it. He was getting desperate to declare his love for her but it didn't come across as he meant it to.

He thought she had affection for him but was unsure, and didn't want to make a fool of himself by telling her he loved her if she only thought of him as a dear friend. He could have got the signs completely wrong.

He could have done with Gail at hand to give him sisterly advice. It struck him he could write to her instead. But then he decided that wouldn't be right and carried on trying to get along as normally as possible. He only hoped fate would step in and resolve it for him.

22

Rachel's parents turned up on a visit. She was distraught as they weren't supposed to know where she was, let alone that she had left Michael.

It became clear to Rachel that they had found out her address when her mother stated, with a slight recrimination in her voice, 'We had a letter from Michael.'

'I see,' said Rachel, just hoping he'd had the sense not to have revealed everything to her parents. But she didn't think he had as they didn't look disgusted, only annoyed with her.

'We're a bit disappointed in you, Rachel. More so, that you didn't let us know what was going on. Are we such ogres?'

Rachel stuttered in amazement, 'Dad said I'd made my bed and I'd to lie on it so there was no going back. There seemed little point in contacting you, only for you to say, 'I told you so!''

'Yes, love, but now Michael has confessed to us about having an affair, it puts a different light on it. It's not as if it's all your fault. Sometimes these things just don't work out.'

Here Rachel felt all colour drain from her face, but to her surprise her mother came across the room to give her a big hug as if trying to offer comfort. At last her mother broke the silence by saying, 'It's terrible, I know love. We only hope the woman he took up with was not a friend of yours as well.'

Rachel heaved a sigh of relief and sent a silent thanks to Michael for, at least, letting her retain her dignity. 'No, I didn't know the person,' she replied honestly.

'That's good, so as I was saying,' but her mother got no further as her father jumped in. 'What she's trying to say, lass, is, I was angry with you at the time, throwing your education and everything away for somebody I could sense was no good for you. But you're not to blame for his behaviour so I don't hold it against you. How can we turn our back on you now?'

Rachel was sobbing with emotion as she said, 'Thanks, Dad.'

Not normally very good at showing his feelings he walked over to his daughter and drew her into his arms. This touched her deeply, and it intensified the crying.

After a moment she pulled back to ask, 'I still don't understand how you know I am here. I didn't tell Michael my address.'

'I mentioned to your Auntie Joan that we

had had the letter from Michael, so she decided it was only right to tell us your whereabouts.'

'Oh!' Rachel said, thinking her mother was probably no longer talking to her sister for sheltering her niece. Now she'd gone and caused more trouble.

But her mother carried on, 'I was relieved to know you were safe and sound and hadn't the heart to tell Joan off for not letting me know what was going on. More so after what she has done for you and she told me it was a safe place you were staying in. I can see what she means,' she added, looking around the room appreciatively.

'Yes, I'm really happy here. More than I have been for a long time. I was a fool when I married Michael. Now I can appreciate what you were trying to tell me. It's all certainly made me grow up.'

'I know, love, but we didn't want you to have to grow up in this manner and suffer like that,' her mother said sadly.

'Oh, I've survived it. Maybe I'm one of those people that only learn by experience. I was sad but felt that I couldn't make contact with you. I'm looking forward to getting my life back together again.'

'So are you going to get your bags and come home with us now,' her mother asked.

'No,' replied Rachel.

'You just tell me when you are coming then and I'll come and pick you up,' her Dad said cheerfully.

'I'm not coming back home,' she said quietly.

'Why not?' her mother cried out in renewed anguish.

'Because I'm very happy here,' she tried to say without hurting their feelings any further.

'But you'll be happy at home. It'll just be like old times,' her mother implored.

'No, there is no going back. I'm sorry. It is difficult to make you understand but, everybody here has gone through some form of trauma. It has helped to put my situation in perspective. That's why I say I think I have not come out of it too badly, considering everything that has happened to me. Here, I feel safe and as if I can find my true self. At the moment I help Auntie Joan around the house, but as soon as I feel I can cope I want to get myself sorted out work-wise.' She gave a small laugh. 'Or should I say education wise.'

'I understand,' her father said gently, which came as a surprise as he was the one who usually put the opposition in her way over everything.

'Thanks, Dad.'

'But we will be able to see you?' her mother implored.

'Of course,' Rachel laughed. 'It's just like I'm living in my own place here, but we live as a family at the same time. I'm totally free to come and go, you know, and have friends and family visit whenever I want.'

'Yes, well,' her mother started to say, still seeming unsure about the situation, as if her daughter was being held there against her will.

'Leave it,' her father said, putting his hand on her mother's arm. 'When she's good and ready, if she decides she wants to come home to us then there will always be a place for her. If she doesn't, she's still our daughter so whatever she does she will have our support when she moves on.'

'Thanks, Dad,' Rachel said again, eyes filling up with emotion.

Her Dad carried on. 'Get in touch when you want to meet again and we will organise something.'

'In fact, is it all right if I come to see you on Sunday?' Rachel said quickly, before her courage failed.

'We'll be in,' her mother said, smiling.

★　★　★

The next morning when her Auntie Joan came to work she looked shamefaced when she met Rachel.

'Sorry, love. I hope I didn't cause too much trouble for you by telling your parents.'

'None at all,' she said happily.

'Really?' her aunt asked with relief in her voice.

'Yes, I should thank you. It was easy after all. Dad amazed me at how understanding he was. In fact, we seem to be getting on better than we have for a long time, even before I left home. I'm going to visit them on Sunday, for my Sunday lunch.'

'You can see the dilemma I was in. If I told them where you were then I knew it would relieve my sister's mind but maybe cause trouble for you. Yet if I didn't tell her, I knew she'd break her heart with worry.'

'It's fine, really, and I do understand. I wrote to Michael as well. He might as well know where I am, and I am sure he won't come looking for me. Now I've made it up with my parents I seem to be able to forgive him as well. Somehow it seemed as if I was blaming him for the split with them, which I realise now was my fault. It's all come out in the wash, thanks to you, Auntie Joan.'

'I shouldn't imagine he'll make an appearance after all he's done.'

'By the way, you did know Mum thought he meant that he'd had an affair with another woman? It will be best to leave them in ignorance, no point in upsetting them further.'

'I won't tell them any different,' her aunt said.

Whilst this conversation was going on Angela's parents were putting all her possessions into black dustbin bags. Once they were happy they had removed all trace of her from the house they loaded them into the car. The receptionist stared in horror as the bags were left with her and she was told, 'Doctor Stringer will know why we brought them here. Just tell him that's all Angela's and we don't want any further communication from the pair of them,' said her father as he dumped the bags onto the reception area floor.

When the receptionist told David his face held a look of disbelief as he said, 'All her things?'

'That's what they said. Oh, and they said one other thing about you and her not making any more contact with them,' she added with reproach in her voice.

Slowly regaining his composure he said, 'It's all right, leave it with me. By the way, Angela will be arriving here after work. Let me know when she's here.'

The receptionist's mind was actively guessing at the situation. She couldn't wait to tell her family what was going on, and him in his early forties and her not out of her teens. It was a disgraceful situation. She realised, with a self-satisfied feeling, she'd have to tell the girl, when she came in, that Dr Stringer could no longer be her doctor.

When 'the girl' announced herself as Angela, she was obviously pregnant, and the receptionist was horrified.

She said in a shaky voice, 'Dr Stringer is expecting me.'

'Yes, well I'd like a word with you before I tell him you are here,' the receptionist replied harshly.

'Oh,' said the girl blushing, making her look even guiltier.

'Obviously Dr Stringer can no longer carry on being your doctor in the present situation.'

'Why not?' Angela asked, with tears in her eyes and fear in her voice.

'Because of your relationship,' the receptionist snapped.

'But he's only found me somewhere to live,' she protested, with a bit more feeling as she was sure she had done nothing wrong.

'And why is that?'

Before Angela could answer a voice broke in angrily.

'The fact her parents don't want her to live at home is none of your business.' Looking at the receptionist's face and knowing her so well, he understood her thinking and said bluntly, 'The baby isn't mine which is what you have assumed. Anything I've done for Angela has been purely as her doctor. Now, is that clear and understood?' he said, leaving no room for argument.

Not waiting for a reply he turned to Angela. 'Come along, my dear, let's remove these,' he said gently and picked up some of the black bags to take with him.

He settled Angela in the car and went back for the rest of her things. He had not had his final say with the receptionist and didn't want Angela listening. 'That girl is under stress already, far too much for anybody in her condition. I would expect you to have more respect and compassion and if I have occasion to hear any more said about this, we will seriously have to consider your position here. A receptionist has to be somebody who can be trusted not to gossip with patients, their circumstances are private. They will not be discussed. Have I made myself clear?' With that he slammed out of the door without waiting for a reply.

The receptionist stood gaping. She felt contrite because she'd meant no harm with her indiscriminate remarks. She realised she had to suppress her urge to jump to conclusions if she was to keep her job.

David turned to Angela. 'I'm sorry about that. It won't happen again.'

She couldn't speak on the short journey, she was choked up with emotion. Seeing all her possessions in those horrible black bags had seemed so final. She couldn't explain the deep hurt her parents had inflicted on her. They had rejected her so permanently. She felt she was in a nightmare world and could only hope she would wake up from it soon.

As soon as Emily saw Angela she noticed that she was upset.

Angela gave a weak smile when she was shown her room. Emily was certain she couldn't have cared less where she was. The poor lass needed her mum and dad and Emily's heart went out to her, knowing what the loss of parents was like, even if hers had been a different situation.

Angela soon settled into a routine, getting herself ready and off to work each day. If Emily had seen her at work she wouldn't have recognised her as the same girl. She was adept at putting on a forced smile and it stayed fixed on her face. She never said a word to her colleagues about the true situation. At home Angela spent a lot of her time in the solitude of her own room. It was as Emily had expected but luckily Ida and Harry had taken to her. Karen had also surprised her. After her initial attitude towards Ida she had expected her to ignore Angela. Instead she'd gone out of her way to be kind to her, making special meals to tempt her poor appetite.

Now it was Rachel who was the enigma. Her home life had been sorted out to everyone's satisfaction. She had received a reply to her letter from Michael. He had asked her to give him a divorce, agreeing he would take the blame for the breakdown of the marriage. With the help of Ida's advice she was waiting for a place on a government training course that would give her the chance of a career in computers. So Emily couldn't understand the hostility towards Angela. Rachel should have felt concern for Angela that her own life wouldn't be sorted out as easily as her own.

It wasn't Angela that was a problem to Rachel. It was the baby she was carrying. It had brought back sharply the loss of her own baby. To see someone who had no apparent interest in the baby, created an unexpected bitterness. She'd have loved her baby and was desperately wanted. She didn't know if she would ever have the opportunity to have another child.

Although, Angela wanted her baby, she hid the fact in trying to recover from her existing hurt and rarely mentioned it.

Emily began to appreciate what was happening when she saw them together more often and realised the animosity was creating an atmosphere.

23

Emily was beginning to feel her group of residents were becoming the family she had never had. The various ages didn't seem to make much difference, they often felt like her children. If she wasn't helping one of them it was another. Her mind was concentrated at present on Angela, she seemed the one in greatest need help.

Angela had been very distant initially with all of them except Ida and Emily decided to have a chat with her. Finding her sitting out on her small patio Emily sank into a chair beside her.

Ida queried, 'You seem tired.'

'I'm fine. It's just nice to rest my feet for a moment. I actually came out here to see you and ask if Angela ever talks about the personal side of her life?' she asked outright.

Seeing Ida's hesitancy she carried on in case Ida thought she was prying. 'I'm not asking out of idle curiosity. I have a reason.'

'I realise that. She has often talked to me but does anybody get close enough to know the true Angela and her feelings? She's an unhappy girl and I could throttle her parents.

They should be proud they have such a lovely daughter. I'm sure all she needs is her parents' support and she would be a lot happier.'

Hearing Ida speaking, Emily realised that Ida was feeling frustrated because she couldn't help the girl more. Help, if it came, had to come from her parents.

'I know,' agreed Emily. 'You just can't imagine anybody behaving in this archaic manner.' She laughed, 'You know me, I can't leave things alone and I have been wondering if there's any way we can help her. It's hurting me to see her so upset.'

'Aye, getting her parents to see sense would be something positive.'

'But they're not going to, are they? What else can we do?' Emily asked sadly.

'Keep on showing her love and affection that's all we can do,' Ida replied.

Emily had a seed of an idea in her head. 'Do you think she really wants to have the baby adopted or is it because it is what her parents want? Is she hoping they will take her back home if she complies?'

'Oh, I know the answer to that one. We were talking about her birthday, the other day and she mentioned she would be eighteen, just after the adoption will be finalized. She said if she had been a few months older she could have made the decision to keep the baby whatever her parents wanted. I reckon if she had a choice she would keep it. At the same time I'm pretty certain, despite all her parents have done to her, that she still loves them and wants them to acknowledge her existence.'

'M'mm. I'll think about it, but we can't interfere,' said Emily, feeling more positive than earlier.

'I don't think there is much you can do to help,' Ida said with a lot of feeling as if she was convinced it was a lost cause.

For one brief moment she thought about suggesting she adopted the baby herself but knew it was not feasible. It was a kind thought but totally impractical. In any case, it didn't solve the problem; it would only mean Angela would know the baby's parent. She still would not be looking after it as her own child.

The answer was so simple that she laughed out loud at her own stupidity. She would have to check up on one or two technicalities, but she was sure there was no legal reason why Angela couldn't just keep the baby — a lot of young girls did nowadays. As long as the other residents were happy she could keep her room in the house. It was large enough to accommodate a baby. Once she returned to work, Emily would look after the baby during the day. The more she thought about it the more Emily was taken with the idea of having a baby around. It was beginning to appear unlikely she would have one of her own.

Whilst she thought of her proposal she forgot about the hard work it would bring with it. Once it was a toddler it would need somebody with a lot of energy to run around after it. Emily saw it as an idea to help Angela and didn't think about the full implications.

She'd have to check with David how the legal position stood. She was sure everybody in the house would be behind her.

David wasn't enthusiastic about her suggestion, but he did admit it was up to Angela to sign the adoption papers, not her parents. Only she could make the final decision whether to keep the baby or not.

'Have the parents asked to be informed once the baby is adopted?' Emily asked.

'No,' he said, feeling by not saying any more he wasn't breeching confidentiality of his patient.

'So they wouldn't know if it had been adopted or she had kept it herself?' she muttered, but really expecting an answer of David.

David tried to reason with her. 'Remember Angela is involved in this and at the end of day it is her decision. Don't influence her to your way of thinking just because you see it as a sensible solution. You will be disappointed if she doesn't go along with your idea. She may insist that the baby is adopted because she is little more than a child herself.'

'I know all that, but I want her to make her own decision and then she won't look back with regret. If she decides to have it adopted then it has been her decision alone and not one that is being forced on her.'

'Point taken, that being the case I applaud your idea and support you all the way.'

Emily was a kind and caring person and David's love grew.

She decided it would be better to tackle the residents individually once she had worked out a plan. Their approval was imperative for it to work.

Harry was the first person she had a chance to speak to and she found him alone in the sitting room. Although he was taken aback at first, he didn't reject the idea out of hand.

'It'll be hard work for you. Are you sure that's what you want with everything you have to cope with?'

'Yes,' she said with more confidence than she was beginning to feel.

'I don't want to sound like a wet blanket but you don't know how many years you will be taking the role on for. It's a very big commitment. You are still young enough to remarry then you don't know what will happen and any future husband may have his own plans which might not include somebody else's child.'

'I know, but surely if that situation arose I could meet the problem then. Things change all the time and you never know, Angela might meet somebody herself. Then she will want to leave here and may not need my services.'

'True, well, I can see you have thought about it.'

'I have.'

'You know I will back you if you are certain that is what you want to do.' He gave a small laugh. 'I could still have my uses, I'm sure I'd be capable of helping you with baby-sitting.'

'There you are then. I said it could work out.'

She discussed it later with Ida with much the same result as with Harry. She was still uncertain of the soundness of Emily's idea and was also aware that despite the fact Angela was a working girl she didn't earn enough money to support herself and a baby, plus to be able to pay for childcare facilities into the bargain if Emily changed her mind about looking after it. Ida was looking at the practical side of the issue.

'One day she will earn better money, then if she wants her own independence she can move into a place of her own and pay a child-minder,' said Emily.

'Yes, but how will you feel if you've looked after the baby and seen it grow then she takes it away from you?' Ida asked, concerned that Emily would be heartbroken if this ever happened.

'I suppose like any other child-minder,' she tried to say in a joking voice.

'Do you really believe that?' Ida asked.

'No,' mumbled Emily. 'But it's all ifs and buts, so whatever comes I'll have to cope with that at the time. None of us ever know how things will work out.'

'As long as you know what you're doing you have my full support.'

Emily flung her arms around Ida. 'Thanks Ida.'

'I suppose I'll be allowed to help you with the baby? Not that I've much experience but it will be something I could enjoy.'

'Of course, Harry's already offered to baby-sit.'

'Has he indeed,' said Ida, laughing at the thought of him changing a nappy.

Emily was convinced Karen would welcome the idea more than anybody. But she was very much against it though not so much for Emily as Angela herself.

'I think it's ridiculous,' she stated boldly.

'Why, it's what she wants, surely?' asked Emily, surprised by this reaction.

'It is what she thinks she wants. She is still a child herself. What does she know about life? Probably even less than anybody else her age having had such a sheltered upbringing. No, she'll grow to resent it as the years go by, blaming it for her missed youth.'

'What makes you think that?' queried Emily, knowing this hadn't happened to Karen to make her so bitter on the subject yet she had said it with deep conviction.

'It happened to my mother. She was forced into a marriage at seventeen to have me.'

'Yes, but she had the marriage to cope with as well. Nobody is forcing Angela into a marriage she doesn't want, only thinking about the ways for her to keep the baby she does want.'

'This may be what she thinks she wants. It'll soon lose its attraction when she has to stay in of an evening and she can't do what her friends are doing. It's a novelty to her now and I think it's a challenge against her parents if she is allowed to keep it.'

'I think that is going too far.'

'I don't. I've spent a lot of time with her

304

and listened to what she has had to say. I think your good intentions are misdirected.'

Emily thought over what Karen had said, but felt the decision had to be Angela's. Whatever she wanted to do Emily was prepared to go along with. She had another hurdle first, Rachel. She was aware how things stood between the pair of them, and the only reason for that was that Angela was pregnant. How would Rachel take to the thought of a baby living in the house? She was sure it would bring memories back of her own lost child.

In fact she took to the idea straight away with no argument put forward against it which left Emily lost for a moment.

Then she laughed, 'I'll help you when I get the chance. You must have noticed I've got rather a hectic social life nowadays.' Before Emily could say anything further, she carried on, 'Must rush, I'm meeting friends in town for a shopping expedition.'

It was Rachel's recovery that had surprised Emily most, of all her residents. She had arrived looking shy, despondent and lonely and Emily had been certain she had been scarred for life with her experience. She now appeared as if she hadn't a care in the world and was confident and self-assured. Most of this was due to the training course she was now attending. She had a small group of friends who were about her own age and single. There was hardly an evening when they weren't out and about and Emily wondered where she got her energy from.

Emily gave a deep sigh; she had given nearly half her existing life to Howard. She would never get those years back, age was against her. Rachel was still at an age to recover from all that and the process had already started. She thought how foolish she had been to stick Howard and her marriage all those years, when Rachel had found the strength and courage to get out of a loveless marriage. She shook herself, this was her life now, she had to concentrate all her thoughts and not look back with regret at the wasted years. That didn't help anyone.

24

Angela had a slight hesitation when Emily put the proposal to her. She was worried and hesitant in going against her parents' wishes. Emily tried to point out as tactfully as she could, 'But they want nothing to do with you, so what does it matter what they think now? They've made that obvious by sending all your things along here with you.'

'I know,' she said sadly, because she was always hoping that she would wake up and it had all been a bad dream.

Emily was aware that Angela was having a difficult time accepting what her parents had done to her and she couldn't believe herself that parents could be so cruel. Human nature is hard to understand.

Angela looked at Emily and said, 'I would like to if you are sure? What about everyone else?'

'Of course I'm sure, I wouldn't have been as cruel as to suggest it if I hadn't thought it all out before I asked you. I have also made tentative suggestions to the others and they have agreed to help out where they can.'

Shortly afterwards Angela finished work

and Emily suggested they get her sorted out with a pram, baby clothes and other things now she'd made the decision to keep the baby. She had managed to save some of her wages, and was insistent she could afford to buy the things herself despite Emily's offer of help.

Emily found there was a Mothercare in Hull and also a baby shop in the town centre, and proposed a trip.

Angela seemed quite chirpy initially but now sat in the car looking pale and tense, with very little to say.

'Are you sure you feel up to going today?' Emily queried, concern in her voice.

'Yes, I'm fine. Just a bit uncomfortable that's all. Must be the way the baby is laying today. But I do want to get the things sorted now.'

'As long as you are sure. I can always come with you another day instead.'

But Angela was adamant she needed to get things for the baby and forced a smile on her face as if she was enjoying herself.

Harry had had a discreet word with Emily, before they set off, asking her to stop Angela from buying a cot, as the residents wanted to club together to get her one when the baby arrived.

Emily tactfully suggested a Moses basket

would suffice for the first few weeks, then she could get a cot later when she was more decided as to what she needed. She saw Angela blanch when she asked the price of a pram, but the lady assistant must have also seen the look as she said kindly, 'We have one in the storeroom we were holding back for the sale. It is now a discontinued style. Would you like to see that one? It's got a good reduction and there's not a thing wrong with it.'

'Oh, yes please,' replied Angela, with a look of relief on her face.

Angela asked, 'Do I have to wait for the sale before I can buy it?'

The assistant laughed. 'By the looks of you I think you might need it before then. Look, seeing as you've bought a lot of other items, I'll let you have it now. But don't tell anybody else otherwise they will all be flocking here before the sale to try to buy reduced items. Do you want the things delivered?'

Angela looked at Emily and asked, 'Do you think if we put some of the things in the pram we could manage to take them all now? Will they fit in the car?'

Seeing the eager anticipation and her flushed face, Emily replied, 'I don't see why not. The pram, after all, is made to fit in a car so we can have a practice run.'

Once in the car and making their way out

of the town centre Emily asked, 'Have you got everything you need now?'

As she turned to look at Angela she noticed the flushed cheeks and wasn't sure if it was caused by the excitement of the day or was more than that. She was unnerved every so often when Angela gave small gasps.

'I'll be glad to get home. To tell you the truth, I'm exhausted.'

When Emily challenged her again later, Angela denied she had any pain and stated she was fine. There was little Emily could do but get her safely back home.

Karen had taken the opportunity to get some baking done while they were out. Harry had gone to stay with a friend for a few days and poor Ida seemed like a lost soul without him. It was a sunny day and she had told Karen she was going to sit outside and catch up on some letter writing.

Meanwhile, whilst Emily and Angela were on their trip to Hull, Alan was on a journey to Hornsea. Just as Karen had predicted her home had been repossessed by the mortgage company. Alan hadn't bothered to put the effort of storing what furniture was left. He had said he couldn't afford it. Instead he had sold off most of the contents to give himself some money but that had soon gone. Anything he wanted to keep he threw into the car. As he sorted through the last of the things he saw a box of old paperwork. He lifted the box throw it out and the bottom fell out, leaving him cursing at the mess and he saw a book with the words 'address book' on the front. A gleam came into his eyes, the book had belonged to Karen. He systematically started to go through it, ringing each number to see if whoever answered knew where Karen was living. He soon came to Emily's old phone number and Howard who had no compulsion in giving the full address to Alan where he presumed Karen to be still hiding out. He had a glint of mischief in his eyes as he read the details out over the phone. Why should he care if he brought trouble down on Emily's head?

Alan had run out of money and was sure Karen must have some by now. She had to have a job and somewhere to live. As he saw it, he'd be able to get around her to help him as she always had done in the past.

When Emily arrived back home she saw the old, battered car in the driveway. Settled, with her past behind her, she never gave a thought that it could be Alan trying to move back into Karen's life. Curiosity getting the better of her she moved quickly to the house with Angela mumbling behind her, 'I think I'll go for a lie down. I feel shattered.'

311

'Give a shout if you want anything,' Emily answered vaguely.

As they approached the house Emily heard loud voices and presumed it must be Ida with the TV on too loud once again. She knew she needed to have a word with her about it, particularly if it could be heard as far away as the driveway. There came a crash of pottery and instinct made Emily realise this was no TV she was hearing. She rushed to the kitchen where the sounds came from. There was a strange man shouting and bawling at Karen and at the same time throwing things at her and Ida was sitting in a chair ashen white, looking barely conscious.

Emily tried to shout above the noise, 'I think Ida is ill.' A plate was thrown at her with the words, 'Keep out of it you nosy cow.'

She ran into the hall, dialled 999 and asked for the police and an ambulance, stating in a mad rush, 'There's a mad man in my house and an old lady has been taken ill.'

Slamming the receiver down she dialled David's number only to be told he'd gone out on an urgent case himself, but the message would be passed on to him via his mobile phone. Emily wasn't sure what had happened to Angela but presumed that she had gone to her room without seeing the fiasco that was going on in the kitchen.

Emily had to brace herself to go back into the kitchen but she couldn't leave Ida alone to cope. There was devastation. Karen was beyond herself with fear, the irate man was totally out of control and was shouting. All his attention was focused on Karen so Emily moved quietly and swiftly to Ida's side. She put her arm around her and whispered, 'How can I help you?'

Ida opened her eyes briefly and mouthed, 'Spray,' and pointed under the table. Emily realised that, in her agitation to take her spray, Ida must have dropped it. Retrieving it she put it in Ida's outstretched hand, who sprayed it under her tongue.

Before Emily had time to wonder what to do next she heard loud footsteps behind her and turned to see two police officers entering the room. She'd never felt so relieved in her life.

'Now then, I'd stop all that if I was you young man, before you do anybody any real harm.'

The authoritative voice startled Alan and he spun round, lowering his arm and dropping the pan he was holding. Emily could feel Ida relax a little in her arms, and hoped the spray was taking effect. The policeman walked over to Alan, put some handcuffs on him and said, 'I think you'd better come this way with us.'

The other asked, 'Does anyone know this man?'

Karen said between sobs, 'He's my husband, we are separated. I don't know how he found me.'

'If I was you I'd get an injunction from the court straight away to stop him coming anywhere near you again.'

She nodded.

There were more footsteps as the ambulance arrived.

The paramedic went across to Ida with an oxygen mask. She'd summed the situation up and realised who needed the most urgent attention. Ida tried to wave her away saying between gasps for air, 'I'm all right now,' but the paramedic ignored her and carried on attending.

Blood was streaming down Karen's face where she hadn't ducked to avoid a flying object. The policeman was saying to her, 'We'll take him into the station. He'll be in the cells overnight as it is obvious he's been drinking. Will we be able to find you here tomorrow if we call back for a statement later?'

Karen looked over at Emily with eyes like a scared rabbit, so Emily answered on her behalf. 'She'll be here.'

Karen felt certain this act of her husband's was going to be the end of her living at Emily's.

Alan was still protesting there was no need to take him to the police station as he was led away, but his protests were ignored.

The paramedic looked at the ambulance technician and said, 'I think we need to get the pair of them to hospital.' She went on to indicate Ida. 'This lady needs to be checked over to see that this is nothing worse than an angina attack,' then she nodded in Karen's direction. 'And I suspect you'll need a few stitches in your cheek. You don't want to be left with scars.'

As she'd finished, a faint voice called, 'Help me, help me!'

Everybody in the kitchen turned around amazed and the technician asked, 'Is there somebody else injured in the house?'

Emily put her hand to her mouth. 'Oh my God, Angela!'

Karen explained, 'She's pregnant and due any day.'

'You two just hang on here,' he said to Ida and Karen, as they made to follow.

'I knew there was something wrong with her today,' Emily said, as she led them upstairs. 'But she would have none of it, said she was just fine.'

One look at Angela with her legs already pulled up and in virtually continuous pain, and the paramedic stated, 'No time to get this one to hospital. It looks like a home delivery. I hope you're up to it Ian?'

'Oh, very funny, I thought that was the females' department,' he joked back.

Once the woman was at Angela's side she was full of sympathy. 'It won't be long now,' she reassured her, then went on, 'But I'm afraid it's too late to give you any pain relief for it to be effective.'

'Just do what you have to do,' moaned Angela.

'I'll just examine you, and see how things are going,' she said kindly, then turned to Emily. 'Do you think you can sort out some towels and something to wrap the baby in to keep it warm once it's born?'

'Of course,' and with that Emily sped out of the room, pleased she'd had the foresight to take Angela to get the baby's requirements that day. She rushed into the kitchen so fast that Ida and Karen panicked and thought that Alan had somehow returned. Seeing the alarm on their faces she quickly tried to reassure them. 'It's OK. Angela's having the baby and it won't be long either. Make some tea, for goodness sake!'

'Aye, that's a turn up for the books,' said

Ida, obviously feeling better by then.

Karen asked with concern in her voice, 'You don't think all this set it off do you?'

'No, I think the little madam's been in labour most of the day and either hasn't realised it or didn't want to say. I don't know what she thought would happen. She must have realised the birth would continue whether she spoke about it or not.' She quickly added, 'Must get back up there with the things they have asked for.'

'Is there anything we can do to help?' they anxiously called after her.

'Just stay where you. There are enough people in the bedroom as it is and they should know what they are doing.' As she said the words she hoped they didn't make her sound too ungrateful, but she'd no time for pleasantries.

As Emily walked in the door she heard a voice saying soothingly, 'That's right, one more big push.'

She quickly moved to Angela's side and took hold of her hand. She felt it gripped tightly as Angela tried to push as directed.

'Good girl, the head's here now. Next time one almighty push and we'll be there.'

As Emily again felt her hand being squeezed she knew Angela was in pain, but working with it and not against it.

317

'That's it,' the paramedic called out, as she gently lifted the baby up for Angela to see. 'A little girl and she looks a good size.' After a moment's pause she added, 'All intact, no problems there.'

She deftly cut the cord and dealt with it before saying, 'We'll just wait for the afterbirth then I think it's hospital for you, young lady, as well as my other passengers. They'll be surprised when we arrive at the hospital for them to see the ambulance full of people.'

'Must I?' moaned Angela.

'Yes, just for a check over. You'll no doubt be back by tomorrow.'

Emily felt drained and deflated. She couldn't believe how much stress she'd had to go through in such a short space of time. Firstly she had felt terror for them all and then excitement at a birth.

'I'll just go and get a chair to take you down, love,' the technician said kindly.

'She will be all right?' whispered Emily to him as he went out.

'Yes, fine. One of the easiest births I've attended. We're only playing safe by taking her in.'

Emily remembered the other two she'd left waiting downstairs and ran down to them crying out, 'It's a girl and they're both fine.'

'Can we see them?' Karen asked impatiently.

'You will in a minute. They're just bringing her and the baby down to take them in the ambulance with you two. I'll lock up and come along to the hospital so I can bring you back home once you've been patched up, Karen. Keep holding that pad to your face.'

Ida grumbled, 'I bet they say I've got to stay in again. My own fault, I should have known better than to run when I heard that commotion going on, then on top of that the shock of it all was just too much for my ticker. That's all it was. There's nothing really wrong with me that a night's rest won't sort out.'

Karen looked across at Ida. 'I'm really sorry, Ida, that I made this happen to you.'

'No, lass, don't blame yourself, you couldn't do owt to stop him,' she said gently.

Emily decided some good, at least, had come out of this — the pair of them were now talking civilly to each other for the first time since meeting.

Ida turned to Emily and beseeched her, 'Harry left his number where he was staying. Will you ring him for me and tell him all what's happened?'

'Do you think you should? I don't want to give him a shock and spoil his break,' Emily queried.

'But he'll be more upset if I don't tell him.'

It was Ida and Karen's turn to get in the ambulance so no more was said on the subject. As the ambulance was turning in the drive, David's car came through the gates. At the sight of the ambulance all colour drained from his face. Emily ran to him in tears with the relief at seeing him.

'What's happened?' he asked, with anxiously.

Emily gave a hysterical laugh and replied, 'Karen's husband has been here and attacked her, Ida's had an angina attack as the result of that and Angela's had a baby girl.'

'What!' he exclaimed in astonishment.

'Look are you off duty now?' she asked, feeling calmer.

'Yes,' he replied totally bewildered.

'Will you take me to the hospital and I'll explain it all to you on the way.'

As they went she told him further details. He was appalled and angry at Alan and queried that she may have been hurt in the crossfire.

'If only I'd got here sooner,' he moaned.

'The police soon dealt with him. He's having a night in the cells to cool off and sober up.'

'Good thing too because it's a good job he's out of my way. I don't think I'd have been able to keep my hands off him.'

Despite the situation Emily felt a small thrill of delight that he cared so much for her and was ready to protect her. She saw the tension go out of his body as he said, 'So, it looks like you're going to be busy helping with a baby a bit sooner than you planned.'

'It would seem so,' she replied quietly.

Now he actually laughed. 'I bet you never thought for one moment when you set all this up that it would lead to such an exciting life for you.'

'I didn't. I thought it was that at college. But it wasn't a patch on what happens around here.'

His face once more took on a solemn look. 'Oh Emily, you could have been hurt.'

A warmth spread through her as these words spoke volumes.

25

It was late by the time Emily and Karen arrived home in David's car. Karen, sitting in the rear of the car, hadn't spoken a word on the journey home. Emily had kept a light banter of chatter up with David on general issues in order to relieve the tension she could feel in the car.

Karen had needed to have some stitches in her cheek but had been assured there would be no lasting scar. Ida had been put to bed in the ward still protesting that she was well enough to be allowed back home. The doctor had been adamant he wanted her to stay to be monitored for the next twenty-four hours.

Angela had been checked over, as had the baby, and all were pronounced fine, although they were staying at the hospital for a day or two. In no time Angela was snuggled down in bed, asleep after her strenuous experience.

Once in the drive David said, 'I'll just drop you both off then get back home.'

'Won't you have a drink before you go?' Emily asked him, with a slight pleading in her voice.

'It's late and you'll want to get to bed,' he

replied, thinking of them.

'I don't think I could sleep yet if I went to bed,' Emily replied.

Karen spoke for the first time since leaving the hospital. 'I'd like you to come in, David. I think I owe you both an explanation.'

'You don't owe us anything,' Emily said kindly to Karen. As she could just manage to see the outline of her arm in the dark, Emily gave it a reassuring pat.

'If you don't want an explanation I would still like to give you one. I'll never sleep with it otherwise,' she said shakily.

In her hallway David smiled as he saw Emily's face turn towards his. They looked bemused at each other as if saying, 'What is to come?'

'It's all right by me,' he stated. 'I'm used to late nights, it's all part of the job.'

'Thanks,' said Karen, looking relieved.

'Now is it coffee or do you want something stronger?'

'An alcoholic drink for me, please,' Karen replied quickly, which surprised Emily slightly as she very rarely drank, except on special occasions. Her excuse had always been that the sight of her husband drunk had been enough to put her off for life. She never wanted to be like that and behave in such a bad manner.

'It'd better be coffee for me unfortunately,' replied David, 'as I've to drive home and have surgery in the morning.'

'Right, I'll just put the kettle on. Can you pour Karen a drink, please, David? I think I'll have a brandy and ginger ale, I feel in need of that more than a coffee,' she laughed nervously. 'I'm still recovering from shock myself.'

'I'm sorry,' Karen mumbled.

'Karen, stop saying that, it's not your fault,' chastised Emily.

When they were all seated Karen went on, 'I was having such a lovely afternoon doing some baking. For once I felt really good about life. Then suddenly I heard his dreaded voice speak behind me. I thought it was my imagination playing tricks to tell you the truth. I nearly giggled at my stupidity but I turned around and there he was.'

She turned to Emily. 'I'm sorry to tell you this but his first words were to say Howard had told him where to find me.'

Emily exploded. 'Just like one of the low mean tricks he'd play to feed his sadistic sense of humour.'

Karen looked slightly shocked herself; having expected Emily to defend her ex-husband saying he wouldn't do anything like that. In a way Karen supposed she had never understood that Emily had suffered an unhappy life like herself. She couldn't see how she could have, not when they'd appeared to have so much, a nice car, beautiful home and expensive lifestyle. It began to strike home how self-centred she'd been, in thinking that she was the only one suffering. There were different levels of suffering and she was beginning to appreciate the fact.

Now she turned to Emily and said once again, 'I'm sorry,' and by the expression on her face Emily could understand why she was saying it, that it meant far more than just for that afternoon.

'What next?' David asked, slightly impatiently.

'I was expecting trouble as soon as I realised it was him,' Karen continued. 'But no, as friendly as you please, like the old Alan. He looked around him admiring the kitchen and asked if the rest of the place looked as good. I told him it did. He wanted to know why I was in the kitchen so I tried to explain the house and its set-up and what my role was in it all. Then he asked where I lived — he was obviously thinking I'd got a place somewhere else. As soon as I told him about my flat upstairs I knew it was a mistake. That was it; he blew a fuse saying there was me living in comfort whilst he hadn't a roof over his head. He'd lost the house as I said he would. He said he had to beg a bed off friends where he could or else rough it in the car. But do you know I didn't feel sorry for him, that's the strangest thing. In the past a tale like that would have broken my resolve to be strong with him, but if anything my heart hardened against him. After all whose fault is it, I ask you?'

'Why his of course,' Emily broke in. Karen was getting angry at the injustice, and she could hear her gasping for breath as if panic was building up inside her.

'He said he was going to stay here with me. He proposed he live in my place and I could keep him. He'd had enough of sleeping rough and as he saw it, I was his wife and it was my duty to support him. I was so angry.' She gave a small, embarrassed laugh. 'Actually, I have to confess it was me who threw the first thing. I wanted to hit out at him, so I threw the dish I was holding. By the way I'll pay for all the damages.'

'Never mind that now. It probably looks worse than it is, we'll sort something out,' said Emily kindly.

'Once I'd done that he was totally demented. Then Ida came in hearing all the commotion. She told him to stop and that did nothing to diffuse the situation. I could see she was very upset and I suspected she was having an angina attack. I made a move to help her but Alan stopped me. You'll never believe what he said.'

'What!' exclaimed Emily.

'Leave the silly old cow alone, it serves her right if she has a heart attack and dies. She shouldn't have stuck her beak in where it wasn't wanted.'

David, seeing Emily's rage, took her hand in his and said gently, 'Emily, temper makes us all say things we don't mean and wouldn't have otherwise said.'

'But even so,' she spluttered.

'Let Karen carry on,' he urged.

Karen said looking gratefully at him. 'It was obvious that Ida was having an angina attack and when I tried to move her he hit me on the face with the saucepan, hence the stitches. Actually there's not a lot more to tell after that. He carried on throwing whatever came to hand and shouting because I was resolute he wasn't moving in here. The more I said no, the nastier and more vicious his tongue became until thankfully you came in and you know the rest.'

'Thank goodness I did. Otherwise what might have happened if he'd been left to carry on?'

'But it didn't and that is the main thing,'

David said calmly, trying to diffuse the tension. He added, 'I think I've gathered the rest of it from Emily so if you don't mind I will leave now, as I've got morning surgery. You will both be okay now, won't you?'

'Yes, I was going to suggest Karen stay here tonight,' then Emily gave a small giggle, 'or should I say this morning, in my spare room rather than over in the house on her own in her flat.'

'I'd really appreciate that,' acknowledged Karen, looking relieved.

She tactfully kept out of the way as Emily went to see David to his car. He took her in his arms. 'Thank God you are safe. I couldn't have stood it if anything had happened to you. No more heroics, please.'

'I never gave it a thought. I just rushed to help when I saw the state Ida was in,' she admitted.

He gave her a long lingering kiss and she knew he was having trouble leaving her, despite the time. It was nearly worth what had happened to hear those lovely words from him.

When she went back in Karen said, 'Would you make me an appointment with Brian Nicholls in the morning? You were right; I should have done it straight away. I guess I'm a slow learner.'

She believed Alan had actually done Karen a favour that night and helped her on the road of recovery.

★ ★ ★

Emily had barely been in the house five minutes checking the damage of the previous evening, when the phone rang. 'Hello, it's Angela,' a voice stated before Emily could think straight. 'Er, I wondered if you could come and pick us up. I have been given the all clear to leave but I've nobody else to ask and I didn't think of my purse,' she said apologetically.

Emily laughed, 'I suppose you mean I've got to tackle fitting the baby seat in the car without your guidance?'

'Yes,' came the hesitant reply.

'Just let me get sorted out here then I'll be on my way. Anything else you need?'

'Some clothes for the baby to come home in.'

'Of course, silly me, not thinking about that. What about for you?'

'Just clean underwear. I don't think I'll fit into a different outfit yet.' Here she moaned, 'It'll be ages before I can wear something decent.'

Emily didn't contradict her but she thought

it would be sooner rather than later, as it had never ceased to surprise her how quickly her pregnant colleagues had got their figure back. She had no sooner put the phone down than the door opened briskly.

'Where is she?' the voice asked.

Emily replied calmly, 'Good morning, Harry. I presume you mean Ida?'

'Yes, is she in her room?'

'No, she's in hospital.'

Emily quickly tried to reassure him, 'No need for alarm. They're just keeping her in for twenty four hours to monitor her. When I left her last night she looked fine, in fact was nagging me to bring her back home.'

Already he was half way back through the door. 'I'll go and see her now.'

Recovering her wits Emily ran after him, 'Wait, Harry.'

He turned at her call. 'Be quick, I'm in a rush to get to her.'

'That is what I'm trying to tell you, I'm on my way to the hospital myself in a few minutes to pick up Angela.'

'Why didn't you say so?' he asked impatiently.

Emily didn't reply because she knew he was really upset about Ida by the way he was behaving in a totally alien manner. Sensing his impatience she put the car seat in the boot and decided to fit it once she was at the hospital. She couldn't do with him breathing down her neck the first time she had a go.

On the journey he kept muttering to himself. 'Oh, I do hope she is all right.'

However hard she tried Emily couldn't get him to converse. She tried to reassure him numerous times by telling him, 'She's fine, really,' but his ears seemed deaf to her words, and she went on to tell him about Angela and the baby.

Emily found Angela agitated and waiting impatiently, just like Harry, as she grabbed her underwear straight off Emily and immediately dressed. Both of them were novices in handling a baby and the tension was released as they giggled as they dressed the poor little mite who continued sleeping through all their fumbling.

Under Angela's direction, Emily fitted the car seat in the front of the car, with less difficulty than she had imagined. She drove back to the house steadily, as if she had a precious cargo on board, glancing across to check the baby was all right every few seconds.

Harry only appeared back home after visiting time had ended later that day. When Emily questioned him he said that he had been with Ida all day. He looked much calmer as he said, 'They have said she can come home tomorrow as long as she takes it easy and nothing else happens. I intend to get straight off in the morning and we'll get a taxi back here, once she's seen the doctor. I'll make sure she looks after herself from now on.'

Emily suggested kindly, 'You could always ring when you know what time she can leave, then I'll come and pick you both up. Save the taxi fare.'

'No, thank you. I'd much rather you kept the home fires burning ready to welcome her back here.'

Emily was a little puzzled by his strange behaviour but said nothing. Angela said that he'd never even asked to see the baby, or Lara, as she was now called.

It had seemed a hectic day for Emily once she'd arrived back home with Angela. She'd been instructed on the preparation of the bottles. She had also checked that Angela was still happy with the arrangement they had agreed upon that she look after the baby. Emily wanted to give her the opportunity to have Lara adopted if she had changed her mind. Angela was adamant she was happy with way things stood.

If anybody could have read Angela's thoughts they would have seen a lot of confusion. As she'd told Emily, she did want to keep the baby but had qualms about what she planned to do. Whilst she had been pregnant she had felt more it would like playing mum to a dolly, as she had done in her childhood. Now the baby was here and already making little meow sounds when she wanted her feed, it all seemed so different and was no longer a game. Her own body felt sore and tender from the birth and now her breasts felt like lead weights and hurt so much. She wanted to relieve the pressure in them but had been given strict instructions from the midwife that the milk had to dry up naturally with the help of the injection they had given her. If she expressed any milk herself to try to ease them it would take much longer to go as her body's natural instinct would be to produce more milk to replace it. She would have to suffer in silence and endure the wet clothing as her breasts seeped milk.

Karen had been delighted when she saw the baby. Angela had been told of the nightmare Karen had to endure downstairs whilst she was suffering her own pain giving birth upstairs. She felt Karen had enough on her mind and couldn't confide in her about any of her own problems. She liked Emily a lot but she felt she was too close to David for her to be told anything in confidence. Rachel was too busy with her own life. She wasn't even home sometimes at night time now. She carried on doing as she'd done so often at home; she forced a smile on her face and they all thought she was delighted with her new daughter.

⋆   ⋆   ⋆

Emily kept her ears open for the sound of the taxi that was bringing Harry and Ida back, because she felt concerned that Harry had left the house that morning in such a strange mood. She was already standing in the hall ready to greet them as they walked through the door holding hands and a great big smile on their faces.

Harry spoke first. 'You can be the first to congratulate us.' Seeing Emily's bewildered look he carried on, 'This lovely woman has consented to be my wife.'

Emily ran to them both and gave them a hug and kiss, pleased by the way events had turned out. It explained so much of Harry's strange behaviour for the last few days. When she could finally draw breath she said, 'I'm so pleased for you both.'

Ida said in a serious tone, 'You don't think we're silly at our time of life?'

'No, why ever should I? I think it's lovely and that you're doing the right thing.'

Emily's face dropped as she thought of something else, 'But you won't be leaving here, will you?'

'No fear,' replied Harry cheerfully.

Ida looked slightly embarrassed as she said, 'We thought we might both move into my room, if that is agreeable with you?'

'Of course it is.' Emily gave a small inward laugh. She should have known this was coming when she thought about the nights she'd heard the stairs creak and the sound of a door opening with a squeak. The kitchen door didn't squeak like that, so she knew it was nobody going for a midnight feast. She'd suspected it was Harry going to see Ida but hadn't said anything in case she had made a fool of herself.

'So where and when is it to be?' Emily asked, then turned around before they could answer and shouted, 'Karen, Angela, come here a minute.'

Both rushed into the hall in panic. Emily seeing their faces quickly said, 'Sorry, I didn't mean to give you a fright. It's some good news for a change. Ida and Harry are getting married.'

Emily couldn't believe her eyes when Karen ran across to Ida, took hold of her in a hug and said, 'I'm thrilled.' At least one good thing did seem to have come from Alan's visit. It had brought Ida and Karen together as lasting friends, something Emily had not managed to achieve herself. She was glad Ida was good natured enough not to hold Karen's earlier antagonism against her and when the hand of friendship had been extended, she'd taken it.

Once they had pulled apart Ida said, 'We're going to ask Bill if he will marry us.'

Seeing Angela's rather shocked expression she went on to explain, 'You see Angela, I have not been married before and Harry is a widower, so there should be no objection.' Then she gave a slightly embarrassed laugh. 'I know you must all think I'm being silly at my age but I still do want to do it properly.' She then looked tenderly at Harry. 'I won't have another chance.'

'You had better not,' he laughed. Then he gave a slight cough and turned to Karen. 'This might seem a rather strange request, but when you get to my age you get rather thin on the ground for who to ask, so would you be my best man?' Then he gave another small cough. 'Or should I say best woman.'

'I'd be honoured,' replied Karen and Emily was thankful that they'd been thoughtful enough to include her in such a way.

Ida turned to Emily, 'Would you give me away?' Then she gave a hearty laugh, 'After all, I can't ask my father.'

'Of course,' replied Emily. 'I can see this is going to be a very unconventional wedding.' Then she gasped, 'Why are we all standing here in the hall. Come into the lounge. I think this calls for drinks to celebrate, even if it is early in the day.'

Once they were all settled, Emily carried on asking questions. They seemed to have thought through everything carefully, which was an amazing on a single taxi trip. 'What about the wedding breakfast?'

'Oh!' Harry replied hesitantly. 'We're not having many to the wedding, there's not that many to invite. We thought all of you here and, of course, David, and even though Bill is doing the service we would like him and his wife to come to the reception. Then an odd friend each or so.'

Emily knew they hadn't a lot of spare money available to them, or certainly Harry hadn't and he'd feel duty bound that he paid for the meal so Emily suggested, 'Why not have it here?'

'Yes,' Karen piped in, 'I would enjoy getting it ready.'

'Actually,' said Harry looking slightly embarrassed again, 'we were hoping you would suggest that, if you can let me know the cost.'

'Oh no, I meant it was on me, my wedding present to you, because I don't suppose there is a lot you need buying in the way of presents.'

'Oh! Isn't that lovely,' replied Ida, looking slightly bemused. Everything was falling into place so easily.

'There you are then, settled. All we need is a date but I suggest that's up to Bill when he has a date available.'

'We don't want to wait any longer than necessary, do we love?' Harry said, addressing Ida.

'No, we don't.'

'So Ida does this call for a shopping trip?' asked Emily eagerly.

'I think it does, I will need a new outfit.'

'Would you like me to take you to York?' she suggested.

'That would be lovely.' Ida turned to Karen, 'Would you come with us as well, love?'

'I will, if Emily doesn't mind?'

'Not at all, I'll probably need your help.'

'What about me?' asked Harry wistfully.

'What about you?' Ida asked, smiling at him.

'Can I come too?' he asked hopefully.

'You most certainly cannot,' replied Emily. 'You are not to see the bride's outfit until the wedding. Actually you are not to see the bride on the night before the wedding. We will have to sort something out there.'

'Next you will be asking me to wear top hat and tails,' he moaned.

'Not a bad idea,' smiled Karen.

'You're joking,' he replied in panic.

'I am but it was worth it to see your face,' she laughed back.

★   ★   ★

Before their trip to York, Karen and Emily had a private consultation wondering what they would be able to persuade Ida to buy for her special day. They knew she now had a little money put by from the sale of her house which had recently sold. It had taken longer than any of them would have supposed, after one set of buyers had messed Ida around for months before backing out of the deal. Luckily a young couple, with plenty of enthusiasm for their own ideas, came along and hurried the sale through.

Emily could sense Ida's excitement when they set off for York and hoped it wouldn't be too much for her. After they had been going for a while and it had fallen silent from the rear of the car, Karen said quietly, 'Ida's asleep, it'll do her good before we walk around.'

Emily had studied the map with Harry and he had shown her where the main shopping area was so Emily could plan the route and keep the walking to a minimum. They were relieved to see Ida's face light up when they took her into a shop that sold Jacques Vert outfits. She usually wore plain skirts or trousers and a jumper or blouse. They'd thought the clothes would be too flowing and fussy for her but she looked through the rails carefully and was enamoured with what she was seeing.

She said she wanted to try on a lilac outfit with a slightly straighter dress with a patterned design and a plain jacket to match. The lilac blended with the steely grey of Ida's hair. She had no need to try anything else on, it was perfect for her. The two women exclaimed with delight when they saw her. 'You couldn't have had anything made to measure better than that. You look lovely.'

Ida laughed, 'I don't know about lovely at my age, but I must say I'm pleased with the effect.'

The shop assistant approached them holding a hat out to Ida. 'This hat was made to go with the outfit if you'd like to try it on.'

'Oh I don't know,' said Ida looking at the rather large and fussy hat.

'Go on,' cajoled Emily.

As soon as the assistant placed it correctly on her head Karen said, 'Look in the mirror, I think it finishes the outfit off beautifully.'

The assistant asked, 'Are you the bride's Grandmother?'

Ida laughed, 'No, I'm the bride.'

'Oh, I'm sorry, I didn't realise. How lovely!'

Ida laughed. 'It's going to be the best day of my life.'

Emily had been looking at a sale rail and said, 'I'll try this on.' She had found a dress and jacket that matched and complemented Ida's outfit perfectly.

Karen said, 'As I'm to be best man I think I'll go for a trouser suit.' Karen wore trousers more often than not and with her tall, slim figure they suited her. Despite being of the generation when many women wore trousers Emily was never comfortable wearing them for a dressed occasion.

They looked for shoes for Ida and Karen found herself a soft, feminine trouser suit. By the time they set off home they were all pleased with themselves.

Bill had given them a date in a month's time, and the arrangements for the catering were in place.

Rachel had got one of her friends from college to come and look after Angela's baby so that Angela could go to the wedding and have a relaxing day. Jane had a small child herself and Angela was happy with the arrangement.

26

Emily had been adamant the correct protocol was going to be adhered to for the forthcoming wedding — whatever their age and however hard they protested. Ida had slept at Emily's cottage and she would get ready and leave from there to go to the church. Emily said she couldn't put a foot out of the door until Harry was safely out of the way. He had spent the night in the big house with Karen seeing to him there.

Emily had set the alarm clock for an early call. She intended to treat Ida like any other bride. She crept quietly downstairs to the kitchen to prepare Ida her breakfast and presented it with a vase in the centre of the tray with a single rose. It was still very quiet upstairs and she gave a small knock on Ida's door before easing it gently open. Ida was still in bed but lay with her eyes open as if pondering.

'What's all this?' she asked as she saw Emily enter the room, holding the tray.

'Breakfast for the bride, of course.'

Ida laughed, 'Give over, you will have me blushing.'

'Eat up, then I'll be back to help you get ready.'

Ida had wanted to go for her usual shampoo at the hairdresser's but Emily had insisted the style was totally inappropriate for a wedding and the clothes she was going to wear. Under a lot of pressure from both Emily and Karen she had finally agreed that Emily could blow dry her hair into a softer style.

Back downstairs Emily picked the phone up and rang through to Karen. 'Everything going okay at your end?'

'Fine, he's just eating his breakfast.'

'Same here with Ida.'

Karen had agreed with Emily to do the same and give Harry his breakfast in bed. The florists delivered a small posy of flowers which they had finally convinced Ida to agree to carry, the buttonholes for the men and a corsage for Emily and Karen. Once more Ida had protested that at her age she would look silly carrying flowers, but this time it had been Harry who had intervened and said he would like her to have some. It was enough to make her agree, although reluctantly.

Emily heard the sound of the shower and knew Ida was up and about and the day begun. Much of the food had been prepared in advance as Karen, with Emily's assistance, had made dishes that could be reheated in the oven whilst they were at church and having a premeal drink. Both Harry and Ida liked traditional food and Karen had made a trifle from an old recipe.

Emily had no difficulty blow drying Ida's hair as it was easy and adaptable to almost any style, and Ida had always had it cut regularly which made all the difference. They were both thrilled with the finished result. 'I'll have to get you to do my hair every week like this. I like it. Now why didn't the hairdresser suggest this kind of style?'

'I think they assume that older ladies want a set and dry. But I'm sure she'll do it like this if you ask her. Now I'll do your makeup.'

'Hey be careful how much you put on. You know I don't usually wear it,' Ida exclaimed, in a panic about. 'I don't want Harry to think he's married some floozy.'

'Don't worry. It will be very subtle.'

Much to her relief Ida admired the finished results. If she was really honest with herself she had to admit, for her age, she looked elegant, if it was possible to say that about a lady of eighty.

Emily sat her down and told her not to move whilst she went to get herself ready. Thinking back she realised her own marriage to Howard hadn't been like this. Sometimes it came over her that she felt both sorry and angry with herself that she had not had the strength of mind to have taken control of her own life at a much earlier age. She gave herself a shake, this wasn't a day for sadness, it was Harry's and Ida's special day.

When she walked back into the room she was carrying two glasses of champagne. 'I thought you might like this for your nerves,' she laughed as she handed Ida a glass.

'I don't know about that but at this rate I'll be tipsy walking down the aisle.'

Her hand was trembling slightly. Emily decided it wasn't surprising, this was her first time walking down the aisle, she was allowed to have wedding nerves.

Karen was chauffeuring Harry to church in Emily's car. There had seemed no point in the extra expense of hired cars as the church was so close to home. David was going to act as chauffeur to the bride and Emily.

As the waited knock came Emily cautiously opened the door and, peering out, asked, 'Is it all clear, have they gone?'

'They have,' replied David.

'Right, I'll get Ida.'

David's was pleasantly surprised when he saw how beautiful Emily looked. She could easily have been mistaken for the bride. When he saw Ida he made the appropriate sounds as she looked lovely.

As they drove to the church Ida's eyes saw none of the familiar sights. She was feeling both sad because her mother wasn't there to see her, and nervous about what she was doing at her age. She had not told a soul, but despite being a spinster, she wasn't a virgin so had no fears in that direction. She had once had a fling on holiday many years before, after her first flush of youth had passed. She had made a decision she didn't want to go to her grave not knowing the delight of making love and once any fears of getting pregnant were past she gave into her body's desires. She had never regretted it and was not the least bit concerned when Harry had found out she was not as innocent as one would suppose. He had already become her lover, although in a more subdued manner due to their age. The nerves were due to the fact of her intense love for Harry and the fear they would not have very long together to enjoy this new love.

She became aware they had arrived and that the guests were waiting outside the church in order to greet her, the bride.

Brian Nicholls had kindly agreed to take the photographs as photography was a passion of his. A few snaps were taken before they entered the church then the organist struck up the chords of the Bridal March.

Emily linked her arm into Ida's and asked, 'Ready?'

'As I ever will be,' she replied, nervously.

Emily felt proud walking Ida down the aisle, and the feeling struck her that it could have been a daughter of her own that she was handing over in marriage, not an eighty-year-old woman.

Harry turned to look at his bride as they came down the aisle and Emily saw his face was full of love and admiration for his bride. It pulled at Emily's heart. She would have preferred it to be her and David here in church. She missed the first few words of the marriage ceremony as she thought about it. The only chance she would have of getting David down the aisle was to wait until Leap Year and propose to him and she knew she could never do that. As the words of the service penetrated her thoughts she pulled herself together waiting to hear the phrase where she had to hand Ida over to Harry.

It was such a rare event, the marriage of two people at their ages and the fact that they were so obviously so in love with each other, that the ceremony was very moving.

Emily was alone with David at the reception. 'It went well, didn't it?' he stated.

'Perfect,' she laughed, 'but look who organised it.'

348

'Oh, little miss clever,' he smirked. He carried on in a more serious tone, 'You look lovely yourself, good enough to be the bride.'

Emily felt her mood change and a slight resentment came over her that he could mention marriage in such a casual way, yet their own relationship was not moving forward. She was relieved when they passed through the gateway and she knew her time would be occupied entertaining the guests.

The meal was delightful and Karen looked pleased that her first mass catering event had gone so efficiently well.

Harry stood up and made a speech, thanking everyone for the wonderful day they had had, and thanking Ida for agreeing to become his wife in the first place. He presented Karen and Emily with a pair of earrings each in thanks for all their hard work.

Emily knew she would always treasure them. Harry had taken her to one side a few days prior to the wedding and had thanked her for taking both him and Ida in, and making it possible for them to have met each other. He had also told Emily that the similarity between Ida and Edna was uncanny. He was careful to stress he loved Ida for herself, not because of her resemblance to Edna.

Emily asked the guests not to rush off as

soon as the meal was finished as she wanted the party to continue. She had another surprise in store for the pair of newly-weds.

Pat, the vicar's wife, approached Emily. 'I know it is not really the time and place but do you think I could have a word with you. It is urgent, otherwise I wouldn't ask today.'

'No problem, that is why this place has been set up and I do need residents. There is also a spare room now,' replied Emily, anticipating what she was going to be asked.

'Thanks,' said Pat looking relieved; she didn't contradict Emily.

'Look, why don't I take you to see my cottage. You haven't had a chance to see it yet and we will be quiet there.'

'Yes, I am sorry I haven't had an opportunity to come for coffee. Bill said you kept asking what had happened to me. I don't know where the time goes to be honest.'

'I know, right, tell me about it.'

Pat enthused at seeing the cottage, envying Emily that she had the opportunity to seek solitude sometimes. But it was only a moment's regret that her life didn't also offer that opportunity because, if Pat was really honest, she wouldn't swap her life.

'Well. You will have already guessed it's about another possible resident. I am really worried about her. They call her Sheila and she's in her late fifties, early sixties. Her husband died recently.'

'Oh, that is sad. Was he a lot older than her?'

'No, about the same age. A sudden heart attack with no previous warning. They have no family and were devoted to each other. I've never known a couple like that. They lived for each other.'

'Sad they hadn't a family,' Emily interrupted.

'Oh, it was their choice. They never felt the need for children apparently because they'd got each other. She has never worked since they married. The husband was the old fashioned type and liked her at home. She never objected as she loved looking after the house and having his meals on the table when he came home from work. They never did anything on their own, when they went shopping they went together. I don't think they had any other friends as they saw each other as their friend as well as partner. You can imagine what she feels like now her one and only friend has died. She's like a lost soul and I mean that.'

'Oh, poor dear,' Emily commiserated.

'Then on top of that the husband was very thoughtless in thinking there was no point in insuring his life as he was convinced they

351

would live to a ripe old age together. With having no children he didn't see the need. Since there were only the two of them they did enjoy the good things in life. Everything they had was the best. Now not only has she lost her husband but she is going to lose her home. She has no skills to offer an employer and to be honest at the moment she would never cope with work. Of course, she is too old for most people to take her on. So you can see why I thought of you. It seems the ideal solution to get her away from her own company, yet she still has solitude.'

'I can appreciate the reasoning behind your thinking and of course she can come here if that is what she wants. Hopefully it will help her to realise she can have friends of her own.'

'At the moment she'll do anything that's suggested to her because she is lost and needs guidance. As I said, she is not used to making decisions, but I must stress it will not be easy with her in the beginning because she wanders around aimlessly with no motivation. In reality I know she has no will to live. I was hoping by coming here she might get that back and start to see there is a life possible for her without a husband.'

'Why don't you sort out a meeting and I'll take it from there.'

'I will and I'll get back to you shortly. Thanks ever so much. I know she will be in good hands.'

Emily looked at her watch. 'Oh, we must get back in there to sort their next surprise out.'

Back in the main house she looked for Karen and asked, 'Are we ready then?'

'Yes. David's waiting outside for them in his car.'

Emily called in a loud voice, 'Ladies and gentlemen, could we have your attention please.'

A hush fell on the room as all faces turned to her, full of curiosity. She spoke again in a loud voice. 'Harry and Ida, would you please come here?'

Space was made for them and they moved across to Emily, looking curious about what was happening.

Emily pointed to two suitcases that now stood in the hall. 'They are yours. You are off on your honeymoon.'

'But we haven't one booked,' protested Harry.

'Oh, but you have. On behalf of all of us: we are sending you on a break to Scarborough. David is waiting outside with his car ready to take you. We decided at your age there was nothing we could buy you so this is our present instead.'

They both looked too shocked for words, wondering how it had all been organised without their knowledge. Emily and Karen had sneaked to their room earlier and packed what they thought they would need. Emily had made the booking at the Norlands hotel where she spent her pleasant break with David.

It evoked some memories that were not being fulfilled as she made the booking. She wished it was herself and David going on their honeymoon. She was sure Harry and Ida would have a lovely time.

Finally Ida found her voice. 'Oh, thank you so much everybody. I have had a simply marvellous day and I'm sure I speak for Harry as well. I will never forget my wedding day.'

'I agree wholeheartedly with my wife,' he replied, looking happy and proud.

'Come on then, out you go,' Emily bossed them.

As Ida went to the car a voice shouted at her, 'Throw your bouquet.'

Emily instinctively put her hands up with everybody else to catch it, but when she felt it actually in her hands she became highly embarrassed.

'You'll be next,' another voice shouted.

Emily felt too choked to reply. She was

beginning to get obsessed about David proposing to her, but it seemed it was just a beautiful dream. Their relationship felt as if it had reached a stalemate situation and she had begun to realise she loved him with a love far different to the one she'd ever felt for Howard.

27

Emily and Karen had made an effort to do some tidying up as they felt it wasn't fair to leave it all to Joan on Monday. Although Emily didn't suppose she would grumble at the extra work, as she seemed to thrive on being at the house and in the hub of things. She had been in almost full time the week before the wedding, helping with all the preparations, refusing any further pay and saying the extra work was done out of love for the job; and, of course, the happy couple. But the coming week, besides the clearing up after the wedding, there was now a room to be prepared for Sheila arriving.

Emily had been shocked on the Sunday, just after they had finished their work for the day and Karen had gone up to her flat for a rest, when a knock had come on the outer door. When Emily pulled it open a woman had been standing there who announced herself as Sheila. She had gone on to say Pat had told her after church that morning that she had had a word with Emily and she was in agreement that she could move into her place.

Sheila then went on to say, 'I don't think I can stand it on my own anymore. I have also got a cash buyer for my house and they are pushing things forward quickly so that they can move in soon. Would it be all right if I moved in here on Wednesday, next week?'

Emily was momentarily lost for words at the speed it was all happening. They had not even had a chat in order to assess each other and whether they could get along together. That was one thing Emily was adamant about, that all the residents fit in with each other. For a woman who was having such tremendous trouble coping with the death of her husband she certainly seemed to know what she wanted to do about her future.

As Emily got to know her better she began to understand that she was petrified of sleeping on her own in a house with no other occupants and that was what had prompted her to act in such a manner on her doorstep.

As far as she could see, it wasn't a problem her moving in then as long as the room was ready, and told her so. The words were hardly out of her mouth before Sheila said, 'I can go back to my house in the day time and finish the packing up then sleep here, if that is alright? You don't mind if I bring a few things along with me? I mean small items that mean a lot to me.'

'Of course not, I always encourage that. But I do think it would be a good idea if you saw the room first,' said Emily, now she had time to catch her breath and get her mind in order.

'Yes of course, how silly of me. You see my husband used to organise everything for me so I had no need to worry. Now I have to do it all myself,' she sighed.

Emily could see tears coming into her eyes at these last words and quickly said in order to distract her, 'Come on, this way and I'll show you three rooms then you can take your pick.'

'Oh, there is no need to do that, just show me one that you think is suitable.'

But Emily stayed resolute on that and in the end she chose one of the front rooms with a large bay window saying the items she had in mind to bring with her would fit in there very nicely. She also praised Emily for her choice of decoration saying it looked very homely. Emily escorted her around the rest of the common areas and then she took her up to Karen's flat to introduce them. Thankfully Karen seemed to have got over her earlier problem of resentment towards some of the residents and welcomed her very warmly.

Angela was out, taking the baby for a walk, and Emily thought it only fair to mention there would be a baby around, but some of the time during the day it would be with her at the cottage.

Rachel was also out with friends, but Emily told Sheila about her. Rachel was finding her feet already and once she had a job she would probably want to move to a place of her own, but that was in the future.

She also mentioned that Harry and Ida were on their honeymoon and she saw Sheila's puzzled face enquiring why a married couple were going to live there. Emily went on to explain their ages and the circumstances in which they had met and how lovely the wedding had been.

Sheila was still as enthusiastic about moving in on the Wednesday and Emily told her she was welcome to start bringing some of her belongings before then if it made the move easier. She went away looking much happier and less nervous than when she had first arrived.

★ ★ ★

Joan was late for work on Monday morning and Emily was surprised, more so because Joan knew there was extra cleaning waiting for her and on those occasions she usually came in earlier than was expected of her.

Despite her large size and her slow way of walking, it never ceased to amaze Emily how she always seemed to be where she intended to be on time and how she got her allotted work done so rapidly.

Joan hadn't missed a day's work without prior warning before, and to do that she had recently had a telephone installed, at the insistence of her daughter. Whenever she had rung, Emily had found she had to take control of herself not to laugh aloud at how Joan used the equipment. She seemed to think she had to shout down the phone line and Emily was sure that she could be heard directly from her house to theirs.

She was musing over what she should do about Joan's absence, particularly with everything else she had to complete to have the room ready for Sheila's arrival, when a loud bang came on the door.

As Emily tugged the door open sharply, she instinctively knew who it was since she looked so like her mother.

'You are Joan's daughter?' Emily quickly asked the ashen-faced woman stood on the doorstep who seemed incapable of speech.

'Yes, I'm Alison,' she replied as she found her voice.

'Look, come in, don't stand in the cold,' Emily ordered her.

Alison moved forward as if in a trance, still not saying anything more.

'Have you come about Joan?' Emily queried, feeling this was the only way to get to a word out of her.

All she answered was, 'Yes,' but did not enlighten Emily any further.

'Is she ill?' Emily probed.

'No,' came the monosyllabic reply.

Emily was really baffled. She began to wonder if the woman in front of her had some mental illness that Joan had not mentioned.

Emily looked closely at Alison to see if she could deduce anything but she realised tears were running uncontrollably down her cheeks.

'Come on, what is it?' she cajoled. 'It can't be that bad that you can't tell me. Have you and your mum had an argument?' she suggested.

'It is that bad, she's dead,' Alison replied like a zombie.

'What!' exclaimed Emily, clutching the chair in front of her for support.

'But she can't be, she was here on Saturday at the wedding. She looked okay then and she enjoyed herself enormously. I have never seen her look as happy, what happened?'

'I know, she couldn't shut up talking about

it all day yesterday. We must have heard all the details at least a dozen times. Dad said she got up this morning and was still very chirpy and talking about it all again. If anything she had more to say than usual, if that's possible. Then after clearing the breakfast things she said she would have a breather for five minutes before she came here. Dad knew that was unusual so he told her to shut her eyes for a few minutes and he would bring her another cup of tea. He thought all the extra chatting had worn her out. When he took the tea in to her he nudged her to wake her up, but she didn't move. Dad called up to me, because I was busy getting the children ready for school. He knew there was something wrong but I don't think he wanted to admit it. As soon as I saw her I knew she was dead. She had died in those few moments that he had been in the kitchen making the tea. The doctor thinks a blood clot must have gone to her heart and that was it. You know she never went to the doctors. I don't think she had seen him for ten years or more.'

'Oh, how terrible, and to think it was going to be her sixtieth birthday next month. She was so excited about that. Only yesterday Karen and I were planning a surprise party for her after seeing how much she had enjoyed

Saturday. She once mentioned she had never had a proper party of her own. I was going to try to get in touch with you today so that we could organise it together.'

Emily suddenly stopped speaking as she realised she was rambling on about things that didn't need to be talked about at a time like this. She supposed she was probably in a state of shock herself.

She realised Alison was shaking with violent crying and Emily drew her into her arms, feeling like a mother, despite being of similar age. Tears were also running down Emily's cheeks at the loss of this woman she had become close to in the short time she had known her. More than she'd ever been to her own mother in her lifetime.

Karen came into the hall to find the pair of them in tears. She jumped to the conclusion that something had happened to Ida, but she didn't know where this strange woman fitted into it. The wedding had obviously just been too much for her weak heart.

Emily said between sobs, 'It's Joan, this is her daughter Alison.'

'Joan?'

'She's dead.'

For a moment Emily thought Karen was going to pass out. She went pure white and swayed with shock.

'She can't be — she was here on Saturday.'

'That's what I said. But she is.'

'Oh, this is terrible, and to think with all the good things that have been happening, who would have expected this?'

Emily remembered one of her mother's old sayings, 'Mark my words, there's never a birth without a death.'

Emily had always laughed at this statement as it had seemed so preposterous but on this occasion it seemed to have been correct.

'Anyway,' Alison continued, after staying silent during the exchange between Emily and Karen, 'I had to come and tell you. Dad won't be in to see to the garden for a day or two, not at least until after the funeral.'

Emily quickly interrupted her, 'Tell him to have as long as he needs, the garden will wait.' It struck her that she should have realised that she hadn't seen Fred around either, as he usually came in to give her a cheery, 'Good morning,' before he got on with his work.

Alison stood looking slightly embarrassed, 'I hope you don't think I'm speaking out of turn and it's not really the right time to ask, but do you think I could take over my mother's job here?' Alison put her hand to her mouth in shock at having even thought of it at that time. She could only assume the shock had addled her brain.

Emily nearly laughed with relief at the absurdity of the situation, 'Of course, you can. That, at least, will be one worry off my mind.'

'Thanks ever so much, I won't let you down.'

'Now what about the funeral?' asked Emily, having recovered herself a little. 'I suppose you will not have had time to get your thoughts around that.'

'Well, actually, Dad has to go to the undertakers this afternoon to finalise things. He has been ever so good but I can see he is heartbroken. He is also tearing his hair out with worry because he has hardly enough money for the funeral never mind a meal afterwards. Like you mentioned earlier, with it being nearly her sixtieth, he feels it only right to give her a real good send off.' She stuttered, looking slightly embarrassed, 'Not that he is mean, he would have given her a good do in any case, but she had been looking forward to her birthday, so he feels even in death he has to celebrate it for her.'

'I know just what you mean and I hope you don't think I'm being too presumptuous but seeing that we were going to have a party here for her birthday how about asking your Dad if he would like us to do the funeral meal instead.'

'Oh thanks, I'm sure when you put it like that he will agree. That will be a great weight off his mind.'

Alison left them saying if she could get in she would come and do some cleaning during the week, but Emily promptly told her to put any thought of that right out of her mind, until after the funeral.

There was nothing for Emily and Karen to do but knuckle down and if they couldn't get through all the house cleaning, at least, they could make sure Sheila's room was spick and span for her arrival.

Emily knocked on Angela's door to let her know what had happened to Joan, but she still looked befuddled from sleep. She said that Lara had kept her awake most of the night, so whilst she was quiet she was catching up herself.

Emily was still worried about Angela, because despite the easy birth, and having kept the baby, she still seemed devoid of emotion. Even the news of Joan's death didn't evoke a strong reaction, she mumbled, 'Oh, what a shame,' with no depth of feeling in her voice.

David had been too busy at work to go back to Scarborough to collect Harry and Ivy after their honeymoon but they were happy to have a train journey to Beverley and get a taxi from there. They seemed to see everything they did together for the first time as a novelty. They came home in a very high and cheerful mood having had a marvellous honeymoon and a good journey home. They hadn't been in the house two minutes before it dawned on them that everything didn't appear as it should have been. The house was too quiet and there were still signs of Saturday's disruptions, which was so unlike Joan. She liked everything smart and ship-shape.

Nobody seemed around to tell them what was going on, but Harry suggested to Ida, 'Why don't we go and knock and see if Emily is in her cottage.'

One knock was enough to produce Emily, but it was a very weary and troubled looking Emily who opened the door, not the bright, bubbly person they had left on Saturday. Ida could only think that it was something to do with David, so tactfully asked, 'How have things been whilst we've been away?'

'Terrible,' replied Emily, as she burst into tears. 'Come in and I'll tell you,' she managed to say between the sobs.

'Now then, what on earth's happened that it can be that bad?' asked Ida, in a kindly voice, still convinced it was over David.

'It's Joan, she's dead,' Emily moaned.

Now it was Harry's turn to look shocked as he stuttered, 'How? When?'

'There will be an autopsy but they think it was a blood clot in her heart. She was as happy as anything one moment, still chatting away about your wedding, then the next, gone.'

'Well I never,' said Ida, in a shaky voice. 'When did it happen?'

'Monday morning,' then Emily went on to recount the tale as Alison had told it to her. Finally she said, 'I'm glad you are back, at least you will be here for the funeral next Tuesday. I have said we will do the meal here after the funeral as Karen and myself were already planning to give her a party for her sixtieth birthday. It seems only right we do this one last thing for her.'

'But why didn't you call us back,' Harry exclaimed.

'There was nothing you could do and we wanted you two to enjoy yourselves. You deserved that.'

'That was good of you. But we will do anything we can to help now we are back, won't we Harry?'

It brightened Emily's spirits a little seeing these two already behaving like an old married couple. She suddenly remembered, 'We also have somebody new joining us this afternoon, to live here.'

'You don't let the grass grow under your feet,' Harry said in a lighter voice.

'Well, actually Pat had a word with me on Saturday at the wedding and there was no chance to tell you before you set off to Scarborough. Sheila, that's her name, came to see me on Sunday. The speed she arrived on the doorstep surprised me, and, as I said she wants to move in this afternoon. She has been coming and going with her things but we seem to have missed each other most of the time, so I have not had the opportunity to tell her what's happened. Karen and I had to get her room ready ourselves, so I hope it is clean enough for her. Anyway I think she should fit in very nicely.' Then she recounted what she knew about Sheila and they were instantly full of sympathy for her situation.

No sooner had lunch come and gone than Emily heard a loud knock at the outer door and a voice shout, 'Emily, I've arrived.'

Emily rushed into the hall to greet Sheila. 'Yes, right. I hope your room is okay, but we've had an upset since I saw you. It has been hectic around here; I think that is why we have missed each other.'

'I did wonder why I hadn't seen you. What's happened? You're not going to say I can't stay?' she asked in panic, not noticing that Emily had already said her room was ready.

'No, nothing like that at all. It is Joan who cleaned for us suddenly passed away on Monday, and we had grown very fond of her and it has upset us all.'

'Oh, how tragic,' she said. Emily hoped she had not reminded Sheila of the recent death of her own husband. Amazingly she took the information in her stride asking quite calmly and matter of factly, 'So I suppose housework and the chores have been a problem for you this week?'

'You could say that,' replied Emily.

'Look, I'll just take my things up, if that's alright, don't worry about looking after my room. I plan to take care of it myself.'

'If you are sure?' Emily asked cautiously.

'I am,' replied Sheila, more positive than Emily had heard her speak before.

Next morning when Emily came into the house she was dismayed to hear sounds from the sitting room. She was even more surprised to see Sheila with an overall on and obviously giving the room a thorough clean.

'What are you doing?' asked Emily, slightly more sharply than she intended because of her dismay.

'Giving a helping hand. Housework is a passion of mine. You see, I've had plenty of years' experience, and it is one thing I can do really well.'

She was at a loss at what to say. She had to admit Sheila did look in her element, maybe it was just what she needed. That was, at least, until Alison arrived to take up the role. That would be another day, she would sort it all out then.

★ ★ ★

The church was packed the following Tuesday for Joan's funeral. Emily knew she was well liked among the community but hadn't appreciated how much. She felt really touched that Harry had insisted he wanted to say a few words on behalf of them all. Emily's attention was taken when she heard the words:-

He Leadeth Me — Joan

In pastures green? Yet not always;
Sometimes He who knoweth best,
In kindness leadeth me.
In weary ways where heavy shadows be,
Out of the sunshine, warm and soft and bright,
Out of the sunshine into darkest night.
I oft would faint with sorrow and affright,
Only for this — I know He holds my hand.

So whether in a green or desert land,
I trust Him, though I do not understand.

And by still waters?
No, not always so.
Oft-time the heavy tempests round me blow;
And over my soul the waves and billows go.
But when the storm beats loudest
And I cry aloud for help, the Master
Standeth by and whispers to my soul
'Lo, it is I'
Above the tempest wild I hear Him say,
'Beyond this darkness lies the perfect day,
In every path of thine I lead the way'.

So, whether on the hilltop high and fair I dwell,
Or in the sunless valley where the shadows lie,
What matter? He is there.
Yea, more than this, where'er the pathway lead
He gives to me no helpless broken reed,
But his own hand sufficient for my need.

So, where'er He leadeth I can safely go
And in the blest hereafter I shall know why,
In His wisdom, He hath lead me so.

UNKNOWN

Emily sensed the whole church congrega-
tion were feeling emotional when Harry had
finished the beautiful words. Harry's eyes

were glistening, wet with unshed tears.

Fred had said it had been her wish to be cremated, but that she wanted her ashes to be put in a garden of remembrance. As she had seen it, if the family wanted to visit a place of remembrance then there was somewhere they could go, yet if they didn't want to go then what did it matter about it being left unattended.

It was a very subdued party that drove back to the house. The meal itself proved to be a sober affair and there was little chatter which seemed an irony considering Joan's talkative nature. Karen had once again excelled in her catering skills but it didn't bring forth the praise it deserved.

Emily tried to will a little bit of life into the proceedings by telling the guests that it should have been a party for Joan's sixtieth birthday.

It was Fred who amazed Emily the most. Joan had given the impression that he had no great love for her. His reaction to her death and his subsequent behaviour contradicted those words. He was bereft with grief and Emily was sure if Alison hadn't been living with him at home he would have sunk into despair and been incapable of rousing himself from the chair. It was Alison who prompted him to move on with his life. She had taken over her mother's role. Despite being as meticulous in her work as Joan, Emily still missed all the little stories Joan recounted to them. Thankfully Alison accepted Sheila's help, even if it wasn't officially her job, and they struck up a strange friendship considering Alison was young enough to be her daughter, yet Sheila had never wanted a family.

28

Emily was beginning to think things were settling down after Joan's death, and wondered how they would have managed without the arrival of Sheila.

In an unobtrusive way she helped out where she saw help was needed. She didn't want any reward for doing any work. The satisfaction of knowing she was needed once more was reward enough. Housework was what she knew best and doing anything connected with it made her feel safe and secure.

Emily didn't object because the small jobs she had always meant to get around to doing were now being done by Sheila. She had to admit they were probably being done better than she was capable of doing them. Sheila saw things that needed doing without either Emily or Karen aware that there was anything amiss. She kept out of the way of anyone else when she did anything but she had blossomed to have enough confidence to do things of her own volition. It was Alison, of all the unlikely people, that seemed to be the one she was most friendly with. She had made her nest for what appeared a long time to come.

Ida and Harry were like a pair of young love birds. There was no doubt in anybody's mind that they were made for each other. Emily knew some people had been cynical, believing it was a marriage of convenience at their age in order to give them companionship. But Emily knew it was more than that. They were genuinely in love with each other and showed it all the time by word and action.

Karen had received a letter from Alan, which she had been reluctant to open. She only did so with Emily at her side. It was actually a letter of apology for his behaviour and for the hurt and unhappiness he'd caused her during the marriage. He was in a rehabilitation centre, both to help him get the gambling under control and also to kick his drinking habit. He now understood he couldn't be cured of these addictions but he could be taught how to control them.

Apparently he had been arrested again shortly after the fight with her, on a drink driving charge. He had lost his car and the one place where he could sleep and he had ended up living rough and a particularly unpleasant incident with some down and outs had sobered him enough to question what he was doing with his life. He realised he had hit rock bottom. He had voluntarily contacted the Samaritans in desperation as he had not wanted to go on living if that was all his future was going to be, sleeping wherever he could find shelter and scrounging and looking in dustbins for scraps of food. He felt totally humiliated by what he had become.

The Samaritans had been a great help to him and he was now getting help. He didn't ask Karen to forgive him because he said he couldn't expect that after the hurt and unhappiness he had caused her but he said he had no objections if she was to instigate divorce proceedings against him. He ended the letter by wishing her well in her new life and he was sure she would make a success of life without him hanging around.

By the time she had finished the letter she was crying and Emily said with a hint of panic in her voice, 'Now don't go feeling all sorry for him and take him back.'

'No worry about that. I was crying with relief really that, at least, he has come to his senses. It's too late for us. That part of my life is in the past but it's nice to think I can now look back without bitterness and fear.'

'I'm pleased it has worked out this way,' said Emily and gave Karen a hug. They could both cope with what life threw at them in the future, they were both stronger.

Fred was causing Emily concern. He had been rather stout before the death of Joan, and the weight was dropping off him rapidly. His clothes hung on him as if they were on a clothes horse. Tending the garden no longer seemed to bring him any joy; he did the task more out of habit than pleasure. Emily didn't think he was seeing any of the beautiful plants, which he had previously nurtured with loving care.

She decided to take the opportunity to have a quiet word with Alison who said it was much the same at home. She admitted it had been a shock to her, the depth of his grief, as she had never taken them to be a devoted couple. He no longer tended his own little garden at home, which he had previously taken so much care of. It now had weeds choking the lovely plants. All he did was sit brooding and reliving the past. She had tried as many ways as she could think of to get him motivated and out of his chair.

Alison had tried saying jokingly, 'I know my Mum used to complain he never moved out of that chair but this is different. Before, he made an effort with his garden and himself and there always seemed a purpose when he sat as he did, doing crosswords or looking at his gardening magazines. Now, he just stares into space with an expression of being somewhere else altogether and he never hears a word I say to him. Even the kids arguing doesn't get through to him, he sits rigid, not moving.'

They were at a loss and realised they could not give him the help he so obviously needed. They only hoped time would ease the pain for him.

Angela had not gone back to work at the original due date she had set and Emily had taken it to mean that she was so besotted with the baby that she did not want to leave her until she was forced to resume work, when her funds ran out.

But Angela was so quiet nowadays nobody really knew what she was thinking. If she had been more open they would have known she was dreading the thought of returning to work. She couldn't face meeting her colleagues again. There were those who knew the truth of the situation, that she had gone and got herself pregnant by a lad who couldn't give a damn about her. Her parents had drummed into her how she had brought shame and disgrace on their family. They had said it would be greater shame if she kept the baby, it was living proof of her stupidity. She had now disobeyed them and kept Lara.

She wasn't able to vent these thoughts so they had festered out of all proportion. She had time to sit and brood about them, despite having the baby to look after. If she had been back at work, amongst her young work colleagues, she would more than likely have found it easier. They would have shown her how ridiculous it was to think like this and would probably have applauded her for keeping the baby. But she didn't want to share her thoughts with anyone. If it had been possible she would have shut herself in solitude away from everything and everybody. Then there was the tiredness and lethargy. She couldn't believe a birth could make anybody feel they constantly wanted to sleep as she did. When she moved her body seemed to resist with a will of its own. But when she shut her eyes the nightmares came back to haunt her. She would see her mother leaning over her and leering and shouting obscenities at her and telling her what an evil person she was. Her father would be in the back ground watching on with equally cold and sinister eyes. In her dreams Angela would hold her arms out to them and beg their forgiveness and ask to be taken back home. They would laugh a cruel hard laugh which would continue echoing a long time after they had left her and she would wake up bathed in sweat and feel worse than ever.

It had become her custom to take Lara out

for a walk in her pram most afternoons. It wasn't that she was taking her out for fresh air as Emily presumed, but so that she could go and find a quiet corner in a small public garden she knew. Rarely did anyone pass through the garden and if they did they hardly noticed her tucked away in the corner. It felt like her own little haven, somewhere she could hide in because she didn't want people to see her and stare at the fat and ugly person she felt she had become. It was as if by just looking at her they would know what she had done, what a sinner she was.

In fact, as Emily had suspected, her youthful figure had come back quickly and as she had so little interest in food she still continued to lose weight. Emily was concerned about her but when she challenged Angela about her poor appetite she replied convincingly, 'Because you saw me eating a lot when I was pregnant you seem to presume that is my normal appetite, but I was eating for two. This is how much I normally eat.'

It sounded plausible enough.

Angela was walking back slowly after her afternoon in the garden. The air had become too chilly for her to sit any longer as the cold penetrated her already numb brain. She made a move to go home. As she walked through the small town centre she saw a figure across the road from her, her mother. For the first time in a long time she was motivated to draw attention to herself by calling out, 'Mum, it's me! Angela, over here!'

The figure turned to look at her and eyes stared that seemed to burn straight through Angela with hate as they moved down to look at the pram. Not a word was said. The woman quickly rushed away into a side road nearby.

Angela rushed after her, hurtling the pram across the busy road; she was sure if her mother saw her granddaughter, her hate would melt and turn to love. By the time she had negotiated the traffic, and she turned into the side street there was no sign of her mother. She ran up the street and glanced down other roads but it was as if her mother had vanished. Heartbroken to be shunned in this manner, she just wanted to get away from the staring faces that were looking at her. She thought she only saw contempt on their faces, but it was looks of concern for the poor lass, and disgust that the person, who she obviously knew, could treat her like this.

Angela had to admit Emily and the rest of the residents were kind to her. Hadn't they bought her a cot for Lara? But she felt as a young woman she should not be there, her place was with her parents. It should have been them who had bought the cot and doing the baby-sitting. They would surely understand how she was feeling if they let her back into their lives. Their love and kindness would help her get better and make the heartache go away.

If she had been thinking sensibly she would have remembered that there had never been a lot of love from either of her parents. When she was small there had not been love and cuddles from her mother to make everything better. These things were forgotten now as she saw them as the people she needed to love her and the baby.

She plodded home very slowly, tears running down her face, getting a few stares from strangers. One kindly woman tapped her on the arm and asked her, 'Are you all right dear? Can I do anything to help you? I do know what having your first baby is like; I have five of my own.'

'No, just a touch of hay fever,' she mumbled. The woman looked in disbelief as she knew it wasn't hay fever time of year for sufferers.

Angela managed to get back to the house, entered unseen, then left the pram in the hall, where it had been agreed she could leave it for convenience. She slipped up to her room without anybody coming out to see her, and quickly entered and locked the door. She couldn't face the evening meal, but she didn't think they would bother unduly, because they knew if she had to see to the baby at meal times she would make herself a light meal on her own stove.

She fed and changed Lara without even realising what she was doing then sat rocking her back and forth as if she got some comfort from the action. Lara seemed to sense her mother's distress and was restless. Eventually once Lara was asleep she laid her in her cot and climbed into bed herself without bothering to get any food or undressing. She buried her head under the sheets as if to hide away from the world. The sound of the baby crying penetrated her mind. It wouldn't stop. Up she would to get from her own cocoon to comfort her, and climbed back in bed when she was quiet. This went on until the early hours of the morning and by that time she felt as if she wanted to shake the baby until it stopped making a noise. Only instinct prevented her.

In the end she went to the cupboard and took a bottle out of it. In her fuddled mind she knew that would solve the problem. She gave a quick smirk when she thought how she had sneaked the bottle from Karen's bathroom cabinet without her noticing. She had anticipated the time would soon be right to use the contents. She took one but the noise didn't stop, so her hand reached out and she took another. She would get rid of that sound somehow.

★   ★   ★

As Karen walked down the steps from her flat in the morning she heard Lara crying and hoped she had not kept Angela awake most of the night. When she listened the cry sounded as if the baby was in deep distress. She had worked herself up as if she had been crying for a long time. She remembered thinking in her sleep fuddled brain that the baby was restless during the night and crying more than was usual.

She tapped on Angela's door several times only to be met with no response.

She rushed downstairs to the phone and dialled Emily's number. As the phone was answered she said with panic in her voice, 'I think you had better come over here with your keys. I'm sure there is something wrong with Angela. She's not opening her door, and she must be in because Lara is screaming the place down.' Then another thought struck her, 'She wouldn't leave her on her own would she?'

'I'll be straight with you,' was the reply before the phone was slammed down.

Karen barely had time to put her own phone back on the receiver before Emily burst through the door looking as if she hadn't even brushed her hair. She made straight for the stairs, saying over her shoulder, 'Come on.'

As soon as Emily opened the door they could smell the sweet, sickly aroma of the baby. But there was something else that was ominous and Karen noticed Emily pause momentarily in pushing the door open before she moved forward. With long quick strides she was across to the bed and touching Angela's cheek. She turned to Karen, who stood hesitating in the doorway, 'Karen, see to Lara,' she said in a sharp voice in order to bring Karen out of her state of shock.

It had the required effect as she heard Lara give a big shuddering sob at being picked up. She turned her attention back to Angela and was only glad she had attended the first aid course at college. She started to try to resuscitate her. She worked as if her own life depended on it and kept muttering, 'Come on, Angela, breathe. Think of Lara,' but nothing happened. She felt herself slowly being pulled away from Angela and shouted in panic, 'Stop it, I've got to make her breathe.'

'Come on, time to give up, dear,' Harry said kindly. 'She is past your help or anybody else's. I have rung for David to come.'

Emily stood staring blankly at Harry wondering how he had got there. She relaxed and Harry led her away but she was crying bitter tears now. 'Why, Harry? She was such a young lass with all her life to live?' She had self recriminations in case it was her fault that Angela had kept the baby, maybe that wasn't what she had wanted at all. So many thoughts in such a short time passed through her head.

Harry took her to Ida who was soon looking after her in their bedroom, whilst Harry took over. Ida talked to her in a soothing voice trying to get through Emily's grief. She stressed to Emily that the trauma in Angela had been brought about by more than the birth of her baby. Her parent's attitude during her short life had built up during the years. She had been a very unhappy, confused and disturbed young woman.

Karen walked slowly into the room holding a contented baby. 'Poor little mite, no mum now, a dad who doesn't want to know and grandparents worse than that,' she said with deep sadness and despair in her voice.

'Oh, Karen,' Emily wailed.

The police were called by David once he

had seen the empty bottle of tablets by the bed. Karen had a momentary panic that they were going to accuse her of killing Angela when they started questioning how many tablets had been in the bottle. The bottle had Karen's name on it. She said she could only remember taking possibly five herself. After Alan's letter her mind had been easier and sleep had come naturally. Then when they asked how the pills had got into Angela's room she went cold with fear. She could only tell the truth. 'I haven't a clue,' she admitted. She did go on to say that she rarely locked her flat door so it would have been easy for Angela to have sneaked up there and taken them out of her bathroom cabinet. She also told them it had been no secret to the other residents that she had been prescribed sleeping pills because she had told them all if she wasn't up getting their breakfast, they had to come and wake her up. The policewoman said she didn't think they would need to question her further and left. Once away from them she let out a sigh of relief that they had believed her. She had only just got rid of one problem, Alan, so she didn't need any more in her life.

The police searched Angela's room thoroughly but no suicide note was found. They were at a loss to know whether it had been an accident or was intentional and handed it over to the correct authorities.

Ida was of the opinion that Angela could have been unaware of what she was doing, as she had obviously been under a great deal of stress with the situation she was in. She tried to suggest tactfully that when the brain was sleep fuddled it was possible to do anything without intending terrible consequences to stem from the action.

Karen was blaming herself, even if the police didn't think she had intentionally let Angela get hold of her pills. She should have made sure they were locked safely away. She vowed to keep her flat door locked in the future. They were trying to console each other as they all had their own doubts that they had not done enough for Angela, forgetting for the moment that she had shunned any help and they had given what assistance she had allowed them to.

David blamed himself more than anybody. He was her GP and that was what he had had all the expensive training for. He had been so certain that by going to live at Emily's she'd gone to the one place that could help her. He was probably right, if anybody could have helped her then Emily and her companions had been the people to do it. But the depth of her hurt had been too deep seated.

Professional help may have worked, but it was doubtful.

A very subdued set of people attended the inquest. The police had notified her parents of her death. They didn't attend the inquest, much to the shock of the people there. Some took it to mean that they were too grief-stricken to attend but in reality they had cut her out of their lives when they dumped her belongings at the doctor's surgery. They had had the intrusion into their life for seventeen years, since her unexpected birth, and felt only relief that their existence could get back to normal.

The verdict was, as expected, 'Accidental Death' — whilst her state of mind was unbalanced. Karen felt a weight lift off her shoulders.

She didn't feel absolved from blame but common sense told her that whilst Angela's mind was disturbed it would have been very difficult for anybody to help her.

David drove her home after the inquest and she was relieved when he pulled up outside her own cottage. She couldn't face the others just then.

'Will you come in?' she asked him pleadingly.

'Yes, please,' he replied, bleakly.

Emily was aware he was suffering as deeply

from the shock of Angela's death as from feelings of tremendous guilt. He saw it as a neglected duty on his part, which was nonsense.

Emily came straight to the point. 'David, stop beating yourself up about Angela's death. I was doing the same, at first, but now I realise she was a really unhappy person. However astute any of us had been we couldn't have known her inner feelings. Her parents couldn't even be bothered to turn up for the inquest so how do you think she had been treated by them during her lifetime? The damage was done long before she became your patient. Sadly, if patients don't want to be helped by you then there is not a thing you or anybody else can do. Oh, you know all this, you don't need me to tell you.'

He gave a long sigh. 'You're right, I know. But I have never become hardened to losing a patient. I always take it badly. This is the worst situation I have had to deal with, but I doubt it will be the last.'

Emily pulled him into her arms to comfort him but soon his lips were searching and found hers. In the state he was in all his inhibitions were lost and passion took over. His hands started roaming over her body, gently caressing her. Looking back Emily was never certain who took the initiative but when her senses surfaced for a moment she realised they were in her bedroom.

David was gently undressing her and kissing each part of her body as he went along. She quickly tugged at his shirt buttons, thankful he had taken his jacket off when he had entered the house. She heard small groans coming from him and felt him tremble with passion.

They were soon in bed naked. It seemed as if their lips had never left each other. He gently eased his leg between hers, to part them, and moved himself on top of her. She felt a slight sensation when he entered her then they were swallowed up in passion.

Howard had simply thrust into her, as a means to an end, to make her pregnant and prove his masculinity. Emily had never derived any pleasure from her sexual act with him but was always left frustrated and feeling dirty. Now David brought her to the very edge of feeling as if the world would explode, then gently drew back leaving her begging for more by pulling him deeper into her. They both reached their moment of ecstasy at the same time, Emily experiencing something she never had before. She felt like a virgin experiencing the art of love making for the first time.

'Oh Emily, I love you so much,' David

moaned, as he came back to his senses.

'I thought you would never say it,' Emily laughed.

'But you must have known?' he asked shocked.

'A lady likes to be told.'

'Sorry,' he said, a sense of relief flowing through him that he'd so obviously satisfied Emily. He wasn't that experienced in the art of love making. During his years at medical school, he had had sex with one or two willing females. None were a great passion but he had never received any hurtful comments. He had also been worried that Emily was already a very experienced woman due to her marriage. But now instinct told him she had never felt anything like that before.

She nestled in his arms with a contented feeling. David broke the silence. 'Will you marry me?'

The question was so unexpected after all the months of her imagination thinking about it that she was lost for words. David was quick to think she was going to reject him.

Relief flooded through him as she said, 'Oh David, if only you knew how much I have longed for this moment. Yes please. I couldn't imagine my life without you.'

Before she knew it she was being kissed and caressed again. This time their love making had less urgency, but no less delight, now they had found and were sure of each other.

29

David and Emily decided that as a mark of respect to Angela they would wait until after the funeral before they openly declared their love for each other, although it didn't take Harry and Ida long to guess. Ida mentioned the good news to Karen. At least they now had something happy to think about after the two recent bereavements.

It was only a very small gathering for Angela's funeral; nothing like it had been for Joan's. When the police had contacted her parents and mentioned funeral arrangements they had said, 'What arrangements? We haven't got a daughter. Let the state organise it.' No amount of talking or trying to persuade them otherwise would change their minds.

The police officer who had broken the news to Angela's parents was distressed himself at such a callous attitude. He could hardly hide his anger at a couple who could denounce their daughter so totally. He said as much to his superior. 'There's something wrong with the pair of them, if you ask me. They want certifying and to think there's a lovely babby left with no parents and they want nowt to do with it.'

'That's the way of the world, Colin. I would have thought you'd been in the job long enough to know that.'

'I have, but in my whole time in the police force I've never met a couple like them. They must be unique.'

'Oh, I don't know. I've met some rum folk and that's no lie,' his superior admitted.

When he went home he recounted it all again to his wife. She had more compassion than his boss and understood how personally hurt he was. They held each other closely, only thankful they had plenty of love for their own children.

Emily and David willingly agreed to do whatever had to be done in the absence of Angela's parents.

Surprisingly, Sheila had insisted on going along with them even though she had never met the girl. But in the very short time she had been at the house she felt part of their lives. Rachel had begged off attending by saying it was an important time for her at college. Emily was disappointed by her response, because if Rachel had thought back to when she came to Emily, she would have seen she could so easily have gone the same way as Angela. It was simply luck which had given her a stronger sense of self-preservation, and Emily, along with the rest of them at the house, had proved a good friend to her. She would have welcomed Emily's support.

Fred had sent his sincere apologies and heartfelt sympathy with Alison but he said he couldn't face another funeral so shortly after Joan's. It would evoke too many unhappy memories. Alison said he was no nearer coming to terms with Joan's death, and she didn't want anything more to upset him that could impede his recovery.

A couple of her ex-work colleagues attended the funeral and Emily guessed that when Angela had taken leave to have the baby she would soon have gone from their minds.

She did feel comforted that the kind policeman, who had dealt with Angela's parents, was there with his wife. She had not expected such consideration.

As they had no instructions for the funeral, David and Emily had agreed with Harry and Ida that they should have a cremation and then, like Joan, have her ashes scattered in a garden of remembrance. It was obvious that her parents would never visit a grave or tend it and, as Karen pointed out, it would be years before Lara could understand about her mother and make her own decision. When she was older she would have somewhere to put flowers in a garden of remembrance.

The vicar didn't have a lot to say about her life, because without her parents' guidance, none of them knew anything about her prior to her arriving at Emily's. David had insisted he wanted to say a few words as he had felt a little responsible for her.

He looked sombre, standing in the Chapel of Remembrance, in his dark suit.

'I've probably known Angela longer than any of you as she had been my patient since I came to the practice, although I rarely saw her as she was a fit young woman. It is only this past few months that I had the opportunity to attend to her more often and, as I thought, to get to know her better. We none of us really knew her, only that she was very troubled. It is not for me to condemn the actions of others, but it does make my heart heavy with grief, that she hadn't parents at her side during a time in her life when she probably needed them most.

'To know she was under Emily's roof for the last few months of her life and had as good a life there as she would have found anywhere has helped me to come to terms with her death. I know Emily, Karen, Ida and Harry tried to get to know and understand her better. It was an uphill battle. The damage had been done long before they met her.

'Lara, when we look at her, will give us a

happy reminder that some benefit came from Angela's short and sad life.

'I would like you all to share in this prayer for both Angela and Lara.

'Our Father, which who in heaven . . .

★   ★   ★

Emily could hear quiet sobs coming from Karen. None of them could have been immune to the words that David had said with such depth of feeling. Emily looked at David, and seeing the emotion on his face her heart filled with pride.

No funeral breakfast had been organised as Emily had been sure there wouldn't be many mourners at the church. Once the coffin had gone through the open curtains to its next destination, Emily made a move to leave the church, and in doing so she approached the police officer and his wife and Angela's two work colleagues. 'Have you time to come back to our place for a drink with the rest of us in memory of Angela?' she asked them in a friendly tone of voice.

'Just a quick one,' the police officer said. 'I'm on duty tonight so I want to get a few hours' sleep before I go into work. This poor lass weighs heavy on my mind.'

'I know what you mean,' Emily said. 'Let's

just hope she's found her happiness.'

His wife laid her hand on Emily's arm and said sadly, with a glint of tears in her eyes, 'Let's hope.'

Her former work colleagues declined, saying their boss had been good enough to give them time to come to the funeral, but they didn't want to abuse his goodwill and needed to get back.

It was a quiet group that entered the house.

On their own again after the visitors has gone, Ida stood up and spoke aloud for the first time since entering the house. She looked directly at Emily and David who were stood together. 'Come on you two. Are you going to spill the beans then?'

Emily felt herself blushing. David sought her hand and gave it a gentle squeeze. Finding his voice David said, 'Emily has agreed to become my wife. We thought with the recent events we would wait until things had settled down a bit.'

Ida gave a smile and said, 'I think it's just the kind of news we need at this moment. There has been enough sadness in this house to last us all a long time. Refill the glasses Harry, and let's propose a toast to the happy couple.'

Ida carried on, 'I've been waiting a long time for this day. I thought the pair of you were never going to get on with it, despite our helping hand wherever we could to speed things up a bit.'

'Ida!' Emily exclaimed.

'It's all right, I don't mind,' said David. 'I wish I'd been a bit quicker as well, but you know what they say, better late than never.'

'To the happy couple,' Harry chimed in raising his glass.

'So when is the wedding to be?' Karen asked.

Emily stuttered, 'I don't really know, we never got around to fixing a date with all this going on.'

Sheila gave a slight cough to catch everyone's attention. 'I hope you don't mind me saying, but what have you got to wait for? I wouldn't delay because you never know what's around the next corner.'

David laughed. 'Thank you, Sheila, my sentiments exactly. Why should we wait?'

'There's no reason at all,' replied Emily in a daze about how quickly events were moving out of her control.

★　★　★

As normality resumed, Emily and David found time to have a chat with Bill. Since Emily was a divorcee there were one or two difficulties and it was finally decided that they would have a quiet ceremony at the Registry Office on a Friday. They would invite Harry, Ida and Karen and would leave it to the three of them to decide which two would be witnesses.

On the Saturday, Bill would bless the marriage and they could have the full complement of guests that they wanted to invite. Emily was pleased with the arrangement, even though a quiet wedding alone would have suited her after the ostentatious affair for her marriage to Howard. She had had no control over organising that but felt that as David had not been married before he deserved the opportunity to invite all the guests and colleagues he wanted.

David was adamant that Karen would not do the catering, despite the fact she had already offered. He quickly went on to explain, 'Karen, your cooking skills are excellent. But if you are at the registry office with us on Friday and then we want you to come for a meal with us to a restaurant, there won't be any time for food preparation. On top of that Emily would like you to help get everything else ready, so how are you going to fit it all in? It is kind of you to offer, but we want you to share our day, not work on it.'

'True, I'd never given a thought about it,' admitted Karen.

'So we're all agreed the reception will be at a hotel?'

'Yes.'

'Good, I just hope we can get a booking at short notice but I'm sure Harry and I will sort something out.'

Harry had happily agreed to be David's best man. David didn't feel close enough to any of his brothers to ask them, but he was going to invite all his family to the blessing and reception. Sadly both David's parents had passed away a few years previously and he felt sadness that his mother wouldn't see him getting married, because she had nagged him for years about it.

Gail was going to fly over for the wedding and he would be delighted to see her. She would arrive late on Friday evening so he would not see her until the Saturday. She was going to stay at one of his brothers' until after the blessing, and then David was adamant he wanted her to move into one of his spare rooms so that he and Emily could spend plenty of time with her. He was sure she and Emily would get on well together.

Emily had few people to invite because she had no family left, but when she counted up the people she had got to know since the start of her new life these made up for the lack of relatives.

Whilst all the wedding preparations were being arranged Emily and David were also busy sorting out Lara's future. Until things were settled and possible adoptive parents found for her, Social Services had agreed that she should carry on living with Emily. It seemed to more sensible than uprooting her more than was necessary. Once they knew of the forthcoming marriage this had helped their decision.

David had put his own house up for sale and had agreed they would live in Emily's cottage, as it was handier for her and no further to his surgery. The cottage was also in better condition than his own home and no smaller.

Emily only hoped he could live with the feminine bedroom she had designed until it was time to redecorate. When she mentioned it to him he looked puzzled. She told him, a bit impatiently, 'You've seen it a few times now!'

'Have I?' he queried.

Emily thought he was joking until he continued, 'To tell you the truth I've never noticed. I've only had eyes for you when we've been in there and I don't care how it is decorated as long as we are together every night.'

Emily felt mean that she had been sharp

with him when he genuinely did not care; his eyes were seeing her, not the surroundings.

★ ★ ★

Much to her disappointment it was a miserable day when she woke to get ready for the ceremony. She remembered what a gorgeous day it had been for Ida and Harry on their wedding day. Her spirits couldn't be dampened, she was so excited. She had decided to buy an outfit in a similar style to the one she had worn for Ida's and Harry's wedding as David had admired it so much. This time it was her turn to carry a posy and she had given into Karen's nagging and bought a hat to match. She felt very pleased with her reflection when she studied the finished effect. She might be older for this wedding but there was a shine about her that had been lacking in her marriage to Howard.

Karen was going to drive Emily and Ida in Emily's own car to the registry office and Harry had said he would go with David.

When Emily arrived David was already waiting outside. One look at his smiling face was enough to quash any nerves or doubts Emily might have had.

Having experienced a wedding in a church before, albeit in the distant past, the actual ceremony in the registry office was a little disappointing to Emily. It seemed devoid of personal feeling. But nothing mattered as the words *I now pronounce you husband and wife* were said.

David didn't need to be told to kiss the bride, as soon as the words ended he had her in his arms giving her a deep passionate kiss and he whispered the words 'I love you,' directly into her ear.

'I love you too,' replied Emily in a voice choked with emotion.

They gave a gasp of surprise as the camera flashed when they moved out of the Registry Office to the waiting cars and Emily saw Brian Nicholls beaming behind it.

'Congratulations, the pair of you,' he shouted and they smiled back at him while the camera flashed again.

'How come you're here?' Emily managed asked.

'Nice way to greet me,' he laughed. 'A little bird asked me to come and do some photos,' and with that he was back to his camera and refused to be drawn any further.

'That's it folks, have a good day. I've got to rush as I've another appointment shortly.' With that he was gone with David and Emily's thanks blowing in the wind behind him.

They had booked a meal at the Beverley Arms and many of the diners were looking at them curiously, guessing it was their wedding day. There were no toasts and they left quietly when the meal was finished to go back to their new home together.

It was their honeymoon night which, if possible, was even more pleasurable for each of them than the previous time they had made love. This time there was no rushing up out of bed to go home, they were home.

Karen was looking after Lara in her flat for the next few days. It seemed strange for them to be waking up together, and then getting ready in the same house to attend their blessing. They had planned it so that they would walk down the aisle together.

There were going to be a lot of guests at the blessing and Emily had bought an ankle length dress very much like a wedding dress. It was in an oyster satin, with thin straps to the bodice, trimmed with beads and sequins. The skirt fitted snugly over her hips with a slight flare and had a small bolero jacket to keep the chill off her arms when they were outside. She had decided on one or two tiny flowers to be woven into the natural curls of her hair instead of a headdress or hat, and completed her overall look by wearing her grandmother's antique pendant.

When David saw the finished effect he grabbed hold of her and gave her a long, lingering kiss. Emily squirmed and pulled away shrieking, 'Watch my makeup. I've only just done it and there isn't time to do it again if you mess it up.'

'Rubbish!' he laughed. Nothing Emily said that day could upset him. But then he added, 'Can I mess it up when we get back?'

'Of course, once the guests have all gone,' Emily laughed back.

Karen stood at the door saying, 'Your carriage awaits.' They walked outside into a blaze of sunshine, totally different from the day before.

Bill had created a lovely service for them and if it wasn't an actual wedding ceremony it didn't feel like they were missing out on anything as he said the words:

David and Emily, you stand in the presence of God, as man and wife, to dedicate to him your life together . . .

As the service progressed Emily had to hold back tears, it was all so lovely and the words were especially for them. In a bemused state they walked back up the aisle and Emily barely saw a face as she walked past the filled pews.

When they came out of the darkness of the church into the daylight there were other well wishers waiting for them. Emily supposed some could be David's patients.

Tickton Grange — where they were holding the reception, was a short distance from the church and Howard had the foresight to hire a coach to take the guests. It gave Emily a chance to meet Gail for the first time and for David to have a reunion with her. As David had thought Emily and Gail hit it off straight away. The atmosphere as they drove along was charged with excitement and the rest of the day was no less disappointing.

Emily had a few moments where she remembered how she had endured but not enjoyed her wedding day with Howard and how the marriage had turned out. Maybe that had been an omen of what had been going to happen. If their blessing day was how the second marriage would turn out, then it must bode for a beautiful life together.

EPILOGUE

Two years later

Emily smiled as she sat looking at the two children playing together. Lara was now just over two years old. She was a loving little girl with a head of fair haired curls that had a will of their own. At times she could have a temper that was as curly as her hair. She was worth all the effort that Emily and David had put into making her belong to them properly. The adoption had been finalized the month before and had called for another celebration.

Once married David and Emily soon got used to Lara being part of their little family. It wasn't such a difficult task with so many willing helpers around. When Social Services, on a routine visit, mentioned they would soon have her off their hands, as they hoped to find adoptive parents in the not too distant future, David and Emily looked at each other with disbelief. They had never forgotten she would eventually be moved but kept avoiding the thought of it

Emily was the first to find her voice, 'Er, do you think there's any chance we could keep her?' Then realising she had asked this without even discussing it with David she quickly looked across at him for a sign of his approval. He gave a nod to show he agreed.

'Well, although it would be ideal, particularly since you have looked after her virtually from birth, there will be a lot of formalities to get through and it may take a long time before you can finally say she belongs to you.'

'But she will be with us during all that process,' Emily asked anxiously.

'Oh, yes, but we will need to keep an eye on her.'

David took the initiative and spoke for the first time. 'Then set the wheels in motion as soon as you can.'

'We are always happy to see a child placed with adoptive parents, particularly people like yourselves that will offer a loving and caring home environment.'

When she had gone Emily turned to David. 'I hope you don't mind, I feel I might have pushed you into something you might not want?' she asked looking shamefaced.

'Come here,' he said, as he took her in his arms. 'That's what I love about you most, your kind and caring nature.'

'Thanks, David,' Emily said, comforted.

'What are you thanking me for; I'll get as much joy as you from having a daughter of

411

our very own.' He said the word daughter with a look of pride on his face.

The Social Services lady, Muriel Kemp, hadn't been joking when she said it would take time to complete the process. It had been a very long haul with a lot of frustrating moments and mountains of paperwork, before everything was completed. Now looking at Lara, it was worth every cross moment and tear shed in frustration to know they had finally got her future secured.

Lara was gently helping David junior to find his feet. He would walk around the room holding onto furniture and clutching at things. Lara, being a very determined lady, was trying her best to get him to run around after her.

When she had married David, Emily had never given a thought to having a child of her own so soon. Looking back she supposed it was all the years she had been childless that had made her presume that was the way she would stay. Tests had proved she could have a child but it had been drummed into her so much by Howard that the fault was hers, that she had come to believe it.

She was amazed when David announced that the sickness she had been feeling each morning was due to being pregnant. She had thought the sickness to be a sign of stress or a bug. When he told her she stuttered, 'But I can't be!'

'Why not?'

'Well I thought I couldn't have children.'

'Didn't you have tests that proved you could?'

'Yes.'

'What do you think happens if you don't use birth control?'

'But I never got pregnant with Howard,' she exclaimed, still in a state of shock.

'Yes, but didn't you tell me Howard was infertile.'

'That's what they said, but he always denied it, said it was me.'

'Emily!' he exclaimed, 'Surely you didn't really believe him, after all the tests proved that it was him.'

'No, I suppose not,' she conceded. 'But you didn't know Howard, how persuasive he could be when he set his mind to it.'

'Now we've got that out of the way, are you pleased?'

'I'm ecstatic. It's more than I could ever have hoped for.'

'What about Lara,' he asked in a concerned voice.

'What about her?' Emily asked, not sure what he was trying to say.

'You'll have two to cope with and there will

barely be a year's difference between them if we carry on with the adoption,' he explained.

'There's no way I wouldn't keep her now.'

'Good,' he said with a sigh of relief.

After an easy pregnancy and birth she produced a perfect son, despite all the fears that she had whilst she was pregnant imagining she was far too old or that something would go wrong.

The little cottage was too small for their rapidly expanding family and David had let her have her own way when they bought a new house. He was happy wherever they lived, as long as they were together. She kept to the old style of house that she preferred, and it was not at all minimalist, but a house that could be called home and was lived in with the usual clutter that two young children bring.

Alison and her two children lived in the cottage. Sadly Fred had not survived long after Joan. They all decided he had given up the will to live without her by his side. Unfortunately never having purchased the house, which Joan had always wanted, it created a problem for Alison on his death. Emily soon came to her aid by offering the cottage to rent as it stood empty at that time. It was ideal having her own cleaner on the doorstep, although she had become much more than that by stepping into any breach where necessary.

With her time taken up by her new home and the children, Karen saw to the business side of things and overall running at the house and had blossomed into the smart self-assured person Emily had first known. When Gail had come over for the wedding Karen and Gail discovered a lasting friendship, both being single and of similar age and years later Karen had frequent trips to Spain to spend time with her. Emily continued to oversee everything at the house but didn't interfere.

As Emily had suspected, not long after her own marriage, Rachel had moved out. She was still a career woman and rented a flat with a fellow student; although the last Emily heard of her she did appear to have another man in her life and was living with him.

Sheila was still in residence and liked to take any part in assisting with the running of the house, where it was needed. She helped Karen cook and when Karen went away she took over. She would help Alison clean, and was available when Alison had her days off or went on holiday. She had finally plucked up the courage to move away from the house environment and went to one or two of the town's activities aimed at people like her, on their own, where she had developed a few friendships.

Other residents had slowly been found to fill the vacant rooms. Anne was a woman in her fifties who had looked after her mother all her life. She had had a job but sadly after her mother's death she had been made redundant and felt she was of no use to anyone. David suggested she move into the house when he found she was talking as if her mother was still alive, addressing the empty chair where her mother used to sit, as if she were still there.

David felt if he could get her away from that house and the loneliness, then she would recover her sanity. He had tentatively suggested a room for her and it had worked over time. Sheila and she became friends and although neither was particularly outgoing they did make the effort to go to the cinema once in a while.

Ida and Harry were still plodding on, companionably, not seeming to age. Ida hadn't suffered any more major angina attacks and Harry took good care of her.

Bert was in his seventies, having recently lost his wife whom he had been devoted to. Although he had a family but he was adamant he wasn't going to be a burden to them. He was far too alert and spry to find a place in a residential home, and it proved an ideal solution for him to move in. For once Harry didn't feel outnumbered by all the females surrounding him and he and Bert became firm friends.

Pat approached Karen about one of her friend's acquaintances who was in a particularly difficult marriage. Her first marriage had ended in a rather nasty divorce after she had had an unhappy time of it and she couldn't face all that again. She was desperate to get out of the relationship and Pat and her friend were deeply concerned what she might do to herself. When she had heard about Emily's it gave her the impetus to leave her husband and move in there. There had been a few bad moments when the husband had called but the other residents had been supportive and he left her alone. She was happy now and even had overcome her fears gradually.

Finally there was Tracy, who had been in much the same position as Karen, but her husband had been drunk almost permanently and physically abusive. He had never bothered to work and ran through her money as fast as she earned it. They had never had a home of their own and she never managed to save a deposit to get a place — even a bed-sit, in order to leave him. When the opportunity came to move into Emily's she grabbed it and left him.

Emily and Karen were aware there were people desperately waiting for vacancies so that they could get out of their problem situations. But Emily was also sensible enough to realise that she couldn't help everybody in need. She was also pretty certain there would be no available room in the near future as all her residents were contented to stay.

★   ★   ★

A big smile came to her face as David entered the room. 'What are you smiling at?' he queried.

'Just thinking how lucky I am and how much, without ever knowing it, my Grandmother has done for me. I love you David, and our little family, and I really am a very fortunate person.'

'I love you too,' smiled David, coming over and giving his two girls and his son a kiss.

We do hope that you have enjoyed reading this large print book.

Did you know that all of our titles are available for purchase?

We publish a wide range of high quality large print books including:
Romances, Mysteries, Classics
General Fiction
Non Fiction and Westerns

Special interest titles available in large print are:
The Little Oxford Dictionary
Music Book
Song Book
Hymn Book
Service Book

Also available from us courtesy of Oxford University Press:
Young Readers' Dictionary
(large print edition)
Young Readers' Thesaurus
(large print edition)

For further information or a free brochure, please contact us at:
Ulverscroft Large Print Books Ltd.,
The Green, Bradgate Road, Anstey,
Leicester, LE7 7FU, England.
Tel: (00 44) **0116 236 4325**
Fax: (00 44) **0116 234 0205**

TOO MANY WASTED YEARS

Susan Shaw

Edith is full of regret when her young man, fighting at the front as the Great War rages, is reported missing, presumed dead. For their last meeting had been quarrelsome when she'd refused his advances to make love . . . During her grief she meets Alfred, a passionate man — and she's soon pregnant. They marry, but Alfred, although a kind man and a good father, lets money run through his fingers, and Edith spends her marriage regretting that he isn't her first love . . . When Alfred dies, Edith becomes a housekeeper, and discovers what love really means — finally realising that she's always been chasing a dream.

DREAMS OR REALITY

Susan Shaw

Laura, a teenager in the 1960s, thought she knew it all in the permissive society. Married very young, she is soon disillusioned, she has three children in quick succession and suffers physical abuse in the marriage. She develops into a person in her own right and believes that material possessions are now the most important thing in her life in order for her to attain happiness. Although she achieves the possessions, her world still collapses around her, so she must finally make the important decision as to where her loyalties lie. Whatever she decides will have a tremendous impact on her future.

ELEANOR

Susan Shaw

It's 1919 and Eleanor is full of the joys of spring because it's her eighteenth birthday and she feels this is the start of an excellent life for her in Kent. But events don't turn out as she expects and she's devastated when her father refuses to let her marry Harry, the father of her baby. She'd wrongly assumed that her father would set them up with a business to give them a start in life, despite Harry coming from a lower class. Forced into a loveless marriage, Eleanor becomes determined to make her mark in the business world . . .

SIGNED, MATA HARI

Yannick Murphy

In the cold October of 1917 Marguerite Zelle, alias Mata Hari, the infamous exotic dancer, sits in a Paris prison cell awaiting trial on charges of espionage; the penalty, death by firing squad. And as she waits, she tells stories to buy back her life from her interrogators . . .

LOVE'S HERITAGE

Louise Pakeman

In response to her mother's dying request, Maggie Townsend is on her way to England, with the address of a grandfather she barely knew existed. However, when Tim Fenton, a fellow Australian she meets on the journey, insists on giving her his contact details in London she begins to have qualms. Maggie finds that her relations are grander and stranger than she imagined. She is shocked when her grandfather refuses to acknowledge her, and by sinister undercurrents in the household. Tim and the aunt he is staying with prove to be true friends when events spiral out of control.